THE HOUSE IN THE CLOUDS

VICTORIA CONNELLY

Cover design by The Brewster Project
Photos copyright © Depositphotos

Author photo © Roy Connelly

Published by Cuthland Press

ISBN: 978-1-910522-16-5

To my dear friends Kerrie and Emilie with love

CHAPTER ONE

Edward Townsend had known the house his whole life. Having grown up in a neighbouring village in the Sussex Downs, he knew it as Winfield Hall although the locals had another name for it – The House in the Clouds. Looking at its lofty position above the village now, Edward couldn't think of a more fitting name. How palatial it looked. Compared to the tiny cottages clustered in the village, it must indeed seem like a palace with its splendid Georgian dolls' house exterior and its large sash windows glinting in the light.

He'd spent the morning walking around the empty rooms of the hall, noting the crumbling plasterwork, the broken balustrades and the general air of decay, but he'd known that he had what it took to restore it to its former glory. It was a house with good bones, and that's what counted. Everything else could be replaced or repaired.

Sitting in his car, Edward glanced down at the catalogue he was holding. The property was to be sold at a public auction which made him anxious. On the one hand, you could get an absolute bargain at auction but, on the other, the price might rocket to way above what you were happy to pay for it. How he wished that he could just put an offer in now and be done with it. Edward didn't like surprises. He liked to know what he was getting and he was buying this place as an investment because he could see a real future in it.

Winfield Hall was a property of untapped potential in a beautiful location within commuting distance of London. What was not to love about that? And he planned to divide it into apartments, renting them out while living in one himself. He wasn't sure for how long. Maybe three to five years, maybe more. He'd have to see how it suited him and his job in the capital.

His doctor had told him to slow down and to take some time off from his job as a financial adviser, but that was easier said than done. Edward was a workaholic and lived for his job, and yet somewhere inside him was that little boy he'd left behind in the countryside of the downs – the one who'd clambered over stiles and gone swimming in the rivers and the sea. Now, he was lucky if he got a once-a-week dip in his club's pool. His punishing timetable meant that leisure time was often squeezed into non-existence.

He rolled his shoulders and cricked his neck, acknowledging that the punishing hours at his desk were taking a toll on him physically and, of course, there was the old problem, he thought, giving his left leg a massage. Just for a moment, he allowed himself the luxury of imagining an alternative lifestyle where he might be able to work from home a couple of days a week and fit some wild swimming into his timetable. Gosh, how he missed that. He still had his wetsuit somewhere, didn't he? It was such a long time since he'd worn it, but he was pretty sure it was in his car.

He smiled at the thought of swimming in the wild again, imagining what it would be like to feel the cold, silky river water welcoming him and that incomparable feeling of freedom and relief he felt only when swimming. But he mustn't get too carried away, he told himself. The house wasn't his yet.

He took one last look out of the window at the pale golden facade of Winfield Hall before starting his car for the two-hour drive back into London. He wasn't looking forward to it and he knew that he would be leaving a little part of him behind in that Sussex village.

Abigail Carey took a big, deep breath of the downland air, revelling in its early autumn purity. It was quite unlike anything she'd ever breathed before and she knew that she had found the one place she wanted to be more than anywhere else, which was a strange feeling for her to have. As a child, Abi had never had a garden beyond a bare courtyard and she wondered where this sudden longing came from now. But, wherever it came from, it was most welcome. She could draw here, she thought, and paint and embroider and ... *breathe*. That's what she wanted to do more than anything else after years of working so hard. It seemed to her that she hadn't had a single moment to breathe in years.

After a spell at art college, Abi had struck out as a freelance designer for a number of companies while working on her own designs in the evenings. It hadn't been an easy existence and she'd lost count of the number of dreadful flats she'd lived in, sharing with strangers in order to make the rent.

And then something strange had happened. Her "doodling" as her sister always referred to it had taken off and she suddenly found herself flavour of the month. Then flavour of the year. She'd been able to pay for her own studio and then her own shop. Suddenly, Abigail Carey was running a business and a successful one too. Her prints and linocuts were featured in all the newspapers and glossy magazines and several of her patterns were bought by department stores for quality bed linen, cushions and curtains. What a whirlwind it had been.

Smiling as she thought about it all, her fingers found a large silver locket she wore on a long chain around her neck. She didn't open it, but it was a comfort to know what was inside: that first doodle of the sunflower that had launched her career. It had seemed like such a simple thing to draw. Everybody loved sunflowers, didn't they? With their happy round faces and those bright fiery petals, they were a symbol of joy and strength, a winning combination, and it was as she thought about them that she determined that she would grow them at Winfield if she made the winning bid at the auction. There was a walled garden and, as she walked around it now, she promised it sunflowers.

She felt sure she should have been asking the estate agent questions, but he'd disappeared a few minutes ago to give her some privacy. After all, this was the kind of property one needed to *feel*. You couldn't really take it in with an estate agent giving you a potted history and blasting you with useless details like the measurements of rooms. That wasn't what Abi was interested in at all. She wanted to reach out and touch the place, running her fingers along the plasterwork and listening to the sound her feet made on the bare wooden floorboards. It was important to get to know a property quietly, especially one that had been empty for the last few years. It needed to be respected, its empty rooms entered silently, reverently and not with the constant babble of an estate agent's voice accompanying you.

And, oh those rooms! Lofty, light and airy – just like the landscape which the large windows seemed to invite inside so that the two seemed indistinguishable. Abi was glad that they were empty of furniture because she could fill each room from her own imagination and what plans she had for the place. Of course, Winfield Hall was far too big for her to have all to herself. As much as she'd relish drifting from room to room and filling each with her art, she knew that this was a place to be shared.

She remembered those long, grim years of rented flats, the dark and dingy rooms, the uninspiring views of rooftops and litter-strewn streets. How her heart had yearned for such a place as this – even a small portion of it. One room or even a small corner would have sufficed as long as it had one of those glorious windows framing the great flank of a down and the wispy clouds in the heavens above. She'd known as soon as she'd seen the house for sale online that she would share it, but not with just anyone. She wanted to share it with fellow artists and creatives – people who would love the place as much as she did. She had so many ideas for the future of the place. Each room had been so full of light and possibilities. Abi smiled, feeling hugely excited at the thought of what the future might hold.

She took out her sketchbook and started drawing. She drew the grand front of the hall with its beautiful pediment pointing into the blue sky, she drew the walled garden with its swaying grasses and she drew the great bulk of the down behind the house, with its dark saddle of trees and the chalky ribbon of footpath which led into the valley. What a special place this was, she thought, throwing her head back and gazing up into the endless blue of the heavens. It was a landscape of air and space, of sky and solitude, and she knew – because she could feel it in the very fibre of her being – that this was the place she wanted to live forever.

CHAPTER TWO

The auction room was horribly crowded. Abi glanced around, wondering how many competitors she had hiding there. A number of properties were to be sold that day, but how many people were there for Winfield Hall, she wondered?

She'd walked up to the house earlier that morning, leaving her car in a leafy lane by the church and taking the footpath up the chalky track that climbed the hill out of the village and skirted the grounds of the hall, giving her a good view of the property. She'd sat on the grassy slope of the down in the September sunshine for a few minutes, gazing at the house and grounds below her and admiring the soft ambers of autumn in a nearby wood. The morning was diamond-bright with great white clouds scudding across the sky and a cool breeze had reminded her that summer was well and truly over, but that hadn't mattered because Winfield was beautiful – whatever the season.

It was, she'd acknowledged, one of those painfully delicious moments in life when things could go either way. She'd looked at her watch, thinking that, in a few hours' time, she would either be the happiest person on earth or the most miserable. But which way would it go? She almost couldn't bear the suspense of it all.

Now, in the stuffy atmosphere of the auction room, she tried to channel the peace she'd felt while gazing at Winfield. Whose home could it possibly be if not hers? Surely there wasn't anybody in that room who felt as passionately as she did about the place.

She shook her head. She mustn't assume she had the monopoly on passion when it came to Winfield. She'd be very surprised if there weren't at least half a dozen people, maybe even a dozen, who loved the old place. It was the sort of house to inspire such feelings after all. But, all the same, she couldn't bear to think of anybody else owning it. Sitting on the slope looking at the property that morning, the wind blowing through her long fair hair, she'd had such a strong feeling that she was gazing down at her future home. She could really see herself there. More than that, she could *feel* herself there. Now, that might be fanciful. Abi would be the first to admit that she had sudden and often wonderful flights of fancy, but this was something more. It was almost as if she'd been granted a glimpse into the future.

She gave a delicious little shiver as she thought of it again and took a deep breath. It was perhaps a little odd that the very first property she was trying to buy was so grand. But she hadn't wanted to buy just any old property and so had continued to rent as her business had grown. To be honest, she hadn't really had time to think about purchasing a house – she'd put everything she'd had into her work and she felt so lucky to be standing here now able to consider such a purchase.

She'd dressed smartly for the occasion, swapping her usual

denim blouse and floral-patterned skirt for a crisp honey-coloured suit which she hoped she hadn't wrinkled when sitting in the grass. She'd chosen a sweet blossom-pink blouse and, as ever, was wearing her silver locket with the lucky sunflower doodle, hoping it would work its magic for her. She touched it lightly as the auctioneer stepped up to the podium. It was time to begin.

Things warmed up with a couple of townhouses, a plot of land with a decrepit bungalow in the middle of it and a thatched cottage that would definitely be a labour of love for somebody. And then came Winfield Hall.

'A special lot this,' the auctioneer began. 'First time on the market in ninety years and a real landmark in the area. A twelve-bedroomed Georgian property with many fine original features, it comes with seven acres of land in splendid downland countryside. Now, who'll start the bidding?'

He opened the bidding at an eye-watering sum and a hand immediately shot into the air. Abi waited, biding her time, watching the room as the price rose slowly but steadily. She could feel her heart racing and, for a brief moment, was fearful that she might not be able to bid at all – that some strange power might prevent her, and so she raised her hand.

'We have a new bidder in the room,' the auctioneer announced. How ghastly, Abi thought, as heads turned to seek her out, but at least she was a part of things now.

As far as she could see, there were four other bidders, one on the telephone, one online and two in the room. Abi had known ahead of time that she could have bid from her place in London, but she'd wanted to be in the auction room itself and had been desperate to visit the hall too so she could imbibe some of its magic beforehand.

The price continued to rise and she noticed that the bidder

on the phone had dropped out. It was getting closer to becoming hers, she thought. She just had to keep going and make sure hers was the last hand in the air when the gavel fell. She'd set a price limit, of course. It seemed ridiculously high to her and she'd seen other similar properties online, fully restored, selling for much less, but she knew that Winfield was special. Its setting made it unique and that would come at a premium, she realised.

Still, the price rose until another bidder bowed out. How many were left now? Abi quickly glanced around the room. It was just her and one other: a man in a sharp, dark suit with neat sandy hair and a gold watch which caught the light each time his hand rose to bid.

For a few tense moments, it was just her and him. She bid; he bid. On it went, the price rocketing, scarily close to her limit. She swallowed hard. What would she do if it reached her limit? Could she risk spending more?

She bid; he bid.

She mustn't forget how much it would cost to renovate. It would probably be as much as the sale price and then there were bound to be a few surprises. She'd heard there always were with older properties.

She bid; he bid.

Then there'd be the auctioneer's fee on top of the sales price.

Abi felt a wave of panic. They were reaching her limit.

She bid and there was a pause. Then he bid. The limit had been reached and the bid was with him.

Tentatively, she raised her hand and bid again.

He raised his and the price shot up.

Once more, she told herself – just once. She touched her locket. One more lucky bid. She raised her hand. There was a pause. The auctioneer looked at the gentleman. He bid again.

'Are we all done?' the auctioneer asked, looking at Abi in case she had another bid in her. But she couldn't do it. She shook her head, slowly realising that it wasn't meant to be. So much for her vision of the future. This, she thought, was where flights of fancy got you.

As the auctioneer's gavel closed the winning bid like a cruel gunshot, Abi's heart broke a little. She picked up her bag and got up to leave the room.

Stephen slapped Edward on the back as they left the auction room together.

'Well done, mate!' he said. 'I know how much it means to you to get this place.'

'Thanks,' Edward said. 'Hey, you know who she is?' He nodded to the fair-haired woman ahead of them.

'Who?'

'My underbidder – over there.'

Stephen looked at the woman who had paused to pick up a catalogue an elderly gentleman had dropped.

'She's that artist, I think,' he said.

'What artist?'

'The one who does the patterns and things.'

'Is she good?'

'Yeah, actually. Bit of a success story,' Stephen said. 'Abigail something. Carrick. No, that's not right. *Carey*! Does those pretty prints that women like. You know – cushions, curtains, aprons – that kind of thing. Got a chain of shops in London and a big factory somewhere up north.'

Edward nodded. He wasn't aware of the world of interior design. When he'd bought his London apartment, he'd hired someone to decorate it for him, writing down two words: sober, minimalist. He'd always had an aversion to feminine florals and anything in a pastel colour.

'How do you know all this?' Edward asked.

'Saw an interview with her in a magazine. My wife was going on about her. She wanted to give our bedroom the Abigail Carey touch, she said.'

'And did she?'

'Yes, she did! There's a sunflower wherever I look!'

Edward laughed. 'I think I'll stick to my nice grey walls.'

'Very wise,' Stephen said. 'There was a rumour going round that she was interested in Winfield Hall.'

'Yes, but she wasn't *quite* as interested as I was,' Edward said, allowing himself a little moment of pride.

'You did well,' his friend told him. 'Congratulations.'

'Now, I think I've got some business to settle,' Edward said. 'Then fancy some lunch to celebrate?'

'Absolutely!' Stephen said. 'You can tell me your plans for that great monster of a house.'

Edward smiled. It had been a stressful morning and he was glad that the whole business of it was over. Still, at the same time, he couldn't help thinking that now was when the real work began.

After leaving the auction house, Abigail hadn't dared drive through the village again. She couldn't bear to look at the house that wasn't to be hers. As she hit the motorway back to her place in London, she tried desperately to be positive, but it was hard. She'd always been able to see the good side of things, but today seemed totally devoid of good sides. She thought of the neat, crisp man in the suit who had placed the winning bid and she sincerely hoped he'd be happy at Winfield Hall and that he'd bought it because he loved it and not because he was some property developer who was simply passing through. The house deserved more than that. It needed somebody in it who would not only nurture it, but cherish it too. That's what had been missing for so many years now – an owner who saw its true beauty and who would love it for years to come.

When she got back to London, her small home seemed even smaller than ever. She loved it, she truly did. With its sweet balcony overlooking the Thames and a tiny yard that received more than its share of sunshine for a London property, she had a lot to be grateful for. But Abi couldn't unsee Winfield Hall and she couldn't set aside the dreams she'd had for the place – a vision of a new life for herself with large, lofty rooms where she could host artist retreats, a garden where she could really indulge her passion for growing cut flowers, and having walks from the doorstep taking in the magnificence of the South Downs. London had its own beauty, it was true, but Abi had tired of it. It had been very handy to live in the capital for the past few years. She'd needed to for her business. But she wanted to stretch and reach out to something more now. She felt she needed open space and an abundance of greenery and fresh air. She wanted to feel earth under her feet rather than pavement and to leave behind the acrid smell of the city and the human crush of it all. She needed a space to call her own.

She sighed. Where was that space if it wasn't Winfield? She'd pinned so many of her hopes on it and she wasn't sure she had the heart to start all over again. She'd been so *sure* about the place.

As she walked into her study, she opened her handbag and pulled out her sketchbook, flipping through the pages of drawings she'd made of Winfield, seeing the autumn colours once again even though she'd drawn in pencil, and feeling the cool breeze that had lifted her hair away from her face.

Slowly, she closed the sketchbook and, opening a desk drawer, placed it carefully inside. She had to try and forget about it. But, deep in her heart, she knew it would be difficult.

You couldn't just switch off a dream, could you?

CHAPTER THREE

If Edward had had his way, he would have moved into Winfield Hall the afternoon of the auction. Unfortunately, the world didn't move as fast as he wished it would and there were endless contracts to sort out and sign.

It was mid-October by the time Edward picked up the keys. The colour of autumn had deepened in the woods, painting the trees in rich ochres and deep ambers, and the first frost had rimed the valley, making the grass verges sparkle. It felt good to be out of the city, he thought, as he drove through the winding lanes. He always missed the country when he wasn't there. Well, the truth was, he didn't really have time to miss it when he was working in London. His head might not have time, but his heart still missed this place. It was like a daily ache he carried around inside him. He often visualised it, feeling sure it was eating him up, molecule by molecule until, one day, there would be nothing left of him at all. Just a hollow husk riding the tube to work, an empty vessel devoid of dreams.

He felt like he'd got out just in time. At thirty-five, he was still young, he told himself, he still felt passionate about his job and still had the energy to pour himself into a project of the magnitude of Winfield Hall. Of course, he'd still be living in his London flat for most of the time, but the fact that he now had somewhere to escape to at the weekends – even if it was a building site for the foreseeable future – was a great comfort to him.

There was just so much to do. Edward had thought he'd prepared himself for it by reading a few books about house renovations and watching YouTube videos, but nothing had prepared him for the enormity of the project. The full structural survey he'd had done on the property ahead of making his winning bid had shown a few key areas that needed work and, on top of that, were the plans for turning the house into leasable flats. That's what Edward had envisaged as soon as he'd seen the place. He'd known it was too big for him to live in alone and that it would be way too ambitious even on his city salary. But he could take a generous slice of the house for himself and make an income from the rest. It was a sound investment, he believed.

Being a listed property, though, meant that you couldn't just start knocking down walls as soon as you took ownership. No matter how keen you were to save the old building and make improvements, things had to be done officially, with the right permissions and that, of course, meant delays. It was very frustrating and Edward had no choice but to hire a manager to oversee the whole project, liaising with builders and workmen and being around to sign for deliveries. He'd given it a go trying to coordinate everything himself, but it was impossible when he was working in London.

But he lived for the time when he could be at Winfield, pacing the rooms and envisaging what it would be like when the work was done. This was what he'd been dreaming of for the last few years and he couldn't help but allow himself a proud little moment as he stood in one of the grand first floor rooms and looked out of the great sash window across the valley beyond. He deserved this, he told himself. He'd worked and saved hard for it, and he was here now, making his dreams a reality.

For a moment, an image entered his mind of the woman who'd been bidding against him at the auction. He hadn't seen her face clearly, just a glimpse of blonde hair tied back. But he remembered the way she'd carried herself as she'd left the auction room. Was it his imagination or was there something defeated about her gait and posture? And was Edward having a glimmer of guilt now because his victory had been at the cost of somebody else's happiness? But that was the way of the auction room, wasn't it? There could only be one winner and he couldn't truly have any regrets because he was that winner.

Still, as he turned away from the window to venture back downstairs, he couldn't get the rather forlorn image of that woman out of his mind.

Abi smiled sweetly at the estate agent, but she wasn't really listening to her patter. The woman was saying something about local amenities in the nearby Oxfordshire town. Apparently, they were second to none. Very popular. Very handy. But Abi wasn't really interested.

She walked around the garden and glanced back at the house. It was pretty enough in that golden Cotswold stone, but Abi didn't feel the need to get out her sketch book. She didn't even want to look around the rooms for a second time when the estate agent offered. She'd seen enough. She was done.

The next week, she viewed a property in Hampshire. It looked like a dolls' house from the front with fine sash windows and perfect Georgian symmetry. The rooms were just as light and lofty as those at Winfield, but they didn't look out onto the downs.

Then there was a house in Kent, close to the coast: a weather-boarded property with lots of character and a small walled garden which was very pretty indeed.

All of these properties were lovely and each would have made a perfect home and, perhaps, Abi might have been happy in any one of them. But they all had one fatal flaw. They weren't Winfield.

Once back in her London home after yet another trip to see a house, she kicked off her shoes and rubbed her eyes. She was tired and not just from the travelling to see all the recent properties. It was more than that. She felt heart weary. It was as if she knew that the home for her was off the market and she wasn't going to find another. She'd have to make do with second best. Which was silly really because there couldn't just be one perfect home for somebody, could there? There were bound to be dozens if not hundreds of places where a person could be happy. That's what she tried to tell herself.

She even thought that perhaps she should stay in London. Maybe the universe was steering her in a direction she couldn't quite make out yet. And then she'd close her eyes and think of those green lanes and chalky footpaths of the downs. There was something about that countryside that had resonated so strongly with her and she simply couldn't fall in love with anywhere else. Not for the time being, anyway.

'You're acting like a spoilt child,' she said to herself. There were any number of beautiful places she could afford. So she couldn't get her first choice – so what? Luck or fate or whatever it was hadn't meant it to be so she needed to pull herself together, that was all.

But, as often as she told herself that, she couldn't help harbouring just a little self-pity over the beautiful home that wasn't to be hers. And so she switched off from property hunting for a while and focussed on her work.

It was a strange, transitory time for Abi because she'd recently sold her company – the company she'd started from a few illustrations of sunflowers she'd idly sketched at her kitchen table. When she thought about it now, she'd had no idea of the crazy times that lay ahead of her. If she had, perhaps she would have torn the illustrations up into a million tiny pieces because, for Abi, it was all about the art. She had never planned on being an entrepreneur, but fate seemed to have plans for her and, within a few short years, she found herself at the head of a company that was making more money than she'd ever dreamed of.

Abi still couldn't believe there was so much money to be made from tea towels, wallpaper and tablecloths, but there had been something special in her designs – something unique and fresh that the world was ready for and Abi had been flattered and had gone along for the ride. She would have been crazy not to. And how wonderful it had been to see her designs in shops. At first, she opened a small concession in a department store, but it had done so well that it soon became apparent that she would need her own shop. So she slowly built a team around her and they had managed very well to begin with, designing a website and handling each and every order themselves. They felt that they knew their customers individually and there was a real sense of family about the business.

Then the crazy times began with more shops opening and more staff being hired, staff that other staff were hiring. Branches began opening all over the country and then abroad, with their first shop in Paris. It had been such an exciting time and Abi had genuinely loved seeing the international appetite for her designs. But things had moved so far away from what she wanted now and, for the past couple of years, she hadn't felt in control anymore. She'd slowly morphed from creator to business woman and it was a role she didn't feel cut out for. On top of that was the fact that she was surrounded by so many people who were there to make decisions for the company – decisions that Abi couldn't make on her own. It all felt so *big*. That might have seemed like a feeble complaint to most people and some might have thought her foolish for walking away from her little empire when it was doing so well, but Abi knew that she had to get out. It didn't feel like *her* anymore. Somewhere along the way, Abigail Carey had gone missing. The young artist who had sat at her kitchen table, lost in her work, had been swallowed up in a company that had grown so fast, that not only had it made her head spin but she was in fear of losing her very mind.

So she had walked away. The newspapers were full of the story and, quite predictably, some had thought her crazy. But was it really important what strangers thought? Abi believed not. In fact, she believed that if she examined her critics' lives that she would think them crazy. For we can't live one another's lives. Each of us, Abi reasoned, had their own vision of what their life should be and Abi's had moved so far away from her vision that she had to do something drastic.

Now, sitting in the home she no longer wanted to live in and with no other home on the horizon, she wondered if she'd made a terrible mistake.

Autumn turned to winter and the Sussex landscape was shrouded in mist and rain. Edward stood shivering in one of the first floor rooms, gazing out over the countryside that was almost unrecognisable from that golden autumn day when he'd moved in. He'd taken a walk earlier in the day while the workmen had been making more noise than he could cope with. He'd followed the path from the hall which wound its way up the grassy slope of the down, the mist wet on his face and the scent of smoke spiralling up from the cottages in the village. Winter was definitely here, he'd mused, thinking of how very aware he was now of the passing seasons. Living in London, it was easy to be sheltered from the changes in the weather. Concrete didn't blossom, and you could go whole weeks without seeing anything green if you were a workaholic as he was. But he was making changes now, wasn't he? He was making time to see things, to hear them and smell them, to absorb them into his very being.

However, tuning into the senses wasn't always such a good idea when you were surrounded by noisy workmen and their power tools. Edward had known that Winfield Hall needed a lot of work and he'd been prepared with a team of surveyors, architects and builders on standby for when all the paperwork was completed but the reality of the work was something else. One could never really prepare oneself for the intense noise and the constant dust in the air.

He made a little home for himself on the ground floor near the kitchen and set up his laptop so he could work and he'd bought an airbed for when he stayed overnight. It was kind of fun. A bit like camping only under ornate plaster ceilings. And it surprised him how very little he needed in order to function. Other than food and toiletries, a laptop, a bed, a kettle and a mug were pretty much it.

October mists turned into November sleet and that revealed the true state of the roof. An army of buckets were deployed as repairs were begun before the worst of the winter weather hit.

'It could be worse,' one of the builders told him. 'But it will mean a delay.'

Of course, Edward thought sagely.

December showed the true horror of the rotting timbers behind some of the walls in the north wing, and there was woodworm, death watch beetle, rising damp and dry rot as well as crumbling plasterwork and blocked chimneys. All had to be fixed before the conversion into apartments began. It was a massive undertaking that came to a complete standstill with the onset of the Christmas holidays and New Year.

And then January came. Edward had been prepared for the extent of the work needed, but he hadn't quite expected the nightmare that was exposed once walls were knocked down. Hundreds of years of horrors which had been patched up and covered over now needed attention. Builders from the past had chosen the wrong materials or taken shortcuts and everything was now being exposed and left for Edward to finance. Of course, he'd set aside a sum of money which he'd thought would be adequate for the restoration of the hall. He'd even topped it up after his second viewing, guessing that there'd be a few of those little unforeseen jobs that older properties had a habit of hiding from prospective buyers even after a full structural survey. Now, he shook his head at his optimism. There were no *little jobs* at Winfield Hall; they were all *massive* jobs.

A whole city of scaffolding had been set up and Edward had lost count of the number of workers who were now coming and going. He was heartily glad that he'd hired a project manager to take care of it all, and he was kind of glad of his commitment in London because he wasn't sure he'd have been able to cope with the stress of all the noise and seeing whole ceilings and walls being pulled down.

It was the end of January when they hit another problem. Max, the project manager, called Edward to give him the news.

'Do you need me on site?' Edward had asked from his office in London.

'Trust me – you're going to want to see this,' Max had told him.

So Edward drove down.

Max was outside, pacing up and down.

'What is it?' Edward asked, almost dreading the answer but needing to hear it quickly.

'Subsidence,' Max said. The word to strike terror in any new property owner.

Edward sighed and Max proceeded to show him the damage. It had come up in a survey as a possibility but Edward had somehow managed to put that to the back of his mind. The whole of the east wing was affected. It could be fixed, Max assured him, but it would delay all the other work on that part of the house and, of course, would mean an extra bill. A very sizeable bill.

'Do what's needed,' Edward told him.

Max nodded. 'Sure thing.'

It was the only option, Edward told himself. You couldn't do half a job on a place like Winfield or start gilding on rotten foundations especially if he wanted to rent apartments to other people. He couldn't let out rooms in a house that was slowly sinking, could he?

He went for a walk after that to try and clear his head. He took the route through the village, passing the huddle of cottages hunkering close together under their thatched roofs as if in an attempt to keep warm. Looking at them now, Edward almost envied their simplicity and smallness. Just think how easy it would be to live in a cottage. How practical it would be to heat and maintain it. You could virtually see the whole property at once, he thought with a grin. There would be very little to surprise you with a cottage, he believed. Or, if there were any issues, they would be relatively easy and cheap to deal with.

But Edward hadn't chosen to live in a cottage. He'd chosen a sprawling Georgian mansion. And he had the bills to prove it. He shook his head. It was only money after all, he told himself, and what was money for if not to spend? He'd just have to make some more. Besides, things were bound to get better soon. It would be spring before he knew it and his energy would pick up then as it usually did, with the promise of warmer weather when he could start to enjoy wild swimming again. And then winter and all the work and the money spent on renovations would be behind him and he'd have the summer to look forward to. He could spend more time outdoors then, enjoying the garden and the countryside. Now, *that*, Edward thought, was something to look forward to.

But little did he know the news that February would bring.

CHAPTER FOUR

There had been no warning signs. Nobody had suspected what was about to happen and it was the very last thing Edward had thought would happen to him.

He was made redundant.

It was nothing personal, his boss had said. Your work is good. Second to none. Only it seemed he *was* second to somebody at the company his was merging with. A number of his colleagues had suffered the same fate too. Within a week, he'd gone from having his own office to being forced to clear his desk. There was a redundancy package, of course, but that would only go so far. Edward was pretty sure some of his clients would come with him in time, but most, he feared, would stay loyal to his firm. A firm that hadn't stayed loyal to him, he couldn't help thinking bitterly.

And what about him? What was he going to do? He'd been at the company for twelve years and had never even considered working for anybody else. How long would it take him to secure another position somewhere? Or maybe even set up on his own? Because that was looking like a very real option now.

But a little voice told him that these things would take time and he needed money now to pay all the people who were working at Winfield. Not only were there wages to pay but there were materials to buy as well as the basic running costs of such a large property. For the first time since taking on the project, Edward felt unsure of himself. It was one thing when you had a full-time wage coming in, but quite another to be cast adrift. Winfield was relying on him and he wasn't at all sure that he could do the place justice anymore. The last thing he wanted to do was to let it down. The old place deserved better than that. So what were his options? He couldn't spend money that he didn't have and Winfield needed a lot of money, not just now but in the future too. Could Edward rely on himself one hundred percent to provide that money and to secure the future of Winfield? He could no longer be certain, and that was a feeling that left him shaken to his core.

After several sleepless nights on his airbed, Edward called Stephen and invited him over.

'Well, you know I've always thought you were crazy to take this place on,' Stephen said as he paced up and down the hallway, glancing up at the grand staircase which swept like a graceful centrepiece in a classic film. Indeed, one half expected Vivien Leigh to appear at the top of it.

'Crazy? You congratulated me for buying it!' Edward pointed out, remembering the day of the auction quite clearly and how chuffed Stephen had seemed.

'I was just being supportive,' Stephen said. 'It was what you wanted, wasn't it?'

'I still want it.'

'You mean, you're not going to sell it?'

'I couldn't. At least, not properly.'

'What do you mean?'

Edward ran a hand through his hair. 'I've had an idea. I'm

not sure if it's just – well – ridiculous or not. But I'm not sure how many options I have.'

'What are you going to do?' Stephen asked.

'I was hoping you might be able to help with that decision.'

'You don't need money from me, do you?' Stephen had turned quite white.

'Don't panic!' Edward told him. 'It's not money I need from you. It's information.'

'Well, that's a relief. What sort of information?'

'About that woman.'

'What woman?'

'My underbidder.'

Stephen frowned. 'The woman at the auction?'

'Yes. What do you know about her?'

'Only what I told you before. She's famous for those sunflower designs. Has quite a few shops. Or *had* a few shops. I think she sold her business.'

'Do you know why?'

'Not really. Just a headline I saw in one of those Sunday supplements.'

'What's her name again?'

'Abigail Carey.'

'And that was the name of her business?'

Stephen nodded. 'What's all this about?'

'Well, it's just an idea at the moment.'

'Oh, yeah?' Stephen raised his eyebrows and grinned.

'Not *that* sort of an idea! A business proposition.'

'Okay,' Stephen said slowly. 'How's that going to work?'

'Well, I've got a bit of background work to do first,' Edward said, 'but let me tell you the rough plan.'

≈

Edward wasn't at all sure that Stephen was on board with his idea but, as with the day he'd purchased Winfield, his friend gave him his full support.

'I guess it's your call,' Stephen told him before he left. 'Let me know how it goes, won't you? Or if you need me to come and bail you out if she turns out to be a mad woman.' He'd chuckled at that, but it did leave Edward questioning his own judgement. This idea of his might not be such a good one after all. Still, he wanted to find out more and there was only one thing you did in the modern world when you wanted to find out about somebody. You googled them.

Edward had to admit that he was surprised how much coverage there was on Abigail Carey. She was quite famous, he realised. And beautiful, with long vanilla-blonde hair that curled down to her shoulders, large blue eyes and what he believed was described as a peaches and cream complexion. Not that that had anything to do with, well, *anything*, but he couldn't help making the observation. And there were plenty of photos of her online – interviews on websites, features in online newspapers and fan sites for her shop and products. It was pretty impressive, he had to admit.

Then he read the news reports of her having sold her business and he frowned. Why had she done that? It was a sound business that was doing well. That concerned Edward for a moment, but then he realised she had money because she had been bidding for Winfield Hall, hadn't she? And maybe she was starting another company. Entrepreneurs often did that, didn't they? Perhaps she was the sort that started one project and then got bored and moved on to a new venture. Yes, he thought, that was probably it. Anyway, he could always ask her. If they were going to be partners, it would only be fair to know where they stood with each other. Perhaps he'd ask to see her business plan. That would put his mind at rest, wouldn't it? But what if she asked to see his? It was all right him sitting in judgement of her, but what if she wanted to know his plans? He'd been made redundant – what would she make of that?

But you also own Winfield, he told himself, and she wanted Winfield.

Anyway, maybe she was retired now. Maybe she didn't have any plans to work again. He wasn't sure how he felt about that. Well, he was actually. He thought it was very strange indeed. A person needed an occupation, he believed. One shouldn't just sit around all day without a purpose. He would have to make sure she wasn't one of *those* types of people. He didn't think he could bear that.

Switching his laptop off, he put the kettle on and wandered through to the hallway, dipping in and out of the rooms the builders had been working in earlier that day. It seemed eerily quiet now that they'd gone, the rooms returning to their natural state of silence. For a moment, Edward wondered what it would be like to live here alone – to have so much space all to himself, but he quickly dismissed the thought. Not only was it impractical, but he wasn't at all sure he'd enjoy the reality of living in such a large place on his own. He wasn't exactly a gregarious person. He didn't need people around him all the time and he'd always valued his privacy, but he liked the idea of people being nearby. In their own homes, of course.

Anyway, it was becoming very clear that he couldn't afford to live in Winfield on his own. Not that he'd ever planned that. It was much too large a property for one single man. And, seeing that he'd always planned to let out a percentage of the space as apartments, where was the harm in taking that idea further?

Abigail had been sitting at her desk overlooking the river. She'd given herself the exquisite pleasure of opening a brand new sketchbook that morning and had been doodling in it ever since, careful to switch her phone off and to ignore her computer. The February light was a soft dove-grey and Abi had had a crisp, brisk walk first thing. Now, she was settling down to some work. Well, not work really. She had allowed her mind to wander and her pencil to do its own thing. She wasn't quite sure which direction she was going in and she didn't want to put any pressure on herself. After the recent sale of her company and the press interest, she wanted to create a safe little cocoon with her work. She needed to get back to basics and remember her first love of drawing. When had she last just sat down and doodled? She really couldn't remember and that made her sad.

Her pencil paused in mid-stroke and she glanced out of the window and then she did something that was fatal: she looked at her computer. It was after eleven. Maybe she should check her email? Just quickly. She wouldn't hang around and get sucked in – she'd just do a quick sweep to make sure she wasn't missing something important, and she wouldn't make the mistake of going to any social media sites. Since people had been tagging her and sending all sorts of hateful messages for leaving her company, Abi had closed all her accounts down. By simply removing them and herself, she'd managed to reclaim a certain amount of peace in her life, but she still couldn't get some of those messages out of her head. Why were some people so nasty? Why did they feel so entitled to jump into her life and give their opinion? She'd never have dreamed of reaching out to others in the way that some had reached out to her. It was truly baffling. But that was the crux of social media, wasn't it? Everyone had their little corner of the universe from where they could shout and be heard. Well, Abi wasn't going to listen anymore.

Trying to put all thought of online negativity out of her mind, she checked her email. There was the usual stuff – messages from friends checking up on her. Another from her sister who was complaining about the latest drama with her children. Then there were the companies reaching out to her hoping to woo her with a job offer or secure an endorsement for their products. The thing was, Abi had signed a non-compete clause when she'd sold her company so her hands were tied for the next few years. She'd wanted freedom and now she had it.

As she scrolled through the messages, there was one that caught her eye. It was from somebody called Edward Townsend – a name she didn't recognise. But she definitely recognised the name in the subject heading.

Winfield Hall.

She clicked on the message.

Dear Miss Carey

I'm the new owner of Winfield Hall and it's been brought to my attention that you were my underbidder. I have a unique proposition for you and would like to invite you to Winfield at your earliest convenience. I don't want to sound overly dramatic, but this house needs you.

Yours sincerely
Edward Townsend

Abi sat staring at the message. The last person she'd ever expected to hear from was the new owner of Winfield Hall and he said he had a *unique proposition* for her. Why would he say something like that? Why not just say, can you help me with the decorating, as most people asked? It was perplexing. She thought about emailing him back to explain that she wasn't really doing interior decorating anymore. In fact, she'd never really done it in the past either. It was just one of those common misconceptions people had about her. She could do it, though. She'd helped many of her friends out, producing mood boards and helping them choose fabrics and papers from her own designs. It was always fun and she couldn't wait to see how she could help the new owner of Winfield. But there was a part of her that wondered if it would hurt too much to see the place knowing that it could never be hers.

Still, curiosity got the better of her and she emailed him back.

Dear Mr Townsend
    Would tomorrow at eleven o'clock suit you?
    Best wishes
    Abigail Carey

Five minutes later, she got his reply saying, yes, that would indeed suit him.

Abigail set off for the drive down to Sussex on a particularly fine morning. It was good to get out of the city and she wound her window down as soon as she turned off the main road towards the village that she'd once thought would be her home. The February air was chilly but delicious and she inhaled deeply as much to calm her nerves as to shake the last vestiges of London from her lungs.

She turned into the steep lane that led away from the village, following it around several bends until it became a track.

Driving over a cattle grid a moment later, the rumble of her car tyres seemed to mark the entrance into another world and Abi could feel her shoulders losing some of the tension from her long drive. She took a long, deep breath, the silver-blue freshness of the air so clear and sharp and heady. The landscape of the South Downs opened up to her right, its proud hills rising up sharply to the very heavens.

And then she gasped as she glanced left. There it was – golden and graceful in the late winter sunshine. Winfield Hall. How strange it was to see it again and to know that somebody was living there. Somebody that wasn't her. It wasn't in Abi's nature to be bitter, but she couldn't help feeling the same sadness she'd felt on leaving the auction room that day. She hadn't got this place out of her system yet, had she? Perhaps she never would.

Slowing her car down as she entered the sweep of gravelled driveway in front of the house, she noted the other vehicles and two large skips, and she could hear the sound of banging coming from inside. It seemed odd that Mr Townsend was thinking about decorating already when the builders were still at work, but maybe he'd found a quiet little corner of the hall to call his own and wanted to get that just right so he had somewhere to escape to.

She sat in her car for a moment, gazing up at the hall's large sash windows. It was a true beauty and she wished with all her heart that she'd been able to make that winning bid. But could she have done it? Should she have risked everything and saddled herself with a massive mortgage just after walking out on her company? As she sat in her car now, gazing at the friendly face of the building that she loved so much, a part of her berated herself for not pushing just a little bit harder to make the place her own.

Abi reached across to the passenger seat where she'd placed

a small portfolio of her work, taking it with her as she got out of the car and walked across the driveway. She remembered the last time she had done so and how she'd had that remarkable feeling of coming home. Well, so much for premonitions, she told herself.

The front door was open and she went inside, mindful of the workmen all around her and wondering if she should be wearing a hard hat. Sure enough, a burly looking man approached her, a frown on his dusty face.

'You can't come in here, love,' he said gruffly. 'It's not safe.'

'I'm looking for Mr Townsend.'

'He's not in here. Try the back.' He pointed with a stubby finger. 'But be *careful!*'

She nodded.

Walking in the vague direction the builder had pointed, Abi passed the magnificent staircase, glancing up just as a shower of dust descended. She coughed and kept walking.

As she left the noise of the building work behind, she could hear the voice of a man on the phone and followed that, hoping it might be Mr Townsend. Sure enough, she saw him a moment later in a large room overlooking the downs which was empty save for a desk with a laptop on it and what looked like an airbed on the floor. She grinned. This was obviously his home for the time being.

She gave a little wave as he glanced up from his call and saw her for the first time. She didn't recognise him from the auction, but he had dark sandy hair and a nice, open face, Abi decided and, despite being surrounded by builders, he looked as neat and crisp as if he was putting in a day at the office, albeit in jeans and a casual shirt. Some people had that ability, didn't they? To look neat and tidy even when slumming it and Mr Townsend, she thought, was one of those people.

She watched as he ended his call and strode across the room, hand outstretched towards her.

'Miss Carey?'

'Abigail, please.'

'Abigail,' he said, an awkward smile on his face. 'Sorry about the call. Chaos here.'

'I can see,' she said, returning his smile only a little less awkwardly, she hoped.

There was a kind of tension in his expression and a furrowing on his brow that spoke of worries and stress.

'I'm Edward Townsend.'

'Yes,' she said. 'And is it Edward or Eddie or Ed perhaps?'

'No, it's Edward,' he said seriously.

'Right.'

'Thank you for coming, by the way.'

'I was surprised to get your email,' she confessed.

'It seems a bit early to be thinking about wallpaper.'

He frowned. 'Excuse me?'

'Wallpaper,' she repeated. 'That is why you called me, isn't it? I've brought my portfolio.' She showed him the folder she was carrying as he was still looking confused.

'I think there's been a misunderstanding.' He glanced around the room. 'Listen, let me get you a drink. Tea? Coffee?'

'Tea, please.'

'Good. Then I'll explain – erm – what's going on.'

Abi watched as he walked across to a little table at the far corner of the room with tea-making things on it.

'Things are a little primitive here,' he said, 'but at least it's clean. The kitchen isn't fit for humans at the moment apart from the new fridge.' He switched the kettle on.

'You've been living here full-time?' Abi asked.

'Er, no. I'm back and forth between London and my work. That is...' he paused. 'Yes. Back and forth.'

Abi nodded, wondering what he'd been about to say.

'Milk? Sugar?'

'Just black, thank you.'

He handed her the mug and motioned to a pair of office chairs by his desk and they both sat down. Abi was growing more and more curious as he closed his laptop and then cleared his throat.

'Were you very upset not to make the winning bid on Winfield?' he suddenly asked.

Abi's mouth dropped open. She hadn't expected such a blunt question.

'Yes,' she told him, thinking it merited a blunt answer. 'I was.'

He nodded as if he'd known.

'Have you been looking at other places since?' he asked.

She sighed. 'I have.' She shrugged. 'Nothing like this has come up again.'

'No. It is a one of a kind, isn't it?'

Abi shifted uncomfortably in her chair. 'I hope you didn't bring me here just to gloat over winning the auction.'

Edward looked mortified. 'God, no!' he cried.

'Because that's how it's feeling at the moment.'

'No, no. You misunderstand. I'd never do that. I asked you here because things have changed for me since the auction. My *situation* has changed.' He sighed and Abi thought that he looked as if he was in pain.

'What's happened?' she asked gently.

He looked directly at her then and she noticed that his eyes were clear hazel.

'Things have got a little bit more expensive than I envisaged,' he began, 'and I envisaged a lot, believe me. I wouldn't have gone into a project like this blindly. I did my homework, but there's only so much you can guess will need doing on a project like this and it isn't until you start physically taking walls down and going up into the roof that you realise the full extent of the work that needs doing.'

'I see,' Abi said, wondering what this all had to do with her and realising that he probably hadn't invited here on the strength of her wallpaper designs.

'No, I don't think you do.'

'What is it you want to talk to me about?' Abi asked him. 'I still don't understand why I'm here.'

He nodded. 'I have a proposition for you. A proposition that doesn't involve wallpaper or decorating or anything like that.'

'You're selling Winfield?'

His face darkened. 'Good lord, no! That is – not the whole place. I've invested too much and I want to see this project through. But I am going to sell half of it.'

Abi frowned. 'Half?'

He nodded. 'I'm afraid I have to. You see, I've just been made redundant. Winfield was already taking all of my money, but I should have been able to manage. What I didn't factor in was, well, this happening.'

'I'm so sorry to hear that,' Abi told him sincerely.

'Thanks, I'm still trying to process everything. But one thing I have processed is that I'm not giving this place up. I'll do whatever I can to keep it and if that means selling half of it then so be it.'

Abi had literally been sitting on the edge of her seat throughout this revelation, but she sat back now, slowly digesting what he'd told her.

'What do you think?' he asked her. 'I mean, you were the first person I thought of.'

Abi placed her unfinished cup of tea on the floor beside her chair. 'You're asking if I want to buy half of Winfield Hall?'

'Yes,' Edward said. 'That's it exactly.' He sounded relieved now that it was out.

'And you've not approached anybody else?'

'I didn't really want to go through the rigmarole of putting the place on the market. Not if I didn't need to.'

'So I can go ahead today and buy half of Winfield – right now – if I wanted to?'

'Well, I thought we could get to know one another a little. Maybe ask each other a few questions? I mean, if this is something you want to do, perhaps it would be a good idea to make sure we get along together.'

Abi nodded. 'This is rather a lot to take in,' she confessed, feeling slightly spaced out by what she'd been presented with.

'I know. I didn't know how else to ask you,' Edward said. 'I mean, it wouldn't have been right over the phone, would it?'

It was then that something occurred to her.

'How did you find me? I mean, how did you know who I was?'

Edward cleared his throat. 'My friend recognised you at the auction.'

'Oh, I see.'

'You're something of a celebrity, I believe.'

'I wouldn't say that.'

'People recognise you,' Edward pointed out.

'Not very often.'

'Well, I'm glad my friend did,' he said, and then he glanced away as if embarrassed.

Abi got up from the chair and walked across to the window, gazing out over the expanse of the downs.

'How do you propose to divide the house?'

Edward got up and joined her. 'It would be pretty straightforward actually. I've spoken to my builder about it.'

'So where would the division go?'

'Well, the staircase is central and it seems that the house naturally divides itself from there into two sides. So everything to the left of it upstairs and downstairs would make up one half, and then the right-hand side both up and down would be the other half.'

Abi thought about this for a moment. 'And do you have a preference?'

Edward smiled as he gazed out of the window. 'I've kind of got used to this side.'

'With the view of the downs?'

'Yes.'

'I suppose it's only right that you get first choice,' Abi admitted reluctantly.

'I suppose so.' He looked back at her.

'And how are you proposing to half the place?' Abi asked. 'I mean, will you be putting up walls and barriers and things?'

'Nothing that restrictive. Nothing that will detract from the character of the place.'

Abi nodded, relieved to hear this.

'Listen,' she said, 'this is a bit of a bombshell, I have to admit, and I'm not quite sure what to think. Would you mind if I took a look around the garden? I often think better outdoors.'

'Okay,' Edward said. 'I'll be here if you need me. Oh, and there's a hard hat on the windowsill by the front door. You'll need to put that on if you're looking around the rooms.'

'Thank you.'

They looked at each other, an awkward sort of silence falling between them. Then Abi pointed to the door.

'I'll be in the garden then. For a bit.'

She left the room and walked back down the corridor that led to the entrance hall, her ears assaulted by the builders' noise.

Escaping out into the fresh air, she took a deep, settling breath as she glanced up at the hills. The bright sky had darkened now and there was a mist hanging over the downs. As she rounded the hall towards the walled garden at the back of the house she thought that it truly was the House in the Clouds today. That was its nickname, wasn't it? The estate agent had told her that and she'd remembered it. Looking back at it now, her heart swelled with love for the place.

And it could be yours, a little voice told her.

Well, half of it could be hers. If she wanted it. And did she? Could she? Would Edward Townsend interview her formally before she was allowed to purchase the half he loved the least. How would this all work? She wasn't at all sure, but she was sure of something – the deep, unsettling, wonderful feeling of excitement, like a great big bubble about to burst inside her. And that told her one thing – she *had* to make this work. Every other property she'd looked at had left her feeling empty and frustrated because she'd known in her heart that Winfield was the one. She'd known it the first moment she'd seen it and she knew it now. Even if that meant sharing it.

Okay, she told herself, *think*. Don't get carried away by this.

She looked up at the hills, now shrouded in low cloud, admiring the dark beauty of the day. It was a true testament to her love of the place if she could adore it as much on a cold, winter's day as she could on a golden autumn one. But adore it she did. Walking around the garden, she noted once again the long red-brick wall and the lean-to greenhouse with its missing panes of glass. How she longed to breathe new life into it and to raise seedlings here and to grow as many sunflowers as she could within the safe, warm walls.

If Edward was making his home to the left of the staircase, that would give Abi the rooms and the garden to the right. As she looked around them now, working out the position of the sun during the day and how easy it would be to grow her beloved sunflowers, she felt her heart flooding with peace. Of course, if she accepted Edward's proposal to buy half of Winfield, it wouldn't be the same as being its sole owner, she knew that, but that wasn't an option, was it? She had hoped to run art courses and to lease rooms to arty types and turn Winfield into a delightful retreat from the world. Would that be an option if she didn't own the whole place? Would Edward become a sort of landlord or boss over her? She'd have to find out exactly how this would work before she let her heart run away with her and she ended up crushed for a second time.

The front door was still open when she returned to the hall and, as she entered, a builder was coming towards her with a wheelbarrow full of rubble. She quickly grabbed the hard hat Edward had told her to wear and put it on.

'Excuse me!' he said cheerily and Abi smiled, wondering if some of that rubble was from what might well be her half of Winfield.

'No,' she told herself. 'Facts first. Fantasies later.'

She popped her head round the doors of a few of the rooms, reacquainting herself with the place, but it was so dusty and noisy that she finally gave up the idea of a proper house tour and returned to the room Edward was in, knocking lightly on the door which had been left ajar.

'Hey,' he said, turning around from his laptop.

'Thank you.'

'What for?'

'Giving me some time to walk around and think.'

'Can I get you another tea?'

She shook her head. 'How much?'

His eyes widened. 'You mean...'

'How much would you be selling half of Winfield for?'

Edward leaned across his table and picked up an envelope, handing it to Abi. She opened it and took out a sheet of paper on which was a neatly typed price together with his contact details. She folded the sheet and placed it back in the envelope.

'Are you going to keep me in suspense?' he asked with a nervous kind of laugh.

'No,' she said. 'I'm interested.'

'You are?'

'But I have a few questions as I'm sure you do of me.'

'Okay, good,' he said. 'You want to sit down?'

Abi shook her head. 'I'm too hyped up to sit down.' She walked towards the window and gazed up into the misty hills.

'What are your plans for Winfield?' she asked.

'You mean my half if you buy in with me?'

'Yes.'

'I'm going to split the place up into apartments.'

'Apartments? You're not going to sell them, are you?' Abi asked. It was what she'd been dreading for the fate of Winfield – to become a collection of second homes for people based in London. They'd be left unloved for weeks on end.

'No, I'm going to lease them. They'll make a good income and enable me to live here.'

'I see. And how will you decide who rents them?'

'Well, I want professional people who appreciate a beautiful space but who aren't going to be partying in it every weekend.'

Abi smiled. 'Good. I value peace and quiet.'

'Me too. And I want to keep the leases short. You know – in case we do need to get rid of anyone.'

Abi noted his use of the word 'we' then. Already, he was thinking of them as co-owners.

'What would you do with your half?' he asked.

'The same. Make a few apartments to rent out.'

'Really?'

Abi nodded, deciding to hide the fact that she wanted artists in her half. She wasn't yet sure how he'd react to that announcement and she didn't want to risk losing the opportunity to live here.

'Then we're on the same page,' he said.

'It certainly looks like it.'

There was a pause, but Abi could tell that Edward had something he wanted to say.

'What is it?' she asked him.

'Why did you sell your company?'

'Excuse me?'

'I'm interested in why you sold your company.'

Abi frowned at him. 'You researched me?'

'Yes, of course. As I would before any serious business transaction.'

Abi bit her lip, trying not to laugh.

'Are you telling me you *didn't* research me?' he asked.

'I might have popped your name into a search engine,' she confessed, feeling her cheeks flush. 'But everyone does that these days, don't they? Even if you're just meeting somebody for coffee.'

'And what did you find?'

'Nothing much.'

'No. My former employer has already taken my details down from the website so I no longer officially exist. So, why did you sell your company?'

Abi decided that there was no use hiding the truth. 'It got too big.'

'What do you mean?'

'The company. It was all too much and too many of everything. Too many shops, too many people, too many decisions. It had got so far away from what I wanted to do with my life that I felt selling was the only decision left to me.'

'And you just walked away?'

'Yes,' she said. 'It was quite easy really.'

Edward looked astounded by her declaration. 'But you're going to start a new company now?'

'What makes you say that?'

'Well, I just assumed...'

She shook her head. 'I need some space for a while. I need to be free again.' She saw the look of panic on his face. 'That doesn't bother you, does it?'

'Erm, well, I've just never met anyone who...' he faltered.

'What?'

'Who didn't want to work.'

'But I *do* want to work. And I'm working all the time. But it has to be on my own terms and what I was doing before really wasn't on my own terms anymore. It turned into something quite different.' Abi stared at him. 'Are you worried I'm not viable as a partner in this?'

'No, no.'

'Because you sound worried.'

'I'm not. I trust you.'

'Are you sure?' she asked him.

'I just wanted to know – well – a bit about you. I have to admit that I was a little bit anxious to hear that you'd walked away from your own company. I mean, will you walk away from this project if you tire of it?' he asked.

'I might.' Abi saw him blanch and realised that it had been the wrong thing to say. 'But I won't,' she quickly added.

'How do you know for sure?'

'Because this place is in my heart.'

'Is it?' he looked surprised.

'Yes! Every damp, dusty, crumbly inch of it.'

He gave a tiny smile. 'Mine too.'

'And the truth is, owning half of Winfield is better than owning the whole of anything else,' she told him candidly.

'I feel the same.'

'I haven't found anything that comes close to this place,' she told him, knowing that she shouldn't be showing all her cards in this way, but she just couldn't help it. This place, this glorious place, had that effect on her. She had to be honest about it.

'I'm glad you've told me that.'

'So do we have a deal? Am I going to purchase half of Winfield Hall?'

He looked a little hesitant for a moment, but then – to Abi's great relief – he held his hand out towards her. 'We have a deal.'

Abi shook his hand and beamed him a smile. 'Well, I guess I'd better get back and start organising things my end.'

'Then we'll keep in touch?'

'Of course,' she opened her handbag and pulled out a business card. 'My number.'

'Thank you.'

'Shall I see myself out? I know the way.'

He nodded and she made to leave. 'Abigail?'

She turned around. 'Yes?'

'Thank you. I mean, I'm glad it's you. You seem... you seem the right sort of person.' He grimaced. 'Sorry, that sounded pompous and condescending. What I mean is, you seem the right sort of person for this place. You appreciate it in the same way that I do.'

Abi smiled. 'Thank you.'

'It is special, isn't it? It is worth saving?' There was that anxious look of his that Abi had noticed earlier as if he wasn't at all sure of himself and needed a little reassurance.

'Of course it is,' she told him. 'It's the most perfect place in the world!'

CHAPTER FIVE

Abi sat in her car feeling stunned. She wasn't sure what she'd expected from being invited to Winfield by Edward Townsend, but it hadn't been this. She had to bite her lip in order to stop herself from screaming with joy at the turn of events. She was going to *live* here. Her heart had known it all along and yet she'd allowed herself to slip into despair when the auction hadn't gone her way. But fate was bigger than any auction. A dream couldn't be stopped, could it? It would find you somehow.

After leaving Edward, Abi had walked around the garden once again, knowing that she needed to burn off some of her nervous energy before she got into her car for the drive home.

Home, she thought, now that she was in the car. *This* was going to be her home. This special place that she loved so dearly. Of course, she was only getting half of Winfield, but that was enough. It was a compromise for sure, but it was one she was happy to make because, until a few hours ago, she wasn't getting *any* of Winfield. The place had belonged to somebody else. Edward.

She thought about Edward Townsend now. She'd liked him

and yet there was something guarded about him. Hadn't he said that today would be about getting to know each other? Well, she hadn't learned a thing about him and he'd only asked her a couple of questions about her business. Was that all he wanted to know about her? Whether or not she was a viable source of much-needed income for Winfield? He didn't need to know about her thoughts and feelings about the world or anything about her family. He hadn't even asked if she was married or not, but perhaps he'd read that she wasn't in an online interview. There was enough about her private life online to sate even the most ardent fan.

And should she have asked more about him? Surely he'd have mentioned if he had a wife and five screaming children? She'd noticed that he hadn't been wearing a wedding ring, but plenty of people didn't. Maybe she should ask him when she got home. Drop him a quick email and say – by the way, is there a Mrs Townsend? Would that sound odd? Would he think she was a desperate single woman in search of not only a country estate but a husband too?

Abi smiled. She'd leave it. They both seemed happy to be doing business with each other and that, surely, was enough. So what would that make them to one another, she wondered? Edward wouldn't exactly be her landlord and he wasn't going to be her boss. And they didn't know each other well enough to be thought of as friends.

Neighbours, she decided at last. Yes, they would be neighbours. Or perhaps something a little more than neighbours with their shared love of Winfield uniting them in quite a unique bond. Together, they would tear away all the rotting bits of the place and help restore it to its former glory. They would breathe new life into the long-forgotten rooms, repair its broken windows, restore the long-neglected garden, paint each beautiful wall and fill it with fine things and happy people.

Partners, Abi thought. Perhaps she could think of her and Edward as being partners in restoration. That was rather a fine title, wasn't it? Yes, she liked that.

As she drove through the village and wound her way through the deep lanes of Sussex towards the motorway that would take her back to London, she knew that she was leaving a little piece of herself behind. A piece which she hoped to join once again very soon.

Edward Townsend looked at the business card Abigail Carey had given him. It was one of the prettiest he'd ever seen, featuring her signature sunflower. Edward was used to being handed dull beige business cards where the only highlight might be a slightly interesting font. This, though, was the card of an artistic soul. He didn't know too many of those. He didn't really get to meet them in his line of work.

His line of work. He baulked at the phrase. He was unemployed. But he was still a financial adviser, wasn't he? He had yet to make any clear decisions on his next move, but selling half of Winfield would, at least, buy him a little time. *Abigail* would buy him a little time. He'd liked her. He was still perplexed by a person who would just walk away from a successful company when it was at the height of its power, but he guessed he was going to have to try and understand that some people just didn't think the same way as he did.

But what a relief she'd said yes. Edward really hadn't wanted to go through the rigmarole of putting the property on the market again, albeit half of it. It would have been taken out of his hands if he'd done that and he wouldn't have been able to choose his buyer so easily. This way, he'd have total say in whom he shared Winfield with and it seemed a strange kind of fate that things had happened the way they had – with his friend having recognised the underbidder at the auction and her not having found another place yet and still being so very in love with Winfield. He'd seen that trait in her straight away. He'd watched as she'd glanced around the room he was in now and he'd seen that glorious glazed look upon her face as she'd taken in the view from the window. Indeed, Edward felt sure he wore the same look himself only perhaps he hid it better than Abigail did. He had the feeling that she was one for showing her emotions through both her art and her speech. It was one of the things he'd warmed to about her – she didn't waste time being cagey. She loved Winfield and she wasn't afraid to admit it. That was to be admired. So often in life, people hid behind artifice, saying things they didn't mean or things they thought others wanted to hear, and what was the point of that? It was hard enough trying to navigate one's way without having to deal with such nonsense. No, he thought, Abigail Carey was open and honest and kind. He could see that shining through her eyes.

He shook his head. Why he was suddenly thinking about Abigail's blue eyes, he didn't know. But she'd had a way of looking at him that had been both mesmerising and disconcerting – as if she could see into his very soul. As if – at the very least – she understood him and his love for Winfield. And that was what bonded them. That was why he was so glad he'd reached out to her and felt as if he'd made a good decision. He wasn't sure if anyone else would see it that way, though.

'You're really going to share Winfield?' Stephen said as he sat down on Edward's office chair.

'You know I was thinking of it,' Edward told him. 'It's the only way I can see of making it work financially. Why do you sound so surprised?'

'I don't know,' his friend said. 'I guess I never thought of you as a sharing sort of a person.'

'First time for everything,' Edward pointed out.

'I guess.'

'Anyway, I think it'll be pretty safe sharing with her. She's one of these artist types. They're usually quiet, aren't they?'

'But what if she plays the bagpipes for a hobby? Or likes to blast rock music while she paints?' Stephen said with a smirk.

Edward smiled at his teasing. 'Funnily enough, that's not the impression I get from her.'

'Well, it's a risk.'

'So is not doing the work that's needed on Winfield.'

Stephen glanced up at the ceiling that was giving him a plaster shower. 'Yes, I see what you mean.'

'She's a good sort,' Edward told him. 'I think we'll get on.'

Stephen had taken his phone out of his pocket.

'What are you doing?'

'Just looking her up again,' Stephen said. 'Ah, right!'

'What?'

'She's *very* pretty!'

Edward frowned. 'What's that got to do with anything?'

Stephen grinned. 'Well, I'd say it would be far easier to share one's home with a pretty girl than with an ugly one, wouldn't it? Oh, come on! That *had* to have something to do with it!'

'It certainly did not. She just happened to be my underbidder and feels the same way about this place as I do.'

'And you'll be very cosy here together, I'm sure.'

'Very funny!'

'Seriously, though,' Stephen added, 'I'm pleased you've found a way through this. I'd have offered to take half this place off you myself, but you know I can't stand big draughty rooms.'

Edward nodded in understanding. It wasn't everyone who

was willing to take on a cavernous old building and he knew his friend preferred his small London apartment with every single piece of technology a modern man could need.

'I love this place,' Edward suddenly declared. 'And I don't want to lose it.'

'Then you won't,' Stephen told him. 'I know you and you usually get what you want when you put your mind to something.'

Edward smiled. 'I do?'

'You *know* you do! Ever since our days at uni. You're always so focussed on what you want.'

He sighed. 'Well, that's good to know.'

'I can't wait to see what you and this woman–'

'*Abigail.*'

'Yes, Abigail. I can't wait to see what you both do with the place.'

When Abigail left her flat, she was surprised to see a paparazzo standing outside on the pavement. It had to be a slow day in the news for someone to bother with her, she couldn't help thinking. Unless he was after the young guy who'd just moved in down the street. Wasn't he some talent show winner? She didn't keep up to date with those sorts of things. Anyway, she disliked this sort of intrusion. Perhaps that was one of the reasons Winfield appealed to her so much. It was so wonderfully cut off from the rest of the world. It was, in fact, its very own world up in the hills like that, half hidden in the clouds during the winter months. She loved that. To her, it was so much more than a house – it was an *escape.*

As she walked to a nearby market to stock up on fresh supplies, she wondered how much of London she would truly miss. There was the convenience of being able to get absolutely anything one wanted within a few minutes, she acknowledged that. There was the theatre and the wonderful shows, the restaurants and the cafes, the colourful street life and the ever-changing window displays of the shops. Was she crazy to leave it all behind for the solitude of a house in the middle of nowhere? There was only one small shop and post office in the village of Winfield. Could that satisfy someone who'd lived in London all her life? Growing up in the suburbs, she and her sister, Ellen, had been aware of the great metropolis just a short tube ride away, but they'd rarely had the money to enjoy it until they were working themselves.

Abi thought for a moment about their slightly unusual childhood. They'd never known their father. He'd left when Abi was a baby and Ellen was just four. Ellen said she had no memory of him, only what her mother had told her and that hadn't exactly been happy recollections. The trouble was, Abi didn't really remember her mother either for she'd died when Abi was only six. It was something that wasn't really talked about, even to this day, Abi had just accepted it because she'd been so young, but she often wondered what had happened. She'd asked Ellen a few times, but she'd always been vague and quickly changed the subject. She'd been ten when it had happened and Abi guessed that Ellen remembered more about it all than she was letting on. Maybe it was painful for her. Abi wasn't sure. But Abi had never pushed her to say more.

After their mother had died, they'd gone to live with her sister. Aunt Claire was a no-nonsense sort of woman who did her job in raising her two nieces, but gave nothing more than she needed to. They were clothed, fed and schooled and then told to get jobs and a place of their own as soon as they were able to. Abi was kind of grateful for that sort of upbringing because it had made her independent. She'd never been afraid to be reliant only on herself and she felt lucky that she'd always had her art as an escape because that had provided a safe haven during those tricky early years.

Perhaps that was what was driving her now, she thought, with the purchase of her dream home and all the plans she had for it. Perhaps she knew that nobody but her was going to help her make her dreams come true. Nobody had knocked on her door and said, we believe there's a talented artist here who can run a brilliant new company. And nobody was going to take her by the hand and guide her to her perfect home. Although she supposed that Edward Townsend had sort of done that, hadn't he? She smiled at the thought. Anyway, Abi had learned that you made your own luck in life. She had discovered Winfield Hall and had made sure she was in the auction room that day. If she hadn't been, Edward Townsend would never have been able to reach out to her.

As she filled a paper bag with some peppers, she wondered how long it would be until she could move into Winfield. A whole month had passed since her visit. She'd swapped a few messages with Edward since then, but hadn't been down to Winfield since. What took so long with a bit of paperwork? Abi was always baffled by it. She was a cash buyer and she wanted to buy as much as Edward needed to sell. It was all agreed. So why did it take so long? It really was very frustrating. In her heart, she had already moved so it was exasperating that the world didn't move at the same pace.

Edward had warned her that work would continue on Winfield for the rest of the year if not longer. Abi was aware of that and of the noise and mess that would mean, but she couldn't wait to make it her home anyway and leave London behind. As much as she'd loved living there and growing her business, it was time for a change – a different pace of life. What was it she'd thought on the day she'd viewed Winfield?

She needed a place to breathe. That was it. She could no longer breathe in London.

Her sister had managed to escape the city when she got married, moving first to a pretty village in Hampshire and then to the outskirts of Brighton. Abi hadn't yet told Ellen of her own plans to leave London. She supposed she'd have to let her know at some point, especially as she'd be living in the same county as her sister.

As she filled a bag with apples, Abi thought of Ellen. When they'd been girls, they'd often been mistaken for twins as Abi had been tall for her age. They'd worn their hair the same – shoulder-length blonde curls, and their clothes were the same because their aunt didn't like shopping and just grabbed two of everything in the appropriate sizes.

But, now, Ellen Fraser wore her hair short. It was what Abi thought of as a busy mother's haircut – a style that you could tumble out of bed with and not pay the slightest bit of attention too. It was a shame, Abi thought, because it made her sister look older somehow, less feminine, perhaps, less soft around the edges. Aunt Claire would have approved, no doubt.

One of the reasons Abi had wanted to move to Sussex was to be closer to her sister. Well, if she was being absolutely honest with herself, it was to be closer to her nieces: ten-year old Bethanne and six-year old Rosie, whom she adored. She loved her role as aunt and spending time with them was always a treat. Something which couldn't be said for spending time with her sister, she mused.

It was a sad fact that Ellen Fraser nee Carey was one of life's pessimists. If there was a downside to anything, she would find it, focus on it and turn it into her reality. Abi, who was an unapologetic optimist, found that being with her sister was so emotionally draining that she tried to limit their time together. Abi had been known to ring ahead to try and gauge her sister's mood before committing to an actual visit. On several occasions, she'd also offered to take the girls out, thus leaving her sister some much-needed time to herself. Ellen always seemed delighted by this. Well, delighted in her own subdued way.

'You've *no* idea how much I need this time,' she'd say in her woebegone way when Abi arrived, her short hair dishevelled and a look of pure resignation to the agonies of life etched across her face.

Abi would grab the girls and sneak out as fast as they could. After all, there were only so many times you could say, 'Oh, no,' or 'Oh, dear,' or 'Well, I'm sure things will get better soon.'

But, oh, those nieces! They were worth a quick run in with their tormented mother. How Abi adored them and she was so looking forward to them visiting Winfield. They would love it, wouldn't they? With its many beautiful acres and easy access to the downs, there would be infinite possibilities for adventures. She'd just have to make sure Ellen didn't follow them around, pointing out rabbit holes where ankles could be twisted and bramble bushes that might scrape a little girl's skin.

Abi was never quite sure how Ellen's husband put up with her. Douglas Fraser worked in training – a job which meant he spent a fair amount of time away from home. This didn't please Ellen who often complained that she was, essentially, a single parent, bringing up their two children alone. Yet, whenever Douglas was home, Ellen would complain about that too. Perhaps he'd chosen his job very deliberately, Abi thought, knowing that it would allow him at least some respite from the constant barrage of complaints he received from his spouse.

Abi finished her shopping and walked back home along the river. The spring air was cool and she could feel strands of winter in it still. She wondered what Winfield looked like today. Would there be primroses opening in the garden? Would it be warmer or cooler up on the downs than in London?

As she reached home and put her shopping bags down, she got her phone out and called her sister.

'Hey, it's me,' she said a moment later.

'Abi. How are you?'

'I'm good. How are you?' she dared to ask.

'Oh, my god! You wouldn't *believe* what's going on here. We've got some guy in the back garden taking a tree down. It's been threatening to collapse for months and our neighbours have been kicking up a stink about it. But the noise, Abi!'

'It won't last forever.'

'And the *mess*! It's going to be left to me to tidy it all up, I know!'

'I'm sure it won't be as bad as you imagine,' Abi told her. She then listened to Ellen as she continued her rant against the tree guy, against the paper delivery boy who'd completely shredded the paper in the letterbox – *again*, and the local supermarket who'd given her the wrong change. Abi let Ellen get it all out of her system before she dared to speak.

'Listen, I was thinking of coming down tomorrow as it's Saturday and the girls will be home.'

'Were you? It's a bit late notice,' Ellen said.

'Oh, are you out?'

'No.'

Abi paused. The fact was that no time was ever convenient for Ellen. There was always some drama happening in her life and everything and everyone was an inconvenience. So Abi played her best card.

'I could take the girls out – give you a break. I mean, if Douglas isn't home and wanting to spend time with them.'

'No, he's still away.'

'And I've something to tell you.'

'What?'

'I want to tell you in person, don't I?' Abi said with a laugh.

'Well, I suppose you *could* come down. Heaven knows I could use a break from the girls.'

'Great! How about mid-morning? I could take the girls out for lunch by the sea.'

'As long as you don't pump them full of chips and ice cream,' Ellen warned.

'Ice cream – in March! You've got to be kidding,' Abi said with a grin, but she could almost smell the hot vinegar of the chips she was planning to buy for them all.

CHAPTER SIX

Abi always got excited about seeing her nieces and it was even more exciting now that she knew she'd soon be living closer to them. The drive from London was never a problem for her, but she'd welcome being nearer to her family in the future.

She passed the turn off for Winfield and it was hard not to make a detour, but it would be weird if Edward caught her there, wouldn't it? The place wasn't hers yet and she didn't want to intrude and so she continued on her way towards Brighton and to the comfortable Victorian home where Ellen lived.

She parked on the street outside when she arrived. Ellen didn't like her taking up the driveway even though there was always plenty of room.

'You never know when someone might call,' Ellen told her.

Abi wondered why her sister never considered that Abi was actually *someone*.

Ringing the doorbell a moment later, she heard the excited thunder of footsteps in the hall beyond the front door which was a smart navy with a small pane of stained glass.

'Aunt Abi!' Rosie, who was six, skipped and jumped her way towards Abi before leaping into her arms.

'Sweetheart! How are you?' Abi laughed.

'Your hair's longer!' Rosie told her.

'Is it? I suppose it is.' It was true that, since leaving her company, Abi had gently allowed her appearance to return to nature – not worrying about having to be quite so neat and pristine and letting her hair grow in just the way it wanted to which, it had to be said, could get a little wild in its curliness.

'I like it!' Rosie declared.

'Well, good – I like it too.'

'You look like Rapunzel,' Bethanne said as she approached for a hug. She didn't skip like her sister. She was ten now, and a very mature ten at that, but now that Abi came to think of it, she couldn't ever remember Bethanne skipping at all.

'Hmmmm, maybe I should get it cut,' Abi mused.

'Nooooo!' the two girls cried in unison.

'Mum's got short hair and it's so *boring!*' Rosie declared.

Abi tried not to laugh. 'Well, maybe just a little trim then. Where's your mum?'

'In the kitchen,' Bethanne said.

'Ellen?' Abi called through and, a moment later, Ellen appeared in the hallway.

'Come here,' Ellen said. Abi did as she was told and stared out of the kitchen window in the direction Ellen pointed. 'Didn't I *tell* you they'd leave a mess?'

Abi frowned. Was it the small circle of sawdust Ellen was objecting too?

'How about a cup of tea?' Abi prompted. She was desperate for one after her drive.

'Of course,' Ellen said and Abi sat down at the kitchen table, noticing the oilcloth on the table that wasn't an Abigail Carey design. Abi had never forgotten her grave disappointment when she'd shown Ellen the first printed tea towels with her sunflower motif.

'I'm not really keen on yellow,' she'd said with a grimace. 'But I guess they're pretty enough.'

And that, as far as Ellen was concerned, was a compliment. Abi had never seen any evidence of her prints in her sister's home despite giving her a lot of freebies over the years.

'So, what's this news of yours that couldn't be told over the phone?' Ellen asked as she made the tea.

'I'm buying a house,' Abi told her. 'Or rather, half a house.'

'*Half* a house!' Rosie cried as she pulled out a chair and sat next to her at the table.

'Well, it's a very *big* house,' Abi explained. 'In seven acres.'

'In the country?' Ellen asked.

'Here in Sussex.'

'You're moving *here*?' Bethanne asked.

'I am.'

'When?' Ellen said.

'Soon as the paperwork's done.'

'I didn't know you were planning on leaving London.'

'Well, I'll still keep my flat, but I want to be in the country now.'

'Will we see you more often?' Bethanne asked.

'I hope so! And you'll be able to visit my new place. You're going to love it. The gardens are wonderful and there are walks right from the door up onto the downs. You should see the views.'

'What's all this costing?' Ellen asked. It was a typical Ellen question. She wasn't interested in what the property looked like or how Abi felt about it. She wanted hard facts. So Abi told her.

Ellen whistled. 'You're doing well, aren't you?'

Abi smiled. Something else Ellen had never quite been able to grasp was just how well Abi had done with her business.

Indeed, Abi had the feeling that Ellen still thought her sister was just a step up from a shopkeeper.

'Well enough to want to invest in a decent property.'

It was then that Bethanne handed her a piece of paper.

'What's this?' Abi asked.

'Oh, that!' Ellen said, crossing the room and taking the drawing from her daughter before Abi could see it. 'She's been doodling. I can't stop her. Doodle, doodle, doodle! Doodling your life away, aren't you? When you should be doing homework.'

'Let me see,' Abi said. Ellen sighed and handed the paper back. 'It's a sunflower!'

'She's been copying *your* designs,' Ellen pointed out.

'Not copying,' Bethanne protested.

'No, I can see that,' Abi said. 'You've got your own style going on here. It's very good, Bethanne.'

'Don't go encouraging her,' Ellen said as she handed Abi her tea. '*One* artist in the family is enough.'

'Is that what you want to be?' Abi asked her niece. 'An artist?'

Bethanne nodded, but her mother was shaking her head.

'I want her to start thinking about a future in science. She's good at science.'

'She's good at art,' Abi pointed out.

'But there's no money in art,' Ellen declared. Abi blinked. 'You know what I mean.' She waved a frustrated hand at her sister. '*You* got lucky. But it's a struggle for most.'

Abi took a deep breath, trying her best not to explain that the success of her company wasn't just a case of being lucky, and that long hard hours of work had built it up.

Ellen could obviously see Abi's annoyance.

'Come on – you must admit that you're the exception to the rule.'

'You don't know that,' Abi said. 'How can you know what Bethanne is capable of? I think her art should be encouraged.'

'You would say that as an artist, but I'm her mother and I think she should concentrate on something solid. Something she can build on.'

Bethanne reached out to take her drawing from Abi.

'It's really good,' Abi told her. 'You keep on drawing, okay?'

Bethanne nodded, but all the light had gone out of her face.

'Right!' Abi said after she'd quickly downed her tea. 'Grab your coats, girls. We're going out for lunch.'

Bethanne raised a smile at that and Rosie squealed.

'Don't forget your hats, girls!'

'I'll get them, Mum,' Bethanne said.

'And remember what I said about chips and ice cream, Abi!' Ellen cried as they piled into the hall together.

'Chips and ice cream – *yum!*' Rosie said with glee.

'*No* chips and ice cream!' Ellen said.

'We didn't hear you!' Abi said, opening the front door and taking her nieces by the hands.

They took the bus into town, which was easier than trying to find a parking space and got out at the sea front, the March wind instantly pummelling them.

'Come on!' Abi said, taking their hands again. 'There's a cafe over there.'

It was bliss to get inside once more and even more blissful to order three lots of fish and chips.

'Don't tell your mum!' Abi warned.

The girls giggled and the three of them devoured their lunch, enjoying it all the more because it had been forbidden.

After lunch, they left the cafe and headed towards the beach.

'You okay?' Abi asked as she gave Bethanne a little nudge with her elbow. She'd been quiet throughout lunch, leaving the talking to her younger sister, Rosie, who always had something to say.

Bethanne shrugged. 'I'm okay.'

'Yeah? You sure? Because you look like something is bothering you.'

They walked on a little, Rosie skipping ahead, the wind blowing her hair out behind her from under her hat.

Bethanne looked up at Abi, a frown on her young face. 'Why doesn't Mum want me to be an artist?'

Abi puffed out her cheeks as she formulated her answer. 'Well, she's anxious about you doing well in life.'

'And I wouldn't do well as an artist? Aren't I good enough?'

'It's not that you're not good enough – it's just that the world isn't always kind to artists. It can be a hard life.'

'Was it hard for you?'

For a moment, Abi wondered what to tell her. On the one hand, she didn't want to crush her niece's dreams before they'd even developed, but she wanted to respect her sister too. So she decided to be absolutely honest, which she knew one always should be with children, especially inquisitive ones.

'It was hard for a while, yes. I couldn't always pay my rent, you know. I had to sleep on friends' sofas and borrow money from them.'

'But you made it in the end,' Bethanne reminded her.

'Yes, in the end.'

'And it was worth it?'

'Oh, yes,' Abi said with a smile.

'Did your mum not want you to be an artist?'

'We lived with our aunt, remember?'

'Oh, yes. Aunt Claire?'

'That's right.'

'And did she not want you to be an artist?'

'Aunt Claire just wanted me and your mum to be working and earning and out of the house,' Abi confided.

'Why don't we see her?'

Abi glanced across at Rosie as she danced across the pebbles of the beach and couldn't help wishing that Bethanne would join her.

'You're coming out with the questions today, aren't you?'

'Does that mean you're not going to answer them?'

'No. I'll answer them,' Abi said. 'Aunt Claire is what you'd call a tricky woman. She's not really a people person and I don't think she was very happy when she had to take care of me and your mother. It's not her fault, not really, but you wouldn't want to spend time with somebody who didn't want to spend time with you, would you?'

Bethanne looked confused that there were such people in the world. 'I guess not.'

'Because that wouldn't make anyone happy.'

Abi bent down and picked a round, smooth pebble up, holding it in her hand, gauging its weight and suitability as a pocket companion.

'It's sad, isn't it?' Bethanne said.

'What is?'

'That Aunt Claire doesn't want to be friends with us. I mean, she'll never know how cute Rosie is.'

Abi laughed. 'Or you!'

'I'm not cute.'

'Of *course* you are!' Abi said. 'Just look at those dimples when you smile.'

'I'm not smiling,' Bethanne said earnestly.

'Yes you are,' Abi said as she tickled her.

Immediately, Bethanne began to laugh.

'There they are! There's those cute dimples!' Abi cried in

victory. Bethanne laughed again and then the two of them caught up with Rosie and walked down towards the sea.

'Are there sharks out there?' Rosie suddenly asked.

'Here in Brighton?' Abi asked.

Rosie nodded.

'She saw a programme about them on TV,' Bethanne explained.

'Well, you don't need to worry. Not that we're going paddling or swimming today. It's much too cold. But it's too cold for the sharks as well. They don't like our water here.'

'So it's safe?'

'Yes, as much as the sea can be safe. You've always got to be careful with strong tides.'

'And jellyfish,' Bethanne added. 'They can kill you too.'

Rosie frowned.

'Yes, they can, Bethanne, but not around here,' Abi told them. 'There's nothing lethal in our water except the water itself. That's why it's important to always be careful and wear your armbands and to have a grown-up with you.'

They all stared out to sea for a moment. It was rough, grey and moody today with a sky to match. And, as she stood there, Abi couldn't help thinking how incredibly lucky she was to be an aunt to these two wonderful girls who were so full of life and passion and curiosity for everything. It was almost overwhelming, sometimes, when Abi thought about how much she loved them. And then her memory would assault her with visions of her childhood and how her relationship with her own aunt had been so very different. There'd been no trips to the seaside, no confidences shared or idle questions asked. Had Abi and Ellen been particularly objectionable children? Abi didn't think so. Perhaps Abi had been a shy slip of a thing back then and maybe Ellen had always been a little sharp around the edges, but they'd lost their mother and it would be inhuman not to have carried a little part of that with them into their new home.

Abi sighed and looked down at Bethanne and Rosie, vowing in that moment with all her heart that they would never be ignored, and that they would always know how very precious they were to her.

'Hey,' she said, as a naughty thought crossed her mind. 'It's getting a bit chilly, isn't it?'

The girls nodded.

'How about we leave the coast and head inland?'

'What will we do?' Rosie asked.

'We could go and see a house up on the downs – if you like.'

'Your *new* house?' Bethanne said.

'Yes. Only it's a couple of hundred years old, but it'll be my new home. Do you want to see it?'

'Yes!' the girls cried in unison.

'Okay then. It won't take us too long to get there, but we'd better check it's okay with your mum.'

'Will she come with us?' Bethanne asked.

'She might.'

They got up from the beach and Abi reached for her phone.

'Well, I wasn't expecting this today,' Ellen said when Abi suggested a trip to Winfield.

'Ellen, what else have you got planned?' Abi asked, finally losing patience with her sister's attitude.

'Well, I can come if it means so much to you.'

'I did think you might want to see the place!' Abi said, 'But don't worry if you don't. I'll drop the girls back–'

'No, no! I'll come with you,' Ellen interjected.

Abi grinned. 'Good.'

~

One hour later and the four of them were on their way to Winfield. Abi was a bit anxious about being seen by Edward. It was the weekend and he was likely to be there. But she couldn't resist seeing the place again when she was so close and she did want to show it to Ellen and her nieces. In fact, she couldn't wait to see their reaction.

They parked in the village by the church. Edward couldn't object to them being in the village and taking a walk, could he? Actually, she was pretty sure he wouldn't object to them calling at the house, but she didn't want to impose. It would be as bad as that moment in *Pride and Prejudice* when Elizabeth is caught poking around Pemberley by Mr Darcy, she thought with a smile.

'Is it in the village?' Ellen asked as they got out of the car.

'Just up the hill,' Abi said. 'We can go up this footpath and get a good view of it from there.'

'Oh, will my boots be all right? I don't want to scuff them.' Ellen looked down at her fashionable footwear in concern.

'I've got some spare wellies in the boot,' Abi said.

Ellen quickly shook her head. 'I'll be all right.'

Abi grinned. Even in the middle of the countryside, Ellen wanted to make sure she looked perfect. The girls, at least, had wellies on and Abi changed into her old walking boots now, glad that she kept them in the car for such pastoral emergencies.

'What do you think of the village?' Abi prompted her sister, keen to hear her thoughts.

'It's pretty enough. But it's a bit remote, isn't it?'

'I've got a car.'

'But won't it be a bit of a shock after London?'

'Shock? You make it sound as if leaving London is some kind of punishment. I'm *choosing* to live here.'

'I just worry about you,' Ellen told her.

'Well, you don't need to. I can't wait to come here. It's going to be a brand new start for me.'

'What about work?'

'I'll be working.'

'Where?'

Abi sighed. Ellen still believed that, in order to work, one should actually leave one's home.

'I'll work from home.'

Ellen frowned, not looking convinced.

'There's plenty of room. I'm going to set up a studio. Actually, I've seen a press I want.'

'A press?'

'To make my prints.'

Ellen shook her head. 'Honestly, Abi, you do baffle me.'

Abi laughed. 'Why?'

'Because you do all these things that other people just *don't* do.'

'And that's bad?'

Ellen seemed to think about this for a moment. 'I suppose not. Not if it makes you happy.'

'It does.'

'*And* if it makes you money.'

Abi smiled. That was the crux of the matter with Ellen and probably the real reason she was worrying about her now.

'Everything is going to be fine. *More* than fine,' Abi assured her. 'It's going to be wonderful!'

The chalk path looked dull today under the grey sky. Abi remembered back to the autumn when it had gleamed so brightly under the sun. How she was looking forward to getting to know this place and seeing the changes that each season brought.

The girls took off ahead of them. Rosie – as ever – leading the way.

'Don't go too far ahead, Rosie!' Ellen shouted after her.

'Wait until you see it,' Abi said, excited herself by the prospect for it felt too long since she'd last seen the place.

They climbed the hill, leaving the village far below them and then taking a turn onto a footpath which skirted the flank of a down and that's when they saw it.

'Welcome to Winfield Hall,' Abi said, gesturing grandly with an arm flung out towards it.

'That's what you're buying?' Ellen looked astounded.

'Well, half of it,' Abi reminded her.

'Goodness, Abi!'

'Is it a palace?' Rosie asked.

'Of course not, silly!' Bethanne said.

'Actually, Rosie, some people call it the "Palace of the Downs".' Abi saw Rosie stick a gleeful tongue out at her sister. 'It's also known as the House in the Clouds because it's so high up. Isn't that lovely?'

'Does that mean it's cold?' Bethanne asked.

Abi laughed. Bethanne did sometimes sound like a born scientist. Perhaps Ellen had a point in nudging her in that direction.

'So, which half is yours?' Ellen asked.

'The right-hand side. Come on, we can get closer to it along this path.'

They set off again, gazing down into the grounds of Winfield.

'Is that your garden?' Rosie cried.

'Yes!'

'It's *enormous!*'

Abi laughed. 'Yes, you might have to come and help me with it.'

'You sure you haven't taken on too much with this place?' Ellen asked.

'Not at all. I'm up for the challenge.'

They walked on a little, the path dipping slightly towards the hall.

'There's a man staring at us,' Rosie suddenly said. 'Look!'

Abi turned around and gasped. It was Edward out in his part of the garden that was visible from the public footpath, and Rosie was right – he was, indeed, staring right up at them.

'Oh, no!' she cried, wishing that the chalk path would swallow her whole.

'*Abigail?*' he called up to them. 'Is that you?'

'Keep walking,' Abi whispered to her family.

'Abi – he's *seen* us!' Ellen protested.

'No, no! Just keep walking.'

'But we've *got* to say hello. Come on!' Ellen grabbed Abi by the arm and the four of them slowly descended the hill towards Edward who was beaming a smile at them as he left the walled garden and walked out onto the driveway. Abi had never felt so embarrassed.

'It *is* you!' Edward said. 'I didn't know you were coming down today.'

'No, it wasn't exactly planned,' Abi said.

'You should have called me. Let me known that you were here.'

'Edward – can I introduce you to my sister, Ellen? And her two daughters, Bethanne and Rosie.'

'Pleased to meet you,' Edward said, shaking Ellen's hand.

'Very pleased to meet you!' Rosie said, coming forward to shake hands too. 'Can we see inside?' she asked, her cheeks flaming in excitement.

'Rosie!' Ellen admonished. 'I'm so sorry. We didn't mean to intrude.'

'No,' Abi said. 'Honestly, I just wanted to show them the village. We didn't want to disturb you.'

'You're not. I'm doing absolutely nothing. Even switched my phone off.'

'Are the builders here?'

'Just one doing something with the floorboards upstairs so it's quite safe to come inside if your family want to take a look around.'

'Oh, please!' Rosie said, grabbing Abi's arm and tugging it.

Abi grinned. 'If you're sure it's no bother.'

'No bother at all.'

Abi glanced at Ellen who gave a little nod.

They followed him across the driveway towards the front door which he opened, ushering them inside.

'Wow!' Rosie cried. Abi glanced at her nieces. Bethanne's mouth had dropped open and her eyes were filled with wonder.

'It's like a film set!' Ellen said.

'That's exactly what I thought when I first saw it,' Edward told her. 'Especially the stairs.'

'Me too!' Abi chimed in.

'Although it's a bit chaotic at the moment with all the builders' things.'

'It's really, really big!' Rosie said, her neck craned back as she took in the ceiling high above her.

'It's certainly bigger than your London place,' Ellen said.

'Yes,' Abi said. 'But this will be split up into apartments.'

'Actually, we're making a bit of progress there,' Edward told her. 'Early days, I know, with all the work that's to be done, but I've got some plans through from the architect and they look pretty good. I'll send copies over to you.'

'Thank you,' Abi said, noticing that, as before, Edward was immaculate in a crisp blue shirt and neat trousers. He was wearing a wax jacket today because it was cool outside and she thought that he looked like he'd stepped out of one of those country magazines one finds in waiting rooms. He was just missing a spaniel by his side.

'Can we go up the stairs?' Rosie cried.

'Is it safe?' Abi asked Edward.

'Well, the roof issue has been sorted,' he said.

'Has it?'

'Thank goodness. We can move on to more interesting things now.'

'This must be costing a fortune!' Ellen said.

'Well, naturally,' Edward agreed. 'But worth doing. Worth preserving a place like this.'

'Not preserving,' Abi said. 'Not exactly. We're not holding it in time like an insect caught in amber. It's more like we're giving it new life.'

'Can we live here with you, Aunt Abi?' Rosie asked as they climbed the stairs.

'I'm not sure your mum would like that! But you can visit whenever you want to.'

Edward led the way, opening a door here and a door there, each leading into sizeable rooms with high ceilings, marvellous views and a heap of issues to sort from crumbling ceilings to cracked walls and the floorboards where the builder was working. In her romantic daydreams about Winfield, Abi had managed to forget just how much there was to do to the place in order to make it habitable. But they'd get there. Step by step.

'We're now in Abigail's half,' Edward said as they crossed the landing.

'How did you choose who'd get which half?' Ellen asked, always practical.

'It was mutually agreed,' Edward said.

'And very lucky too,' Abi confessed. 'Edward wanted the views towards the downs and I wanted the rooms that overlooked the main part of the walled garden.'

Bethanne tugged at Abi's sleeve. 'Can we see the garden?'

Abi smiled. Just like her, Bethanne preferred exploring outside, and it was pretty dusty inside. It would be lovely to get back outdoors.

'Listen, Edward – we don't want to keep you,' Abi told him as they went back downstairs. 'We'll just have a quick look at the garden and then be on our way.'

'Okay,' he said.

'It's been good to meet you,' Ellen said. 'I didn't even know this place existed until today.'

Edward smiled. 'Been keeping it a secret?'

Abi could feel herself blushing. 'Just waiting for the right time to tell everyone.'

'Well, listen, I'll get those plans over to you. See what you think.'

'I'll look forward to it.'

They held one another's gaze a moment, and Abi could feel Ellen's eyes upon her.

'Garden!' Rosie yelled, breaking the spell.

'We're going,' Abi promised.

'I'll see you, Abigail.'

She nodded and they left the hall.

'Well, you were certainly keeping *him* a secret!' Ellen said.

Abi could feel her cheeks flushing again. They had a horrible habit of doing that. 'No I wasn't!'

'So what's the deal with him?'

'What do you mean?'

Ellen leaned in closer to whisper so the girls wouldn't hear. 'Are you getting half of *him* with the house?'

'We are merely business partners,' Abi declared, but Ellen's raised eyebrows showed that she didn't wholly believe her.

Rosie and Bethanne had run across the driveway now and

were heading into the walled garden and Abi was glad of the distraction.

'Just look at this space!' Abi enthused as they joined the girls.

Ellen looked around. 'There are brambles everywhere!'

'I know. It's been horribly neglected.'

'It'll take weeks of work, Abi. *Months!*'

Abi sighed. Ellen always saw problems rather than potential. 'Well, I've got months ahead of me, haven't I?'

'You're talking as if you've retired.'

'I've not retired. I'm just resting a while. Catching my breath.'

'Having a fling.'

'What?'

Ellen gave a tiny smile. 'You know, you *should* have a fling. And this – what's his name?'

'Edward?' Abi frowned. Did she mean him?

'Yes – he's flingable, isn't he? Is that a word?' She nodded as if it was.

'Whether he is or he isn't is irrelevant seeing as that's the last thing I'm thinking about.'

'The *last*? Surely not!' Ellen said. 'I mean, you have noticed how handsome he is, haven't you?'

Abi didn't reply.

'Come *on!*'

It was clear her sister wasn't going to let this drop.

'He's easy on the eye,' Abi said at last, 'but that's not what this is about. I came to Winfield to find a home, not a husband.'

'Who said anything about a husband?' Ellen cried.

Abi could feel herself blushing again.

'Anyway, I don't know anything about his situation,' Abi told her.

'Well, he's not married, is he?'

'No, but he could very well have a girlfriend. Why are we even talking about this? I wanted to show you the garden!'

'Okay, okay,' Ellen said. 'Show me this garden.'

They ventured further into the walled garden, passing through a small orchard of fruit trees where the girls were playing tag. The grass was overgrown here, and there were nettles and the stalks of dead ragwort that would have to be dealt with.

'God almighty. Will you look at the state of that?'

Abi followed her sister's gaze as they passed through the orchard. 'You mean the greenhouse?'

'You're going to pull it down, I hope!'

Abi's mouth fell open in horror. 'I'm going to restore it.'

'You're kidding!'

'It's an original Victorian lean-to. It's beautiful.'

'It's an eyesore.'

'Well, it's missing some of its glass and is a little battered, but it's going to be absolutely glorious once it's all fixed up. Just like the house.'

Ellen shook her head as if Abi's plans were a personal affront to her.

'Girls!' Ellen called. 'Don't go near those brambles! Honestly, Abi – it's a terrible mess.'

Abi did her best to hold her tongue. Could her sister really not see the beauty in the place?

After the girls had burned off some of their energy, they returned to the village.

'You do like it, don't you?' Abi asked as Ellen got into the cars.

'Of course I do. I'm just surprised, that's all,' Ellen said. 'It's all so big! I didn't know that's what you wanted.'

'I didn't know either until I saw a photo of it,' Abi said as she pulled out into the road for the journey back to Brighton. 'It was like it was speaking to me.'

'Houses don't speak!' Bethanne said from the backseat.

'I know! But it *seemed* to speak to me,' Abi said with a laugh. 'I remember looking at the photos of it online and it felt as if a part of me was already living there. I couldn't stop thinking about it. I knew I had to try and make it mine, but then I didn't make the winning bid at the auction. The price rose and rose and – well – you met the winner today.'

'So how come he sold half to you?' Ellen asked.

Abi told her the story as they headed towards the main road.

'You mean, he's redundant and you haven't got a job, and you're taking on this money pit?' Ellen sucked in her breath. 'Forgive me, but this sounds like a disaster waiting to happen.'

Abi couldn't help smiling at that because, to her, the word disaster was the very last she'd choose to describe the situation she now found herself in.

Reaching Ellen's, they all got out of the car and, once inside, Ellen made tea and put some biscuits on a plate for everyone.

'Listen, Abi,' Ellen said as the girls grabbed a couple of biscuits each and left the kitchen, 'I'm really pleased that you're going to be closer. Heaven only knows I could use your help with the girls every so often, but it's good what you're doing.'

'You think so?'

'Yes. It's good you're taking some time for yourself. But don't overlook a bit of romance, will you?'

'Ellen!'

'I mean it! When was the last time you went out on a date? Was it that Italian bloke?'

Abi quickly finished her tea and got up.

'You're going?'

Abi crossed the room and kissed Ellen's cheek. 'Better hit the road before rush hour.'

'But it's Saturday!' Ellen called after her as she ran into the hallway.

'Even more important,' Abi said, making her escape through the front door.

'Abi!'

'I'll call you soon.' Abi got into her car and waved a hand from behind the safety of a closed window, blowing kisses to her nieces who were waving from the living room window.

She would have liked to have stayed longer, maybe joining them for tea and spending some more time with Bethanne and Rosie, but it was a relief to get away from her sister's probing questions. Heaven only knew that Abi didn't need reminding of her past relationships and she certainly wasn't going to think about them now. All those awful dates she'd been on over the last few years. All the embarrassing set-ups through work, through mutual friends, and all the dead-end relationships that had started so well and then just fizzled. Perhaps it was her fault. Perhaps she just wasn't meant to be with somebody. Not everybody was, were they? And Abi had always been married to her art. That was enough for her. She was fulfilled in herself and she certainly didn't need a man to make her feel complete.

So she drove home, back to her London flat where she lived on her own but never felt lonely. Pouring herself a glass of wine, she sat in the armchair which she'd placed by the window overlooking the river. She pulled out the sketchbook that she'd taken to Sussex on the day of the auction and flipped through the pages now, smiling as she gazed at her pencil drawings of Winfield. Then, putting her glass down and picking a pencil up, she drew some more, her pencil gliding over the page quickly and skilfully, almost subconsciously.

It was only when she looked back at her sketches later that evening that she realised that one of the pictures was of Edward.

CHAPTER SEVEN

April and May were Abi's favourite months in London. It was usually mild, sometimes even warm, but it rarely had the same energy-sapping temperatures of summer, when the heat of the pavements and the crowds would make one irritable and fatigued within minutes of leaving home. But Abi barely noticed that magical time this spring. She hardly saw the unfurling of the vivid green plane tree leaves or the diamond-bright morning sparkle on the Thames. Abi was already living somewhere else in her mind.

All the paperwork was completed by the end of May. Abi had been keeping in touch with Edward and had even had a couple more visits to see the work that was being done. He'd also emailed many photos, keeping her abreast of the progress.

'You know it's going to be a building site for months to come – maybe even another year,' he reminded her.

'I know,' Abi told him. But she hadn't wanted to postpone her moving in date. After all, he hadn't, had he?

Finally, the great day arrived and Abi woke to a London dawn of pearly-grey, promising sunshine and warm weather.

The removal men arrived and her flat was slowly emptied, her boxes of books and art materials far outnumbering anything else. She took a second to bid the place farewell, thinking of all the special moments she'd had there – all the sketches and plans she'd made for her business, all the dreams she'd dreamed, and all the heartaches she'd nursed too – both business and personal. There was so much of her tied up in this place's four walls, but she knew it was time to let it all go and that she couldn't start her new life until she'd left her old one. So she took one last look around the empty rooms, knowing in her heart that she'd never spend another day or night there even though she'd go on renting the place. And then she whispered goodbye, locked the door for the last time and left.

The drive down to Sussex was quick and uneventful and Abi sighed in relief that she'd made it safely, arriving shortly after the removal van so she was able to supervise her things being taken inside. It was a little chaotic with the builders working, but they all got on with things.

Edward hadn't been exaggerating when he'd said there was still a lot of work to do. It was soon obvious to Abi that they'd both be living with builders for the foreseeable future. But that was fine with her. She was at Winfield now and that was all that mattered.

One thing Edward had made sure of, though, was that her apartment and his were the first to be tackled and Abi was thrilled with the results. Where there had once been only one large room on the ground floor, there was now a living room, a kitchen diner, and a spacious study that she was going to use as her studio. A staircase had been built which allowed Abi to live on two levels in this part of the wing and, walking up it for the first time, she saw that it opened into a large airy room with stunning views across the walled garden from its three sash windows. There were also two bedrooms and a bathroom. She couldn't have been happier with it. Edward had done his best sending her photos of the progress as it had happened and consulting her on fittings and fixtures, but nothing could have prepared her for seeing it herself and she took a few minutes to drift from room to room, looking out of each of the sash windows and standing by the double French doors which opened out into the garden, taking it all in with slow, happy breaths. She was really here, she told herself. She'd done it.

It was just as she was about to sit down once the removal men had left that there was a polite knock on her door.

'Come in!' she called.

It was Edward. 'Okay in here?'

'I am!'

'Welcome to Winfield.'

'Thank you.'

'So, what do you think?'

She beamed him a huge smile. 'I think it's amazing. I can't believe how much has been done since I visited in March.'

'Yes, well, I got my whip out and made sure it was all done for you here. At least so you could move in comfortably. There's still the odd thing to sort out and no doubt there'll be a few teething troubles, but you know where the builders are if and when you need help.'

'Thank you. It's more than I ever imagined could be done in the time and thank you for paying for it all before I bought in,' Abi said, knowing that Edward had taken a huge risk in doing so.

'My apartment's still got no stairs or ceiling between the upstairs and downstairs so I'm living on the ground floor.'

'But you've got everything you need?' Abi asked.

He looked amused. 'If I've learned one thing in all this, it's that you'd be surprised by how little you really do need in life.'

Abi nodded. 'I had a good sort out before moving. I'd accumulated so much stuff! I honestly don't know where it all came from. Papers, folders, and books and music I no longer read or listened to. All these things come into our life and just seem to *stick*. But I made a decision that I didn't want to bring all that with me. This is a new start.'

Edward glanced around the room.

'Can I get you a cup of tea? I was just about to make one,' Abi said.

He shook his head. 'I'll let you get settled in.' He made to leave, but then stopped. 'I was wondering if you'd like to go out to dinner tonight. Nothing too fancy – just a little pub I've discovered that does the most amazing food. My treat. A kind of welcome to Winfield.'

'That would be lovely. We should celebrate this, shouldn't we?'

'And maybe we can talk about this old place then? Where we are now and our plans for the future.' He looked awkward. 'Nothing heavy,' he added, as if afraid he'd scare her away.

'No, that's a good idea.'

'Okay, then. I'll call for you at seven?'

Abi nodded and watched as he left. It was a kind suggestion of Edward's, which she hadn't expected, but it would be good to get to know him a little bit better and the last thing she wanted to worry about was what to cook for herself that night. She was exhausted. So she made herself a cup of tea, sat in one of the armchairs that faced the garden and let herself daydream until it was time to take a shower and change for her evening out with Edward.

≈

The Swan was a couple of miles away and was postcard pretty with its low, thatched roof. Edward parked his car and the two of them got out and walked into the pub. Abi smiled as she took in the old wooden floorboards that creaked underfoot and a huge fireplace dressed with horse brasses and copper kettles.

'This is lovely,' she said.

'Wait till you taste the food,' Edward told her.

They ordered drinks and then, while still at the bar, glanced over the menu on the board and chose what they were going to eat. They then made their way to a corner table by the window which looked out over the garden at the back of the pub and towards the river beyond, and Edward filled Abi in on all the work that had been going on at the hall and told her the funny stories he had about the builders and some of the things they'd discovered about the building.

When the food arrived, Edward asked, 'How are you settling in? If it's not too early to ask such a question?'

Abi smiled. 'It's really funny, but I feel at home already. Is that a strange thing to say?'

Edward shook his head. 'Not at all. I felt the same when I spent my first full day and night there. It was as if I'd found my one true home at last. Like the search was over.'

'Why is that, do you think? Why does Winfield have that effect on us both?'

Edward looked thoughtful. 'I don't know. It's just a feeling, isn't it? Like finding the right job or the right partner, I guess. You just... *know*.'

'Talking of knowing,' Abi said, 'we don't really know that much about each other. Well, you've met my sister and nieces. But what about your family?'

Edward's fork stopped half-way to his mouth and he put it back down onto the plate. 'My family?'

'Yes. Brothers, sisters? Parents?'

He shook his head.

'None?' Abi said in surprise. 'No family at all?'

For a moment, she thought she saw a look in his eyes as if he was trying to recall the information, but he merely shook his head.

'No. No family.'

Abi wasn't quite sure what to say. She'd thought her own situation was odd enough, but to have no family at all seemed like a pretty hard blow.

'I don't have much in the way of family either. My sister and I were raised by my aunt. Aunt Claire. She doesn't really bother with us much these days.' Abi gave a tiny smile. 'She didn't really bother with us much when she was bringing us up either.'

'How come?'

Abi shrugged. 'Just one of those people, I guess. She had her own interests and they didn't include us. I mean, I think she had her own interests. She never really talked to us so I can't be sure.' She laughed, but it was a hollow sort of laugh even to her own ears.

'What happened to your parents?'

Abi took a sip of her drink. 'Our father left when my sister and I were really small, and Mum died really young. I can't remember much about her.'

'I'm sorry.'

'It's okay. What about your parents?'

Edward looked awkward again, but then he spoke. 'My mum died and then Dad... Dad's dead too.'

'I'm sorry.'

'Yeah, well. Families are difficult,' he said. 'They can get in the way.'

Abi wasn't sure she agreed with that. 'Maybe some do, but not all, surely?'

Edward gave a wry smile. 'I guess I'll never know now.'

'But surely you'd like your own one day?'

He looked confused by this. 'My own what?'

'Your own *family*,' Abi said. 'A partner and children? Winfield would make a pretty amazing home for a family.'

'That's not why I bought it,' he told her.

'Maybe not, but it would still be a wonderful place for children to grow up in.'

He didn't reply and, for a few moments, the two of them got on with the business of eating.

Edward had been right about the food. It was delicious and it was good to know about the place. She could bring Ellen, Douglas and the girls here sometime.

'So, did you leave many friends behind in London?' Edward asked, breaking the silence at last.

'One or two,' Abi confessed. 'I had a bit of a party with them when I left the company. But I don't suppose I'll see much of them now.'

'No?'

She shrugged. 'Oh, you know how people move on. You always part with good intentions when leaving a job or moving house, don't you? You always *mean* to keep in touch or visit one another and, for a while maybe, you might post a Christmas card. But then the slow fizzle happens, doesn't it?'

Edward gave a wry smile. 'I suppose it does.'

'And I've got my sister nearby.'

'You two are close, then?'

'Oh, yes.' Abi felt a naughty smile dance across her face. 'She can be...' she paused, knowing that she was probably confessing far too much about her personal life.

'What? What can she be?' Edward pressed now that she'd fed him such an enticing titbit.

Abi could feel her face flaming in embarrassment. 'She can be a little tricky,' she told him, deciding that was a fair word to choose to describe Ellen. 'But she has a good heart and she's always looked after me. She was kind of like a mother to me growing up. Big sister, you know?'

'No. But I can imagine.'

They ate some more of their dinner.

'You were in London before Sussex?' Abi asked.

'Yes. I had a place in Richmond.'

'Nice.'

'It was. It's a shame I couldn't keep it.'

'You sold it?'

'Last month. I was hoping not too, but Winfield...' his voice faded. 'Anyway, I don't really need a place in London anymore. I just shoot in and out for the day now. But you know I grew up here – in the next village?'

'Did you?'

'Yes!' He laughed at her surprise.

'Whereabouts?'

'Not one of the pretty cottages, I'm afraid. One of those dull box houses from the eighties just off the main road.'

'I didn't know. So you're kind of coming home.'

'In a way. Although everything feels different now, you know? That old me and that old home don't really exist anymore. I left them both behind years ago. The new me – the London me – was quite different. And now I'm back. I've left London and everything's changed again.'

'A new version of you?'

'How many incarnations do we get in one life?' he asked, staring at her as if he genuinely wanted an answer.

'As many as it takes to get it right?' Abi suggested. 'I feel like I'm getting another one here at Winfield.'

'A place for new beginnings.'

'Yes,' Abi agreed.

They both finished their meals and took a sip of their drinks.

'I know it's early days,' Edward said, 'and that it'll be a while before the apartments are ready to be rented out, but I was wondering if you had any particular plans for that. Short-term lets? Long-term?'

Abi nodded. 'Actually, I have been thinking about that.'

'Oh, yes?'

'I'd like to rent mine to artists.'

'Artists?'

'Creatives of all type really. Writers, painters, potters, healers–'

'Healers?'

She shrugged. 'We'll have to wait and see who applies. As you said, it's early days.'

'So you mean New Age-type people?'

Abi bit her lip and did her best not to laugh at Edward's anxious expression.

'I don't think we should start categorising people. You don't have to be New Age to be a healer or a creative.'

Edward was frowning. 'But you will be charging rent?'

Abi sighed. This was something she'd given a bit of thought to. 'Yes. But not much. Let's call it a peppercorn rent.'

'Peppercorn.' Edward tried the word on for size and his expression told Abi that he didn't like it. 'Can you afford that?'

'Oh yes. It's something I'd very much like to do. I've always been fascinated by almshouses,' Abi confessed.

'Wait – aren't they for poor people?'

'Well, yes. Traditionally. But I'm not specifically targeting poor people with my apartments – just those who are maybe struggling.'

'You mean those who don't have a job?'

'No! I think you're confusing artists with... with unemployed people. Artists do sometimes make a living, you know.'

'But you're talking about those who aren't?'

'I'm talking about those who are struggling, perhaps. Those who need a bit of help. A bit of space and time somewhere beautiful. The people who give to the world through their art, but who, for one reason or another, don't always get much back. Writers who are struggling to find a publisher or an audience for their work, artists who need a little bit of help while they're finding their way, or healers who are learning how to reach out with their skills. These people matter to me because I could so easily have been one of them. I got lucky with my art and my timing. I won't say it was easy for me. It took years of hard work to achieve what I did, but I'm very aware that I could have worked all those years and not achieved the same result. So many don't, you know. I've seen them – talented designers who just haven't had a lucky break. Artists whose work is good – *really* good – but who have been placed with the wrong gallery or whose exhibition came at the wrong time when the world's focus was elsewhere. By doing this – by renting to these people – well, it would be like I'm investing in them. Kind of like my way of paying my good fortune forward.' She paused, anxious that she'd said too much and scared Edward even more.

'You're really passionate about this, aren't you?' Edward said.

She smiled. 'Does it show?'

'Oh, yes!'

She laughed and she hoped that Edward understood what it was she was hoping to achieve at Winfield.

'Of course, that part of the house is yours to do with as you wish,' he said.

'Yes. As yours is.'

'Then I hope we can all be happy there – whoever comes to live with us.' He lifted his glass and Abi clinked hers against it.

~

Edward Townsend was not, by nature, a liar. Yet he'd sat in the pub that evening with Abigail and told her lie after lie. Why had he done that? He felt awful about it now, but it had seemed the only option he'd had in the moment.

He paced up and down his living room as a builder banged in the hallway outside. He should go out, he told himself, picking up his car keys. But, once outside, he gazed up into the blue sky above him and decided to go for a walk instead, taking the path that led directly from the grounds of Winfield up onto the down. It would be quiet up there. He'd be able to think. The walk would do him good too. He was feeling particularly stiff after a restless night. Worse than normal. The pain was usually worse at night for some reason, but was it the guilt about lying to Abigail that had made him sleep even worse than normal? He wouldn't be a bit surprised. Lies didn't become him and yet he'd managed to come out with so many of them the night before.

First, he'd told Abi that he had no family. No siblings. Nobody. He'd then said his father had died. Well, he had in a round about kind of way. He was as good as dead. To Edward at least. But saying that out loud to somebody else, somebody he was growing to like and respect. Well, he hated himself for it.

He strode across the white spine of the chalk footpath, breathing deeply and trying not to think about the pain in his left hip. It would loosen a little as he walked. He wondered if he should have brought his walking stick with him just in case he got into trouble, but he hated the blasted thing. It made him feel like an old man and he wasn't anywhere near the age to accept that role yet. But he did, on occasion, use it – when his balance was so poor because of the pain and he had little choice if he wished to remain upright.

He cursed. It was three years since the incident and he had

hoped that the pain would have gone by now, but he was beginning to realise that it probably never would. This, he thought, as he struggled along the path, was something he was going to have to learn to live with.

He stopped walking and looked down onto the rooftops of the village. It gave one a wonderful feeling of grandeur gazing down from above. Not that Edward felt godlike or anything. It was more a feeling of appreciation – that he could see the whole of the village in one sweep – the church and the huddle of cottages at its centre, the little shop, the brilliant red of the post box, the narrow footpaths that wended their way up to the downs, and the curves of the lanes that slowly made their way to the main road. Edward could see his old family home in the next village from up here too. He looked at it now and realised that he felt absolutely nothing for it. He'd completely separated himself from the old place. Maybe that was one of the reasons he felt able to come back here. He could still walk the footpaths he'd adored in his youth although he probably wouldn't climb quite so many trees these days.

He continued his walk, his mind drifting once again over the events of the evening before in the pub with Abi and he felt himself heating up in anger about the lies he'd told. He could go and apologise to Abi immediately, he supposed. If he was truly sorry, surely he should do that. But he knew that he wouldn't. For one, it would be way too embarrassing, but he also knew that things were simpler this way. It was easier to write-off his entire family rather than trying to explain them to somebody else.

Doing his best to push his family to the back of his mind – the place where he managed to keep them for most of the time – Edward thought of what Abi had told him about her plans for the hall and how she wanted to share the place with creatives. It was a lovely idea even if it was one he wasn't totally sure he approved of. Yet. But, looking at the landscape around him with its verdant fields in rich yellows and lush greens, the hills that rose so majestically and the ribbons of chalk that danced across them, it wasn't any wonder that she wanted to share it with like-minded people – people who could not only see the beauty around them, but who could translate that into something equally beautiful. Edward envied artists that talent. He didn't have an artistic bone in his body. Well, other than being able to see the potential in Winfield Hall and helping to bring it back to life – that was sort of creative, wasn't it? But he didn't have that lightness that Abi seemed to exude. He'd watched her when she'd talked with such passion about artists, her blue eyes lit up with excitement as she told him about her future plans. If only he could express himself with such ease and enthusiasm. He had passions: for his job and for Winfield, but he always had trouble expressing such things. He'd always admired those who could just talk. Perhaps it was because his job was one where he talked about dry facts and dull figures, although they weren't dry and dull to him. But you couldn't get as excited about those in the same way you could about a beautiful painting or a heart-stirring piece of music, could you?

But Edward knew it was more than that. He wasn't the kind of personality to enthuse. He was reticent, an introvert, buttoned-up even. Yes, he was all those things that were frowned upon in a world that rewarded extroverts who shouted their opinions whenever and wherever they could. But that didn't mean he didn't feel things because he did, very deeply. It was just that he didn't always express them and that sometimes meant that he came across as abrupt and a little distant. He didn't mean to be, but that's just the way people interpreted him and he wasn't comfortable or confident enough to explain.

Perhaps that was another reason why he'd fallen in love with Winfield. It was the perfect place to escape to. Of course, he and Abigail would be renting out some of the space to other people but, for the most part, it would be theirs. A space – a very spacious space – in which to hide away from the world, to shut oneself off, to retreat far from the madding crowd, and lick one's wounds, to contemplate nothing but the sky, the hills and the trees. Everyone should have the luxury of such a place, he thought, and he could see why Abigail wanted to share it with those who might not be able to afford it ordinarily. He liked that quality in her – that willingness to share. She was comfortable reaching out to people, wasn't she? Whereas he wanted to shut himself away from others.

He turned back. As much as he wanted to stride out and lose himself in the fields and woods that surrounded Winfield, he really should be tackling one of the many jobs that needed doing. He could walk another day, he told himself, knowing that he'd made a vow that his move here was going to coincide with him being kinder to himself. He'd promised that he was going to take more time off from work and learn how to relax. Well, that was all right in principle, he thought, but not when you had a massive house to renovate and still had to find employment. He'd relax another time – at some vague point in his future. But not today.

CHAPTER EIGHT

Abi hadn't seen much of Edward. If she thought about it for too long, she would think his behaviour a little strange. After that first evening when they'd had dinner in the pub, he'd been a bit distant. Not that she expected them to behave like roommates. That was the last thing she wanted, but she'd kind of thought he might be a little more chatty. No, that was the wrong word. She had a feeling that Edward was simply not the chatty type. But she'd imagined them running into each other more, swapping funny stories about their new experiences living there together, discussing their plans for the future, discovering a little more about each other perhaps.

It was as Abi was taking a bag of recycling outside that she saw Edward on the other side of the hall talking to one of the builders. He caught her eye and she waved at him and, for a moment, she thought he was going to come over to say hello, but he didn't. She sighed and returned to her apartment.

Abi got on with making her corner of Winfield truly her own. It was such a delight to have doors on the ground floor that she could fling open into the garden, and a garden she could really move about in – a luxury she hadn't been afforded in London.

As her half of Winfield included most of the walled garden, she'd decided that she should try and tackle that as soon as she could. After all, she wanted to get planting and enjoy it over the summer months and already had a tray of sunflower seeds germinating on one of her windowsills. Luckily for her, as she was talking to one of the builders, he mentioned that his son had a gardening business and that he could ask him to make a start as soon as possible. The man in question had just had one of his jobs cancelled so the digger moved in the very next day, turning over the rough ground, pulling out clumps of the unholy trinity of brambles, nettles and thistles. It was a job that would have taken her weeks if she'd been foolish enough to attempt it on her own with a fork and a pair of secateurs, but it was all done in a matter of hours, and what a difference it made. As she paced out the space after the digger had left, she realised how very big the garden was. A part of her couldn't help feeling a little daunted by the prospect, but a larger part of her was delighted by the challenge and couldn't wait to start making plans.

Abi had designed all sorts of things in her time from tablecloths and bed linen, to shop windows and floors, but she'd never designed a garden before. How hard could it be, she wondered? Perhaps it would be like one of her tea towel designs only with slightly more flowers – and flowers that would depend on her for life. It was a big responsibility.

The thing that was most important would be to enjoy the process. This garden, this special place, was not to be a place of stress. Abi wasn't going to let it make demands on her that would make her feel unhappy. After all, wasn't a garden meant to be a place to unwind and forget about life's troubles? That's what this place symbolised to her – it was an escape, a place to breathe and dream and create. She could feel its power even now as she walked around it and she quickly learned that one of the loveliest things to do was to walk to the far end of the walled garden and then look back at the hall. It was a secluded spot and provided a gorgeous view of her half of the property and she knew what she had to do. She would have a bench here – a wonderfully comfortable bench in the sort of wood that always felt warm and reassuring. It would be a place she could come to with her morning cup of tea. A bench not only for comfort but for inspiration. It was such an exciting thought.

It was as she reached the far end of the garden that she saw Edward at one of the windows in his wing. She waved up to him, beckoning him to come downstairs so she could tell him of her plans for the garden. For what was a garden if not to share?

A couple of minutes later, they met at the front of the house.

'I know you can see some of my garden from your part of the house, but come and see the rest,' she said excitedly. He followed her through the gate that led into the walled garden.

'Oh,' he said.

Abi smiled at his reaction, seeing the look of surprise on his face.

'You've been busy.'

'Well, I got a man in with a digger,' she admitted.

'But you're going to be busy filling it, aren't you?'

'I was just thinking about all that when I saw you. I've never had such a big garden. To tell you the truth, it's a little daunting.' She paused, looking at the great space before her again. 'But exhilarating too!' she added. 'Have you time for a quick cuppa? I could tell you my plans for it.'

His face seemed to cloud over. 'I should be getting back,' he said. 'Things to do.' He turned away.

She nodded, wanting to ask him exactly what it was he had to do, but she resisted. She could see that he didn't want to talk and she tried not to take it personally.

'Actually,' he said, turning back towards her once they both reached the gate, 'there was something I meant to show you.'

'Oh?'

'If you have a moment,' he said.

I have nothing but moments, Abi thought to herself, but she didn't say anything as she followed Edward into the house and up the stairs.

They entered one of the rooms on the left which overlooked the downs. It was a beautiful room, or rather it would be one day. It had two large sash windows, and the high ceilings which every room of the house boasted. But it was the ceiling that was the problem.

'This is the last hole,' Edward said, glancing upwards. 'The others have all been repaired now, but I thought you might like to see it. See what we've been up to on this side of the property.'

'All that lovely ornate cornice has been ruined,' Abi said, peering up into the void.

'And you can see the steel girders and timbers that were installed in the sixties. I'm told that was in a desperate effort to stop the effects of the dry rot.'

'Oh, Edward. I had no idea it was so bad up here.'

'Now you see why I had to sell half of the place. Not that I'm regretting that decision,' he added hastily. 'It's good to have someone else on board with a big place like this.'

'I feel guilty coming in towards the end of all the really hard work.'

'Don't be. I was the one who took all of this on.'

'You'll let me know if you need any help, won't you?' she told him.

He looked surprised. 'But you have helped.'

'Yes, but in addition to that.'

He shook his head. 'You've done your bit buying into this place. I didn't mean to insinuate anything showing you this. I just thought you'd be interested to see a bit of this old place's history.'

'Oh, I am.'

'I've never owned an old place before. Always had modern. So this is all – well – a bit of a surprise to me.' He gestured for them to leave and it was as they were walking out of the room that she saw something in the corner.

'What's this?' she asked, walking towards it.

'Some of the old wallpaper we had to take down.'

Abi took it out of the cardboard box where it had been dumped with all manner of other bits and pieces. It was dusty, but she could still see the beauty of it even though it was ripped and frayed around the edges and creased down the middle.

'It's lovely,' she said.

'Is it?' Edward asked.

'Look!' Abi said, shocked that he couldn't see its innate beauty. The delicate lemon yellow rose pattern intertwined with pale green vines.

'I suppose it is, but it was in the way. It had to go.'

'Can I have it?'

He frowned, obviously wondering why on earth she'd want a dusty bit of ripped paper that had seen better days fifty years ago.

'If you want it.'

'I do.'

'What will you do with it?'

She shrugged, her head cocked to one side as she examined the pattern again. 'I'm not sure yet, but it's too lovely to throw out and it's a little bit of this place's history, isn't it?'

'I hadn't thought of it like that.'

She picked up a few torn pieces of the paper to take with her.

'Come outside with me,' she asked him again as they

reached the stairs. 'I know you're busy, but I'd love to tell you my plans.'

He hesitated, his hand patting his pocket as though there was something in there that meant he couldn't possibly spend any more time with her on frivolous things.

'Okay,' he said at last.

'It won't take long,' she reassured him. 'We'll go through my place then I can drop the wallpaper off.'

Abi led the way, noticing that Edward stopped for a moment before entering her apartment, a look of vague surprise in his eyes as he took it all in.

'Okay?' she asked, casting a look around her, trying to see what it was that had caught his attention.

'You've got a lot of... stuff,' he said.

Abi glanced at the living room walls which were now home to two very large white-painted Welsh dressers, each crammed full of crockery. And that was just the beginning of her collection although she didn't tell him that now.

'Come on through,' she said instead, placing the wallpaper carefully on a coffee table and opening the French doors into the garden. The sun was full upon it at that moment and Abi released a long sigh of contentment as they both stepped outside.

'Isn't it wonderful?' she said.

'It's a big space,' he replied, 'and I'm kind of glad it's your responsibility if you don't mind me saying.'

'I don't mind at all.'

'How are you going to fill it all?'

'With plants. All kinds of plants. Trees, shrubs, flowers, fruit and vegetables. I'm going to have a fruit cage and raised beds and I'll get the old Victorian greenhouse repaired. And flowers – there are going to be all kinds of flowers. Roses, jasmine, honeysuckle, sweet Williams –

anything that smells wonderful. And sunflowers. *Lots* of sunflowers!'

'Ah, that's right – sunflowers are your thing, aren't they?'

She smiled. They were having a conversation just like she'd imagined they would do.

They walked further into the garden, the sun warm on their backs.

'I've got somebody coming in to fix the lean-to greenhouse, put in some nice brick paths and build some raised beds. I wish I was handier with construction, but it would take me forever to make a start on any of those things, and I'm desperate to get the planting underway.'

They crossed the bare earth, walking to the point where they could see Edward's half of the house.

'You don't mind being overlooked here?' he asked, gazing up at the windows.

'Gracious, no!' Abi cried. 'There's plenty of privacy at the other end of the garden. Besides, I like looking at the whole length of the house from this point.'

'It's a fine view,' Edward said, and they both took in the splendid architecture with the fine sash windows winking in the sunshine. 'But I'll kind of miss the thistles,' he added, looking back at the garden. 'The finches favoured them over the winter.'

Abi felt herself drain of all colour. What had she done? Had she just gone and bulldozed something precious?

'I'm joking!' Edward added quickly, obviously seeing her discomfort. 'Well, half joking.'

'But I'll be planting plenty of flowers and they love sunflower seeds, don't they? I'll make sure they'll have lots to eat.' She saw that he was smiling.

'I'm sorry. I shouldn't have worried you like that,' he said as they started walking back.

'The last thing I want to do is to chase the wildlife away, but

I couldn't start to make a garden until those thistles were gone. It's a bit like that room you're working on. I guess you have to do a bit of damage in order to repair something.'

'That's a very nice way of putting it,' he told her and she felt relief flooding through her as they entered her apartment once again. And, just like when he'd entered before, Edward's eyes took in the huge dresser filled with crockery. 'I've never seen anything like this before. My family never had pieces out on display.'

'I always think it's a shame to hide beautiful things away in cupboards where they can't breathe or be admired,' she confessed. 'I like to see the things I own and each one of them is chosen carefully and deliberately so that they're not only functional but lovely to look at too.'

'"Have nothing in your house that you do not know to be useful..."'

'"Or believe to be beautiful",' Abi finished for him when he hesitated.

'That's right!' He grinned. 'You believe that, don't you?'

'It's a rule I live by. William Morris is a bit of a hero of mine.'

He took a step towards the dresser.

'You can pick things up,' she told him. 'Nothing's too precious that it can't be handled.'

But he didn't pick anything up. Instead, she watched as his eyes moved methodically from the top shelf to the bottom and from left to right, taking in each individual piece and each pattern.

'I'm afraid there are a few chipped and cracked pieces now, but I can't bear to part with anything once they come into my home. They kind of feel like family. Is that silly of me?'

'No, I don't think so. A touch whimsical perhaps.'

'Yes. And it's a family I keep adding to. I can't stop, you see.

I collect things wherever I go. For years now. Or ever since I started earning my own money. I would go into charity shops but, instead of buying something useful that I could wear, I'd buy something in a size that didn't fit me. A child's dress, perhaps, or a man's shirt because I liked the fabric and needed to have it. Inspiration comes from all sorts of places and, although I didn't really know what to do with them or how I could use them, I could see that they were beautiful and that they would somehow work their way into something.'

'Do you still do that?'

'What?'

'Buy things you can't wear because you like the pattern?'

'Oh, yes, all the time,' Abi confessed with a laugh. 'I have bin bags full of things I'll never wear, but which I'll occasionally dive into. It's rather magical to pull something out you've forgotten you own and to see its colours and patterns as if for the first time. Something happens in my brain. Perhaps it's my synapses snapping away, but it's a lovely feeling of excitement.'

'A bag of inspiration,' Edward said.

'Exactly. Everyone should have one. Because you can get so much from the past whether it's your own or other people's. That's why I love a good charity shop or a jumble sale or village fete. They're treasure troves waiting to be plundered and you never quite know what you're going to find,' Abi enthused. 'And old things are so special. They have heart and soul. They've lived a life – several lives sometimes. So often, our modern designs seem so empty and lifeless. They're very often created by a committee instead of one person with a beating heart full of passion and a vision for what they want to create.' She paused. 'I'm sorry, I'm wittering on now. Boring you to tears no doubt.'

'Not at all. It's good to hear someone who is passionate about what they do.' He glanced at the dresser again. 'And you made a living from all this?' He turned back to face her and Abi couldn't tell if his question was serious or not. 'Your business,' he added when she didn't reply.

'Yes,' she said. 'I made a living from all this.'

They stared at one another for a moment.

'I'm sorry,' he said at last. 'That sounded rude, didn't it?'

'Just a bit, but I'm used to it.'

'You are?'

'I'm afraid a lot of people – usually men – find it hard to believe that a creative woman can make money from what they perceive as doodling and colouring in.' She gave a tiny smile, remembering many a dinner party when she'd been cornered by some bore who mocked what she did. The irony was that she was very often earning a lot more than they were and having a great time doing so.

'I'm sorry. I'm just surprised.' He shook his head. 'I'm not expressing myself well. I'm not very good at this sort of thing, you see.'

'What sort of thing?' she asked, noticing how awkward he suddenly looked standing there in her living room.

'Talking to creative people,' Edward said, his gaze lowering. 'My world is a very dull one full of facts and figures and, well, I don't normally get to meet people like you.'

'I'm very ordinary, I assure you.'

He shook his head. 'You're not. You're – well, you've got something. You see things other people don't see. People like me. Like with that old bit of wallpaper I was going to throw out. I glanced at it, sure, but I didn't really see it. Not like you did.'

'I don't think it takes much skill to see a pretty piece of wallpaper,' Abi said.

'But it's not just the seeing, is it? You see something and then you create something else.' His gaze had softened now and he was nodding. 'I bet you were one of those kids in art class at school who just picked up a paintbrush and produced something wonderful whereas I'd be paralysed by that piece of shiny white paper in front of me.'

'Yes, but I bet you were one of those kids who couldn't wait to use the computers whereas I'd find all sorts of excuses not to use one.'

He gave a little smile. 'I guess we have unique ways of working.' He cleared his throat, suddenly looking awkward in her space again. 'I'd – er – better get back. Things to do.'

She nodded. 'Edward?' she called as he reached the door.

'Yes?'

'Let me know if you find any more wallpaper, won't you?'

He grinned. 'I promise not to bin anything beautiful without consulting you first.'

She watched as he left and then she turned to look at the dresser which she loved so much and which had caused such fascination in Edward. There hadn't been anything as frivolous as a dresser in Aunt Claire's house. Plates and mugs were put neatly away in cupboards. The very idea of having them out on display would have been preposterous. But Abi loved arranging her pieces and she'd collected so many over the years. Once she'd filled all the shelves in her small London apartment, she'd vowed to stop buying, but that decision was impossible to fulfil and so she'd simply hired a carpenter to build more shelves, getting creative and placing them above door frames and up the stairs. She'd also begun double stacking on her dresser, placing smaller jugs and cups in front of plates and saucers. There was so much space she'd overlooked and the jumbly, jostly look she created was reassuringly beautiful. It was almost alive, she thought, filled as it was not only with china but with postcards she liked, photos she'd printed out, bottles for single flower stems and shells picked up from beach walks.

She'd also realised that, if she stopped collecting, she may just stop inspiring herself for who knew where the next nugget of inspiration would come from whether it be an old chipped piece of Staffordshire pottery or the latest Emma Bridgewater design. Everything fed into her imagination and that was necessary and priceless. Discovering new pieces was an important part of her creative process.

Perhaps that's what she needed to do now, she thought, knowing that she hadn't created anything new for a good long while. She'd been so caught up in creating a new home for herself that her art had been forgotten. But maybe a spot of shopping was just what she needed to get things moving again.

With that in mind, Abi grabbed her car keys and headed out in search of inspiration.

Edward saw Abi's car as it left Winfield and breathed a sigh of relief because at least he wouldn't run into her for a little while. Not that they did run into each other all the time. With Winfield being the size it was and with them both being busy people, they rarely met at all, but Edward's face was still glowing with embarrassment at his earlier encounter. What was wrong with him? He just wasn't good around people especially people like Abi who were so naturally easy and open. There was a part of him that wondered why he'd chosen her as the co-owner of Winfield, but perhaps, subconsciously, he'd known he needed somebody like her in his life.

She certainly fascinated him, he had to admit. Her apartment was already so completely a home and so very *her*. While she'd retained the white walls which gave it that lovely light, airy feel, she'd also filled the place with colour in a way that Edward knew he'd never be able to do. He was still getting over the trial of shopping for curtains and cushions for his flat in London. He'd walked into a huge department store and had been completely baffled by it all. There was so much choice. Too much. And it was made even harder when you didn't know what you liked in the first place. He'd walked around for a bit, getting progressively hot and uncomfortable and, when an assistant had approached him, he'd hightailed it out of there. In the end, he'd hired somebody to sort everything out for him. It had cost a small fortune, but it had taken the pain out of the whole process.

What would Abi make of that, he wondered? Would she be appalled? She probably wouldn't understand how painful a task he'd found it because, to her, interior design was a joy.

Sitting down at his desk, he opened his laptop and was just about to contact a former colleague when a massive crash was heard from the room above him, startling enough for Edward to leap up from his chair and slam his laptop shut.

'What the blazes?'

He left his room and had just started climbing the stairs when one of the workman's heads popped over the banister above him.

'Everything all right?' Edward asked.

'All good here, but it's going to be a bit noisy for a while. You're not trying to work down there, are you?'

'No, not trying to work,' Edward said, resigning himself to taking the rest of the day off which wasn't such a punishment, was it? After all, the sun was shining. Sighing, he returned to his apartment, tidied his desk, ate a hastily put-together salad sandwich and then grabbed his car keys. He had an idea for exactly what he should do. It was one of the things he'd promised himself when he'd moved to Winfield only he'd been putting it off. But if not now – on one of the warmest days of the summer so far – then when? His gear was in the car, always ready for him to grab an opportunity. But opportunities had rarely been grabbed during what he now referred to as his

London Years, and he hadn't had a chance since he'd bought Winfield. No, that was a lie. He'd had umpteen chances, but he hadn't grabbed them, had he? Well, today he was well and truly going to grab one.

It was as he was leaving that he saw his walking stick by the door and hesitated. He hated taking it with him as it was like predicting the pain he'd be in and he was hopeful that what he was about to do would actually alleviate it like it used to. But was it better to be safe than sorry? He thought it was and so he grabbed it on the way out.

He knew exactly where he was going, taking the road out of Winfield and heading further into the countryside, passing rolling fields, hot and blonde under the summer sun, climbing steadily until he reached the top of the downs with views that stretched for miles before dropping down a winding road into a shaded valley. There was nobody around here. In fact, he'd only passed a couple of hikers and one dog walker in the last three miles which was just as he'd hoped for he was after a little bit of privacy for what he wanted to do. He only hoped the place was as he remembered it. That was the thing with memory – it was so easy to gloss over reality, editing out the bad bits and remembering only the good. Perhaps he'd done that over the years with this place.

Parking his car by an ancient church whose front was obscured by a large yew tree, Edward got out and opened the boot, pulling his gear onto the ground a moment later.

Suddenly, he became nervous. It was years since he'd done this. Would he still have the nerve? Well, there was only one way to find out, he supposed as he looked up and down the lane, making sure a walking party wasn't about to appear. But there was nobody about so he closed the boot and locked the car before picking up his bag, heading for the public footpath sign a little further down the lane. It was shaded there and a little overgrown. Edward's legs sliced through the long grasses which threatened to swallow up the path completely, using his bag when he came across a patch of hungry-looking nettles.

After a couple of minutes of walking, the footpath dipped into a wood before opening out into a field the colour of dark honey. The path then skirted this field before ending at a stile which the young Edward had climbed over many a time, excitement fuelling him on as he entered the lush green meadow beyond, catching that first, tantalising glimpse of the river. Now, he felt no less excited than that young boy as he saw the water sparkling in the afternoon sunshine. How beautiful it looked. Just as he remembered it. It was one of those rare and wonderful chalk streams that were so clear and pure that you could see all the plant and animal life.

He looked anxiously around the field and up and down the stream as if anticipating company but, as before, there was nobody around and so he began to undo the buttons of his shirt, revealing a dark v-shape where he'd already caught the sun that summer and tanned arms too which had been exposed while walking the downs. Next were his boots and trousers, but he kept his boxer shorts on. Skinny dipping was one thing when you were a young boy, but quite another when a grown man. Anyway, as a galleon-like cloud passed over the sun, he made the decision to put on the wetsuit he'd brought with him.

It was a bit of a struggle to get it on, but he was relieved that it still fit him. He'd been anxious after spending so many years sitting at his desk. He did his best to keep himself fit with his gym membership and walking, but he'd worried that his job might have meant an increase in his weight. Luckily, it hadn't and, doing up the zip, he sighed in relief. He then wriggled his feet into his waterproof boots which fitted oh-so-snuggly and prevented all manner of cuts and bruises when navigating one's way down a wild stretch of water.

Next, he reached inside for the bottle of sun cream and covered his face with the cool lotion remembering, as he always did whenever he applied sun cream, the time he'd spent a day swimming in the river, thinking he was safe with the water covering his body. He'd woken the next morning not only with the world's worst headache, but with skin that looked as if he'd jumped into a vat of red paint. Ever since that day, he never ventured forth without his factor fifty.

Finally, it was time to greet the water and he walked towards a drop in the riverbank where there was a mini pebble beach. Here, he waded into the water. It wasn't very deep at this point, even in the middle, and he walked upstream where he knew it got deeper.

After the initial shock, the water felt glorious. He'd forgotten how good it felt to have the silky cold of another element envelop him. There was nothing else in the world quite like it. Indoor swimming pools just couldn't compete with this. There was a freedom he found in wild water that wasn't perhaps afforded him in his normal day to day life. It was something which you surrendered to completely and where the mind yielded to the body. He liked that. He liked the fact that he became a physical being in the water and that it allowed him to forget everything else that was going on in his life. He soon found that everything was slipping away beautifully – his worries about Winfield and his anxiety about his future work – it all melted away as he focussed on his strokes and his breath.

He swam, warming his muscles as he moved upstream, pushing against the gentle current until he came to a deeper part of the river where he stopped and corkscrewed around so that he was floating on his back, weightless as he gazed up at the sky. And there it was: that sense of peace that was hard to put into words, but which often comes from strong exercise followed by total relaxation, and he found that nothing relaxed him so much as being in the water. The old him had slowly dissolved away – washed away perhaps. Swimming was a kind of meditation, he thought, and the only sort other than walking that he was happy to participate in, for Edward wasn't one for joining classes. The last thing he'd want to do was to stretch out amongst a group of chanting strangers. Besides, where else but a river could you be at eye-level with the moorhens and frogs? Certainly not in any indoor class.

He floated there for a while longer, the warmth of the sun on his face and the cool embrace of the water on his body. He would have happily stayed there until dusk, but he thought it wise to get back and check on the progress of the builders.

He climbed out up the bank and took off his wetsuit before sitting on the short summer-burnt grass, feeling the beat of his heart. It was one of the best feelings in the world – second only to that first icy plunge into wild water when the body was shocked into existence. And he smiled as he noticed something. His pain had gone. His time in the water had worked its magic once again and he knew its effect would last for at least a couple of hours. In fact, swimming was the only time when he was completely pain-free. Physically, that was.

The emotional pain – as much as he wished – never left him.

CHAPTER NINE

Abi hadn't really expected to see any of her old work colleagues once she'd left her company and then moved out of London, but Dana had always been someone who surprised her from the moment she'd walked into Abi's first shop and asked if there were any jobs going. She'd been by Abi's side ever since those early days, growing in confidence until she was putting forth suggestions for designs and new lines in the collection. Since Abi had left, Dana had been more instrumental than ever in realising the vision of the company and that pleased Abi intensely.

For her friend's visit, Abi had made some flapjacks earlier that morning and, after picking her up from the station in Lewes, the two of them sat on a bench Abi had recently bought for the garden, tea and flapjacks on a tray beside them. She'd placed the bench just outside the French doors so that she could enjoy it on summer mornings when she was having her breakfast.

'I still can't believe you're here,' Abi said, looking at her dear friend, noticing that she'd had her long dark hair cut into a neat bob. It had used to spiral over her shoulders and Abi had loved it, but it looked sweet yet professional this way.

'And I still can't believe you're *here!*' Dana said. 'This place is amazing, Abi. To have all this space!'

'It's a bit of a change from London,' Abi agreed.

'The garden is wonderful.'

'It will be,' Abi said. 'I've just had the paths put in and the raised beds built and I've cheated with the grass. Had it all rolled out instantly. It was incredible to watch the transformation. Just got to get more plants in now.'

'I can see you've got your trademark sunflowers,' Dana said, nodding towards the giants at the far end of the walled garden.

'Yes, the recent rain has really given them a boost.'

Dana smiled. 'I often wonder what would have happened if you hadn't doodled that sunflower that day.'

Abi smiled back, touching her silver locket. 'I wonder the same thing too!'

'What if you'd drawn a sausage dog instead?'

'Do you think that would have launched a career?' Abi asked.

'Possibly not!'

'I guess I got lucky. I drew from the heart. I drew something I loved and I suppose that's what resonated with people.'

They sipped their tea and nibbled their flapjacks, looking out over the garden together, watching as a pair of goldfinches landed on a silver birch, their light twittering song filling the air with joy.

'So, how's work?' Abi asked at last.

'Good!' Dana said all too quickly and with far too bright a smile on her face to be convincing.

'Dana?'

'What?'

'What's going on?'

'Nothing! Everything's fine. I just miss you, that's all. It's not the same without you there.'

'Is that all?'

Dana licked a finger and picked up a few stray golden flapjack crumbs from her plate before answering. 'I didn't know whether to tell you or not.'

'What?'

'They've pulled the handbag range.'

'Really? But why? They're doing so well for other designers.'

'Yes!'

'And every woman needs a bag. *Several* bags!'

'I know and I kept saying that,' Dana told her.

'But that's a crazy decision!' Abi declared. She'd promised herself that she wouldn't get worked up over decisions made after she'd left the company, but it was proving hard when she heard news like this.

'I'm going to keep fighting it, but I think the decision's been made,' Dana told her. 'It's so frustrating. They were beautiful bags.'

'Beautiful and useful,' Abi said, remembering her William Morris.

'A rare combination,' Dana agreed. 'So often, you'll buy a bag because it's pretty and you can only fit your lipstick and credit card inside.'

'I designed those bags so that you could fit at least one good-sized paperback book, a bottle of water *and* your lipstick and credit card!'

'I know!'

Abi took a big deep breath and sighed it out, trying to calm herself. She wasn't the boss of the company anymore. She wasn't in London. She was unemployed and she was sitting in her garden in the middle of the day. She had no right to pass judgement on decisions that were being made by the people she'd handed power over to. And yet, it hurt, she had to admit. Something she'd put every fibre of her being into was being changed. It wasn't hers any longer. She wasn't even being consulted. But wasn't that what she'd agreed? She'd signed her rights away when she'd sold everything.

'I knew I shouldn't have told you,' Dana said, pouting.

'No – I want to know,' Abi insisted. 'Well, I *thought* I did. Maybe I shouldn't, though. If things happen in the future, maybe you shouldn't tell me. I mean, what can I do with that kind of information now?'

'Do you miss it all?' Dana asked.

Abi stared deep into the garden, her gaze softening slightly as she focussed on a sunflower whose petals had only just opened to the summer. She looked at the vibrant yellow, the unadulterated beauty of it and then she turned to Dana.

'No, I don't miss it.'

And she knew she was speaking the truth of her heart even though her answer surprised both her and Dana. But Abi didn't miss the sleepless nights worrying about staffing issues and whether or not she was going to be able to come up with new designs each season, and what the trade would think of them, and how the public would respond to them. She didn't miss the noise of London with the crush of the tube, she didn't miss the neighbours in the house opposite who loved to throw parties starting at ten in the evening which would only end once the dawn chorus started.

'But I do miss you,' Abi confessed to her friend.

Dana grinned. 'And how are you?' she asked Abi. She'd

already asked the question before when Abi had picked her up at the station and Abi had responded casually, but Dana's voice was serious now, needing more than a quick and flippant response. 'Abi? Have you been okay?'

'I've been fine.'

'Yes, you said that before.'

'And it's true.'

There was a pause – the first awkward one between them since Dana had arrived.

'Have you slowed down at all?' Dana asked after a moment.

'Yes, of course I have!'

'Because this place looks like a lot to run.'

Abi shook her head. 'It's a pleasure to take care of. Honestly – it's been a kind of therapy restoring this garden.'

'But you need to take care of yourself, Abi. Not just the house and garden. You know what the doctor–'

'Yes, I know,' Abi interrupted, and then she felt bad. Dana was only showing her love for her so Abi reached out and placed her hand on her friend's arm. 'I'm taking things slowly, I promise you. Early nights, plenty of fresh air and exercise. There's nothing out here *but* fresh air and exercise.'

Dana laughed. 'Well, you do look good, I have to say. Retirement suits you!'

'Cheeky! I'm not completely retired, you know! Just resting between amazing projects.'

They both laughed and Abi had to admit that she missed the happy sound of the laughter of a friend.

They walked around the garden after that, Abi telling Dana her plans for the place – the flowers she was going to grow and the fruit and vegetables she hoped to harvest later in the year.

'You know, I always kind of thought that your designs were those of a natural gardener,' Dana said. 'I mean, I knew you didn't have a garden of your own in London. Perhaps you were creating hundreds of different gardens in your designs.'

'Yes, perhaps,' Abi said with a smile. She'd never thought of it like that before.

After she'd dropped Dana off at the train station and returned to Winfield, she stood by the French doors looking out into the garden again. As she'd hugged Dana goodbye, her friend had whispered, 'Take care,' and it was said with great meaning and emphasis as if Abi hadn't always taken good care of herself. And perhaps she hadn't. She did her best to push to the back of her mind what she referred to as her little wobble. But she had definitely been in a bad place for a while not so long ago. The years of designing and the constant pressure of travelling between shops, the exhaustion of trade shows both in the UK and abroad had all taken their toll. When Abi thought about it now in the peace and tranquillity of her new surroundings without a timetable to keep to, she realised how exhausting it had all been. No wonder she'd had her little wobble. Anybody would have. Being creative was enough of a physical drain without the added pressure of running an international business.

To say nothing of the other little thing she'd had going on at the same time, she thought, closing her eyes for a moment, but trying not to sink into the sadness once again because it would be all too easy to do that.

The truth was, Abi had burnt out. Her doctor had said she'd had a breakdown, but she thought that was a little melodramatic. But she'd realised she'd been stressed and exhausted and an emotional wreck. She knew she had to stop what she was doing, rethink things and start again.

And that's what I'm doing now, she told herself as she walked out into the garden again, the early evening sun warm on her bare limbs and the promise of the rest of the summer to comfort and heal her.

~

But it wasn't just Abi who had plans for her summer. Her sister Ellen had plans for them too. Abi had just placed a large sheet of paper on her table, weighted down with pretty stones from a recent trip to the beach as she had the French doors open and there was a slight breeze, and was about to attempt to plan her garden in more detail. But the phone interrupted her and caller ID told her that her day had been robbed from her already.

'Douglas is home,' Ellen blurted without any sort of preamble when Abi answered.

'How lovely!' Abi chimed. 'For long?'

'No, not for long, but we need to spend some time together.'

'That'll be nice.'

'So I need you to take the girls.'

Abi bristled. Not that she didn't want to spend every moment she could with her nieces, but it was the tone the demand was made in that irked her. She'd known that moving closer to her sister would have its downsides as well as its ups, but she sincerely hoped that she wasn't going to be roped into the role of babysitter every five minutes.

'Okay,' Abi said.

'Can you come and get them? I don't have time to drive over and you're not doing anything, are you?'

Ah, Abi thought – the great misconception that, if you work from home, you're never really doing anything.

'Of course I can come,' Abi said meekly, setting a dangerous precedent for herself in the future. 'When?'

'Now.'

It wasn't a question. Abi was just expected to drop everything and be there.

'I'll see you as soon as I can,' Abi said, ending the call and glancing down at the blank sheet of paper that was going to remain blank for at least another day. She walked towards the French doors and, taking a wistful look at the garden beyond, closed them.

When she reached her sister's, she found a house full of chaos. Douglas had left a pile of bags in the hallway which Abi promptly tripped over after Bethanne had let her in.

'They're fighting in the kitchen,' her niece told her matter-of-factly.

'I can hear,' Abi said, giving Bethanne a hug. Rosie ran into the hallway from the living room.

'Are you taking us for chips again?' she blurted.

Abi shushed her quickly.

'Don't worry, they won't hear us,' Bethanne said as Abi gave Rosie a hug.

'How would you two like to spend the day at Winfield with me?'

Rosie looked confused. 'But Daddy's just come home.'

'I know, sweetie. But I want to spend some time with you – just for a few hours. Then I'll bring you back in time for tea with Daddy, okay?'

Rosie nodded, knowing she was defeated, but in the nicest way possible.

'Come and see Daddy,' Rosie said, leading her by the hand towards the kitchen where voices were still raised.

'Ellen?' Abi called ahead, warning of her approach.

The raised voices stopped.

'Abi?'

As Abi entered the kitchen, Ellen crossed the room towards her and they hugged. Abi wasn't used to such a welcome.

'Thank goodness you're here!' Ellen said. 'The girls are ready, aren't you?'

Bethanne and Rosie both nodded.

'Do I get a cuppa first?' Abi joked.

'Yes, of course,' Ellen said, turning to switch the kettle on.

'Hi Douglas,' Abi said.

'Hi Abi.' He looked tired, Abi thought, and his skin was pale against his dark hair. They embraced. 'You okay, Abs?'

'Very well. How about you?'

'Can't complain,' he said. 'How's the new home?'

'Amazing! I'm just working on the garden now. There's so much to do and I'm not quite sure what I'm doing, but it's fun learning.'

'I'll have to come and see it sometime.'

'Yes, please do! When you've got some spare time.'

He laughed at that. 'Yeah, I wonder when that will be.'

'You've been busy, haven't you?'

'Yes. They're keeping me entertained, that's for sure.'

'And he's only here for the weekend,' Ellen said pointedly, handing Abi her mug of tea. 'Can you make sure the girls have everything they need? They've had brunch, but will need something to eat in the afternoon.'

'I *do* know how to feed children, Ellen,' Abi said, trying to sound light-hearted, but she could see the strain on her sister's face so drank her tea quickly. 'Okay, we'll be off. Douglas, it was lovely to see you again.'

'Short but sweet,' he said with a knowing smile.

'We'll catch up soon, okay?'

'You bet.'

'Come on then, girls,' Abi said, rounding up her nieces and making sure they had everything they wanted to bring.

'It's not fair that we don't get to see Daddy,' Rosie said as they left the house and got into Abi's car. 'Mummy's keeping him all to herself.'

'Well, sometimes mummies and daddies need alone time together,' Abi said, making sure they both put their seatbelts on in the back.

'Why?' Rosie demanded as Abi got into the driver's seat.

She sighed, glancing in the rear-view mirror at her attentive nieces who wanted answers. How was she going to explain to them, she wondered?

'Have you got a best friend, Rosie?'

'Yes.'

'What's her name?'

'Annabel.'

'And do you like spending time alone with her?'

'Yes because she's my best friend.'

'And you don't always want to be in a big group and share her with others?' Abi suggested and Rosie nodded.

'Well, it's kind of like that with mummies and daddies. Only different.'

'*How* different?' Rosie asked.

'You'll find out when you're older.'

Rosie sighed. 'Grown-ups *always* say that!'

Abi grinned and they drove in silence for a while with the girls gazing out of the windows. Abi was glad to see them doing that and not glued to some electronic device as soon as they were settled. She grieved for the youngsters who were always plugged into some device or other and had no concept of the pure joy of simply gazing and letting the mind drift. They were missing out on whole worlds of wonder – thoughts and feelings that lived deep inside them and that might never be awakened because they were always being overridden by external stimuli. Abi often wondered what sort of a child she would have been if she'd been growing up now. Would she be addicted to social media and the world of gaming? Would she have missed her true artistic calling or would she still have grown to be the same person she was today?

As they left the main road and drove along the winding lanes across the downs, Abi pondered these thoughts a little longer, glancing quickly at her nieces on the backseat who were still staring happily out of the windows.

'So, what do you want to do today?'

'Can you teach me how to paint designs?' Bethanne piped up.

'In one afternoon?' Abi said with a laugh, but then she bit her lip. She could see that Bethanne was in earnest. 'We can certainly do something. Let me have a think.'

Bethanne looked happy at that. 'Mum keeps tidying my paints away and telling me to concentrate on maths.'

'Oh, dear!' Abi said, screwing her face up and knowing just how painful that was to a fellow creative. 'Well, you can take up as much space and make as much mess as you like at mine. It's what I do all the time.'

'I'm definitely going to live on my own when I'm older,' Bethanne said.

Abi smiled. 'Well, it certainly has its advantages.'

They reached Winfield Hall and, as soon as the girls were out of the car, they ran through to the walled garden to let off some of the steam that Ellen probably didn't always allow her girls to release.

Abi went in through the front door, carrying the bags her nieces had brought with them. She switched the kettle on and reached for the biscuit tin. Jammy dodgers were another thing Ellen frowned upon, but they were exactly what young girls loved after a run around, Abi thought. She put a few on a plate of her own design featuring a pattern called *Strawberry Jam* which, after her iconic Sunflowers, was one of her personal favourites – and then she opened the French doors.

'Come on in, girls!'

They both arrived panting a moment later and Abi gave them a tumbler each of iced water and then grabbed her own cup of tea before sitting down at the table which overlooked the garden.

'Mummy called Daddy a plonker,' Rosie suddenly declared.

Abi spluttered on her cup of tea, only just managing not to spill it.

'What's *plonker* mean?' Rosie asked.

Abi's mouth dropped open and she looked across to Bethanne who simply shrugged as if she either didn't know or just wasn't sure how to help Abi answer.

'Erm, I think it means your mum was tired.'

'Oh,' Rosie said.

'He's been away a lot,' Bethanne said.

'He's *always* away,' Rosie droned.

'And the first thing he says when he comes home is that he's going away again.'

'Oh, dear, that's a shame,' Abi told them. 'But it's difficult for him too, you know. He wants to be at home as much as you want him to be home.'

'Then why does he keep going away?' Rosie asked.

'Because he has to work. That's what grown-ups do,' Abi said. 'You have to have a job to earn money to pay for everything. Like your home and your new clothes and food.'

'I don't need new clothes,' Rosie declared. 'Well, not all the time. Just sometimes.'

The three of them polished off the jammy dodgers and then Abi tidied the table.

'Now, you wanted to paint, didn't you?' she said to Bethanne. 'Rosie – do you want to join us too?'

Rosie nodded. 'I've got a book I can paint in – look!' She ran across the room and grabbed the book from her bag. It was a beautiful colouring-in book of the natural world.

'Perfect! I'll get you some paints.'

Once Rosie was happily sitting at the table with a box of paints, making a glorious mess in bold primary colours, Abi heaved a wooden box into the centre of the living room.

'What's that?' Bethanne asked.

'Shall we open it?'

Bethanne's face lit up and she nodded.

'This is my box of inspiration,' Abi said. 'Well, one of them. I have quite a few. Bags too. And cupboards.'

Bethanne giggled and then gasped as Abi opened the lid.

'This is the one I fill with fabric,' Abi explained. 'Every little piece of fabric from my childhood that I couldn't bear to part with is in here. I would cut out pieces from favourite dresses and things I'd find in jumble sales – whatever they were – I never had a preference. I loved everything from florals and tartans to spots and stripes.'

Abi watched as Bethanne's hand tentatively dipped into the box, her eyes fixed in concentration.

'Don't be afraid. They're not too delicate to handle so you can pick anything up you like the look of.'

Bethanne became braver and Abi watched the emotions flick across her face, recognising each and every one of them as those which she had experienced herself on seeing the pieces of fabric for the first time.

'Why not pick a few out for inspiration before we start painting?' Abi suggested.

Bethanne nodded and rifled through the heaps of fabric with purpose now.

'I like this piece,' she said a moment later, holding up a piece of pink and white chintz, 'with this piece.'

Abi looked at the pairing she'd made – the chintz next to the sky-blue check was an inspired choice.

'That's good,' she said.

'Is it?'

Abi nodded and smiled her encouragement because she knew in her heart that, even though Bethanne didn't fully acknowledge it yet, and even though Ellen passionately discouraged her, Bethanne was a natural artist.

'You have a good eye.'

'Just one?'

Abi laughed. 'It's an expression. Of course, both your eyes are good, but having a good eye is more to do with being able to recognise something. Not everyone has that, you know.'

'And you have it too?'

'I hope so. I *think* so.'

Bethanne gave a tiny smile. 'You do!'

Abi plunged a hand inside the box and pulled out a torn piece of fabric covered in tiny forget-me-nots.

'Oh, look! I'd totally forgotten this was in here.'

'What is it?' Bethanne asked.

'This is from the skirt I wore to a friend's birthday party. I must have been about your age. I loved that skirt, but it wore away to a whisper over the years and I couldn't bear to part with it so I cut this square from it so I could keep it forever.'

'That's a really nice thing to do,' Bethanne told her.

'Maybe you could start your own collection,' Abi suggested. 'It doesn't have to be fabric either. It could be paper prints like wrapping paper on presents or pictures from magazines with interesting patterns.'

Bethanne looked thoughtful. 'How many patterns are there in the world?'

'What a *gorgeous* question!' Abi said with a laugh. 'As many as humans can think of, I suppose. It's infinite.' She thought for a moment. 'Here, take the humble polka dot.' Abi grabbed a sketch book that was lying out and the two of them joined Rosie at the table. 'You can have a single colour dot like this.' Abi picked up a paintbrush and dipped it in Rosie's red paint. 'Or multi-coloured dots.' She whisked her brush in the jar of water and dipped it into the green paint and then repeated the process with blue. 'You can space them out equally or have them just touching each other like dodgem cars. Maybe even interlinked so that their colours merge.' Abi illustrated, turning a yellow one orange by adding red. 'Or you can shade one slightly like this.' Abi added some more red to one side of a dot. 'You can even place a mini dot inside one. But there's something else that would make your dots different from mine and mine different from Rosie's if she painted some.'

'What's that?'

'Our style,' Abi told her. 'You see, each of us is different and so, when we paint or sketch, we're going to bring a bit of ourselves to what we do. Our personalities.'

Bethanne seemed to be taking this in.

'Can you add other shapes to the polka dot pattern too?' Bethanne asked.

'Of course. Here.' Abi handed her the brush she was using. 'Add away!' She watched as Bethanne studied the polka dots Abi had painted and then she dipped her brush into the blue and added some straight lines through each of the yellow dots, turning them into stars and making the lines look half blue and half green where they crossed the yellow.

'That's gorgeous!' Abi cooed.

'Is it? It's not too messy?'

Abi frowned. Bethanne sounded so unsure of herself when there was absolutely no need to be.

'Look at it. What do you see?' Abi asked her.

'They're like little stars. Coloured stars.'

'And how do they make you feel?'

Bethanne chewed her lower lip, her hair falling over her face as she studied the painting.

'Happy?'

'Are you sure? Because you don't sound sure to me,' Abi said.

Bethanne nodded. 'They make me happy.'

'Yes?'

'Yes!' Bethanne gave a laugh.

'Well, good.'

'Is that the right answer? Should patterns make you happy?'

'Absolutely! What's the point of creating a pattern that makes you miserable? Or dressing in something that doesn't make you feel wonderful?'

'Mum sometimes makes us wear ugly clothes,' Rosie piped up from the other side of the table.

'But you'll be able to choose your own clothes one day.'

'Yes, when I'm older,' Rosie said with a sigh. 'Everything will happen when I'm *older*.'

Abi tried not to laugh because she could still remember the frustration of being too young to be allowed to do anything really interesting.

'How do you choose your designs, Aunt Abi?' Bethanne asked, drawing her attention back to what they were doing. 'There are so many patterns to choose from.'

Abi thought about this for a moment. 'I suppose what I'm trying to do with my patterns is to create a feeling of happiness, of joy and welcome. When people look at things I make, I want them to feel at home. I want them to get that lovely cosy feeling that comes from being in a home one truly loves. So I guess most of my designs start with a feeling you get when you see something. Like how did you feel when you picked up those pieces of fabric?'

Bethanne turned to the pink and white chintz and the sky-blue check. 'They made me smile inside.'

'That's the feeling exactly! Now, keep that feeling locked inside you for when you're creating something.'

Abi glanced across the table at Rosie. She'd been very quiet.

'You okay, Rosie?'

Rosie nodded, not looking up from the bird she was painting a vivid red.

'Aunt Abi?' Rosie said as she dipped her brush in the jar of water before dipping it in the green paint.

'Yes?'

'Why haven't you got a husband like Mummy has?'

'Ah, well your mummy got the best man in the world,' Abi said light-heartedly.

Rosie laughed.

'Do you think you'll get married one day?' Bethanne asked.

Abi took a moment before answering. 'I don't know,' she said honestly. 'You have to meet the right person first.'

'And you haven't?' Bethanne asked.

'No.'

'So you can't have children?' Rosie asked.

'You don't need to be married to have children,' Bethanne said.

Rosie frowned, obviously confused. 'Yes you do, silly!'

'No you don't. Chloe Meadows hasn't got a dad, has she?'

'Hasn't she?' Rosie said. 'That's sad. I think everyone should have a mummy *and* a daddy.'

They continued with their artistic pursuits for a while and then Rosie started up again with the questions.

'Do you want children, Aunt Abi?'

Abi gasped at the bluntness of the question, feeling the heat of both Rosie and Bethanne watching her for her response.

'I... well...' her voice petered out and her throat felt dry, her breathing becoming fast and ragged.

'Aunt Abi?' Bethanne leaned forward and placed a hand on Abi's arm, but Abi withdrew, standing up so fast that her chair fell over behind her.

'Get your things together, girls,' she managed to say.

'Are we leaving?' Bethanne asked, her face full of surprise.

'I've not finished my painting!' Rosie complained.

'Never mind that,' Abi said quickly. 'It's time to go home.'

CHAPTER TEN

Abi didn't often have nightmares or, if she did, she didn't remember them. But, sometimes, they would creep up on her in the middle of the night, twisting their tormenting visions through her mind until she woke up in a cold sweat. And she wasn't a bit surprised that she had one the night after she'd seen Bethanne and Rosie.

She hated that she'd been so mean to her nieces and regretted the drive back to their home in silence. Rosie seemed to have forgotten all about Abi's awkwardness and had fallen asleep on the backseat, but Bethanne had looked pale and anxious as if she'd known something was wrong with Abi. But how could she even begin to explain to them?

Still hung over from the disorientating feeling of having been lost inside her own head, Abi switched her bedside lamp on and took a long, cool drink from her glass of water and then got out of bed. She was wearing a long T-shirt and felt uncomfortably warm so she padded downstairs and opened the French doors, letting the cool night air circle around her bare limbs, caressing her gently and making her feel calmer.

Why was she still having nightmares after all this time? Abi had hoped that leaving London behind and all the memories of her old home would mean an escape from her nightmares too, but you couldn't outrun your fears, could you? Even hiding away somewhere as beautiful as Winfield couldn't guarantee banishing one's past. Because the past had a way of creeping up on you when you weren't looking, catching you at your most vulnerable and assaulting you with its memories.

Abi took a few deep breaths, contemplating going out into the garden and sitting in the cool darkness or maybe even walking up onto the downs and cooling off under the stars, but she'd always been a little afraid of the dark and so she closed the doors instead and made herself a cup of herbal tea, sitting down at the table a moment later. It was still littered with the papers and paints left behind by Bethanne and Rosie. She hadn't had the heart to tidy them away when she'd got back from dropping them home. She'd felt bruised by her ugly behaviour towards them and keeping their friendly mess out had seemed a kind of apology to them, making her feel as though they were still with her. She wished they were here now so that she could hug them closely to her and kiss their warm cheeks and tell them how much she loved them and how sorry she was for the way she'd reacted.

Looking down at the beautiful dots that Bethanne had painted, Abi wondered what had gone through her nieces' heads when she'd suddenly bundled them up and taken them home without giving them any sort of reason. She suspected that Rosie wouldn't have made that much out of it. But what of Bethanne? How much had she read into Abi's actions? She might only be ten years' old, but she felt things very deeply and Abi had seen the wounded look in her eyes and the concerned expression on her face a moment later. She'd known that Abi was acting out of character and that it wasn't just about being a grown-up as Rosie might have thought. There was something else going on.

Abi drank her tea, smelling its fruity perfume and hoping it would bring sweeter dreams to her when she went back to bed. It was as she was rinsing her mug at the sink a few minutes later that she heard a loud banging. She frowned. Was someone at Winfield's front door? It was after three in the morning. She moved towards the front door of her apartment and listened. Yes, there was definitely somebody there, banging and shouting now too.

'Edward! Open up! Come on – I know you're in there!'

Abi's hand hesitated on the lock of her door, but the caller obviously wasn't for her so she refrained from venturing into the hall, just opening her door a crack so she was able to hear a little better.

'Come on, Ed! Let me in for pity's sake!' the stranger cried from outside, banging yet again.

Interesting, Abi thought. Edward had clearly told her he wasn't an 'Ed'. So perhaps this was a close friend of his.

At last, she heard Edward's voice. She blinked in the bright lights of the entrance hall which he'd put on.

'You took your time,' the man was saying now that the front door was open.

'What are you doing here? It's the middle of the night!' Edward said angrily.

Abi wondered whether she should go out into the hallway and see if Edward needed some back up, but would he appreciate her poking her nose into his business? Probably not. He seemed to be an intensely private man. Yet, at the same time, she thought she had a right to know what was going on in her home during the middle of the night. But she didn't venture forth. For one thing, she didn't have the courage to wearing only a T-shirt, and Edward seemed to be handling things now.

'You shouldn't be driving,' Edward was saying, his tone angry.

'You letting me in, then?' the other man said.

'No.'

'I'll have to drive home if you don't let me in.'

'You should sleep in your car if you've got any sense,' Edward said.

'I don't need to sleep. I've hardly drunk a drop tonight.'

'Why do you do this?' Edward asked.

'Do what?'

'Act like this?'

'Oh, god – the last thing I need right now is a lecture!'

She didn't quite catch what Edward said next. It was some kind of mumbled curse which seemed to irritate the stranger even more because he started cursing too.

'Shut up!' Edward cried. 'There are people trying to sleep here.'

'People? What people?'

'You know what people. I told you.'

'Told me what?'

'That I sold half of the place.'

'Oh, right.' The stranger made an exaggerated hushing sound and then laughed.

'Sleep it off in the car, okay?' Edward said.

'But I want to talk to you.'

'I've got nothing to say to you.'

'Don't be like that!'

'You shouldn't have come.'

Abi flinched at Edward's tone, wondering who on earth this unwelcome visitor was.

'Why are you like this?' the stranger said. 'Why do you treat me this way? What the hell have I ever done to you, huh?'

Abi leaned forward, but she couldn't hear Edward's reply as

he was muttering under his breath, probably in a vain attempt not to wake her. It wasn't like Abi to eavesdrop, but she couldn't help wanting to hear the whole conversation and not just snatches of it. Then she felt guilty. She really shouldn't be listening in on what was obviously a private moment.

She was just about to close her door when she heard the front door of Winfield slam shut. She waited until she was quite sure the stranger had gone, hearing the screech of his tyres on the driveway outside. Hesitating, not quite knowing what the right thing to do was, she opened her door a little wider and saw Edward standing in the hall, his face dark with emotion.

'Edward?' she whispered as she approached him.

His head shot up in surprise.

'I heard a commotion. Is everything okay?'

He nodded. 'Go back to bed. I'm sorry if you were disturbed.'

'Are you sure you're all right?'

He sighed and it was such a pitiful sound that her heart bled for him.

'Go back to bed, Abigail,' he said, before walking across the hall towards his own apartment.

The next morning arrived as a blessed relief for Abi. Still shaken by her nightmare and the odd behaviour of Edward after the episode with the stranger, she decided to leave it all behind and stride out into the countryside. Wearing a brand new pair of walking boots, a straw hat and a lot of factor fifty, and carrying a backpack in which was a flask of water, a strawberry jam sandwich, an apple and her sketchbook, she felt ready to conquer the downs and was excited to have the whole day to explore. That was one of the joys of working for yourself, she thought – the hours lay ahead of you to be filled by whatever you fancied. You could plan things in detail or be spontaneous and just see what the weather was doing and how you responded to it. There was so much freedom and Abi loved that. So much of her London life had been timetabled and scheduled. There'd been very little room to be spontaneous when running her company, and that had definitely been a factor in her little wobble. But today was hers to do with as she wanted and, with the sky a clear and happy blue and the July sun promising golden limbs, she was going to spend it outdoors.

Slowly, Abi was getting to know her environment, walking the chalky footpaths, exploring the beech woods and following the streams. There was nothing more satisfying than a day spent in the countryside and she was beginning to regret the years she had lost by not spending more time away from her work. But then she had to remind herself that the time at work had been in pursuit of the thing she loved most in the world: her art. She was a creative soul and sometimes, by giving that creativity free rein, it meant giving other things up.

Dana would definitely approve of this, Abi thought, as she hiked up one of the hills outside the village, her eyes devouring the colours of the South Downs. Everything seemed so bright today. The barley fields were a vivid yellow-green when the sun was full upon them, the chalky paths were blindingly bright and the little woods that dotted the hills were wearing their deep emerald colours, glorying in the peak of life. Abi took it all in, her artist's mind thinking about the juxtaposition of the blue sky and the green hills, the silvered and weathered wood of a stile she climbed over, the rich magenta of the common knapweed which danced majestically on its long stalks, and the lacy beauty of the yarrow. There were so many colours and patterns and textures. And what joys would autumn bring, Abi wondered? What would the palette be then? And winter's hues, and then spring before another summer came to enrapture her again. She had so much to look forward to.

After walking for about an hour, she found a shady place underneath a great oak tree with a view into a valley village with a fine church she promised to visit another day. She unpacked her bag, taking a long cool drink of water and devouring her jam sandwich before munching on her crisp apple. It was as simple as lunches got but, eaten outdoors with the trees and sky above her and the landscape of the downs rolled out before her, it was elevated to something very special indeed.

After she'd finished, she lay back, making a pillow of her backpack and gazing up into the dappled light through the deep green leaves of the oak, seeing little patterns of blue sky beyond and hearing the piercing song of a skylark. Her eyes closed in a drowsy daze and she allowed herself to drift off for a few minutes, feeling the warmth of the breeze on her bare arms.

When she awoke, she grabbed her sketchbook and pencil and drew the scene before her, not wanting to forget its beauty. After she'd finished, she walked further along the path, stopping to sketch the wildflowers and the Marbled White butterfly whose distinctive black and white pattern looked as though it had been designed by an Art Deco artist.

Abi was still in that wonderful fallow stage where she was only half thinking about how she was going to make her way in the world in the future. She was lucky that her business had provided her with a sizeable nest egg and she could afford to take time off. A lot of time if she needed. But nest eggs didn't last forever, she was aware of that and she couldn't help wondering if this endless sketching of her new environment would lead to anything particular.

Popping her pencil end in her mouth – a terrible habit she'd had since childhood and one which her Aunt Claire had abhorred – Abi tried to banish her worries about the future because something would come up. It usually did. She just had to trust the passage of time and her instinct because that had worked pretty well for her in the past.

In the meantime, she had the Sussex countryside at her feet and she would walk just a few more miles of it before returning home.

It was as Abi was coming over the ridge of the hill and caught sight of Winfield Hall in the distance a couple of hours later that she realised, once again, how lucky she was to have made a home here. But it wasn't until she was descending the hill that she saw a car in the driveway that she didn't recognise. Perhaps it was a surveyor or someone restoring the hall. So many people came and went, she lost track. But it soon became apparent that the stranger wasn't anything to do with the building work.

It was a tall man in a white T-shirt and dark jeans which looked far too hot to wear in the summer, and he was walking out from the walled garden. *Her* walled garden. Abi felt herself stiffen.

'Can I help you?' she called over to him, wondering what he wanted and how long it would take for the police to get here if he meant no good.

He strode towards her across the driveway, shielding his eyes against the sun. 'Is Edward here?' he asked.

Abi wasn't sure whether to answer him or not. After all, she didn't know this man.

'I notice his car isn't here,' he continued and then he smiled and his eyes crinkled in a way that reminded Abi of a small boy and something in her softened at his sweet demeanour which was very silly of her really, she berated. Any psychopath knew how to smile in a way to charm.

'He's probably in London,' Abi told him.

'Oh.' The man looked a little crestfallen by this news. 'I was hoping to apologise. For last night. I – erm – might have made a bit of noise. Sort of in the middle of the night actually.'

'That was you?'

'Yup! Did I disturb you?'

'Well, I did wonder what was going on,' Abi admitted.

'I was a bit worse for wear, I'm afraid.'

'You'd been drinking and driving?' Abi asked, unable to hide her disapproval.

'Not really, no,' he said, giving a little smile. 'Well, a bit. But not a lot! Really, I would never put anyone else at risk. I'm one of the best drivers around.'

'And who did you say you were again?'

'Oscar. Oscar Townsend. I'm Ed's brother.'

Abi's mouth dropped open.

'He hasn't told you about me, has he?' Oscar laughed. 'Typical. For some reason, he prefers to have nothing to do with his family.'

'Oh, dear,' Abi said, looking more closely at Oscar and noticing that he had the same dark sandy hair and hazel eyes as Edward although his features were slimmer and sharper.

Oscar reached into his pocket for his phone and frowned. 'No signal here?'

'It's a little temperamental.'

He shook his head. 'What on earth is Ed doing living in a heap in the middle of nowhere?'

Abi frowned. 'But he said he grew up in the next village.'

'Yeah, and I thought he couldn't wait to get away from it. He moved to London as soon as he could.'

But wasn't it telling that he'd moved back, Abi thought, but she didn't say anything.

'Will you tell him I called? I mean, I could hang around for a bit...' Oscar said, a little boy lost look on his face now. Abi wondered if he was fishing for an invitation inside.

'I'll tell him you called,' she said.

He nodded. 'Sure.

Well, it was very nice to meet you, erm?' he paused, eyebrows raised enquiringly.

'Abigail,' she said, thinking no harm could come of her revealing her name to Edward's brother surely.

He took a step closer and reached out to take her hand in his.

'Pleased to meet you, *Abigail*,' he said, a twinkle in his hazel eyes that made Abi smile despite herself, and she watched as he walked towards his car, got in and then tooted the horn as he drove away – an act that seemed about as far removed from his brother Edward as she could imagine.

That evening, as Abi was admiring the pinks, purples and blues of the cornflowers she'd planted in one of the raised beds, vowing to paint them as soon as possible, she heard a car pulling up in the driveway. She made her way to the gate and saw that it was Edward arriving home. He was wearing a dark suit, but was carrying the jacket over his shoulder, his briefcase in his other hand. He looked tired after his day in London. Abi didn't envy him that. The journey alone in the summer heat would take it out of her these days, she thought.

She pottered around the garden for a little while longer, admiring how quickly things were growing after the rain the week before which had had the good grace to fall during the night. She marvelled at her sunflowers, glorying in the vibrant yellow petals and the thick stems. Had they really only been seeds just a few months ago? And she looked lovingly at the rows of lettuce and chard she'd planted in another of the raised beds, delighted that she'd done something as simple as growing her own food. It really did give her enormous pleasure.

Finally, she went back indoors, washing the salad leaves she'd picked for a light supper and then brushing her hair quickly before making her way across the hall towards Edward's apartment. It was still an odd feeling to share this large space with a relative stranger – to live so closely and yet so very separately. And she felt a little awkward calling on him like this. It felt like a kind of intrusion. But, then again, she had been asked to pass a message on and so she knocked on his door.

'Abigail?' he said a moment later as he answered. 'Everything okay?' He looked behind and around her as if it might not be. As if, perhaps, something was amiss with Winfield because why else would she be disturbing him?

'Hi Edward. I have a message for you.'

'Oh?'

'Yes. Your brother called by earlier today.'

He frowned. 'My brother?'

'Yes. Oscar,' Abi said as if Edward might need reminding.

'I see.'

'He didn't leave a message, but wanted you to know he called by.'

'Right.' Edward stood awkwardly at his door and Abi stood awkwardly in front of him.

'You told me you didn't have any family,' she dared to say after a moment.

Edward glanced at her, not looking happy that she'd remembered such a detail.

'I know.'

'So you lied to me.'

She saw him swallow hard and then he sighed.

'I did and I'm sorry. It just seemed easier at the time.'

'But why?'

He glanced down at his shoes and Abi wondered what he was thinking. 'Things are... complicated with my family.'

'Aren't they with everyone's?' Abi pointed out.

'I shouldn't have thought so.'

Abi placed her hands on her hips. 'Edward, I hate to break it to you, but you aren't the only person on the planet with a complicated family.'

He grimaced. 'It kind of goes beyond complicated, I'm afraid.'

Abi frowned. 'Like how?' she asked, and that's when she saw him almost physically withdraw from her.

'It's not something I want to talk about, okay?'

'Okay,' Abi said. 'Listen – the light in the garden's wonderful right now. How about joining me. I can make us some tea. I've just picked some salad.'

He shook his head. 'I've had a busy day. I'm just going to crash.'

'You could crash in the garden with me?'

He gave a tiny smile. 'Another time. Maybe.'

It was the word *maybe* that signalled to Abi that she really shouldn't push him. He didn't want to be sociable. Not today and maybe not ever.

Edward was just about to close his door on her when she spoke again.

'He seems nice.'

'Who?' Edward said.

'Your brother!' She laughed, but Edward's expression told her that he was not in a laughing mood.

CHAPTER ELEVEN

The next day, Abi was still smarting from Edward's behaviour. The more she thought about it – and she really had tried hard *not* to think about it – she believed that he'd behaved unreasonably. She'd had a message to relay to him and he'd been most unwelcoming when he'd opened the door and then been rudely evasive when she'd pointed out the fact that he'd lied to her that evening in the pub.

Then she'd felt bad because it seemed obvious that Edward was hiding something and perhaps that something was painful and it was wrong of her to push for details. She mustn't forget that they were only sharing a living space. That didn't mean they automatically became best friends and confidantes.

She smiled as she tried to imagine that. Edward as a confidante. The idea was outrageous. And yet, there was something deeply appealing about his reticence. It was unusual and dignified. Perhaps she'd been too harsh on him, thinking him rude. Perhaps he was just a very private man and she should do her best to leave him alone.

In the apartment across the hall from Abi's, Edward was pacing. He regretted speaking like that to Abi, but he really hadn't been in a chatty mood. Not that he ever was, but perhaps he'd been even less chatty than normal when she'd called round with the news that his brother had called at Winfield.

Oscar. Just the name sent Edward into a tailspin. He hadn't yet got over his brother's visit in the middle of the night and was angry that it had disturbed Abi. But the fact that Oscar had visited again and had introduced himself to Abi was really maddening. He'd had no business to do that. Indeed, Edward had contemplated not telling Oscar about his purchase of Winfield Hall. He'd seriously thought about just disappearing, only Winfield was such a small community and it wouldn't take Oscar long to track him down to the very village they'd grown up next to. After all, Oscar did still live in the neighbourhood.

Maybe he'd made a mistake in coming back to Sussex. Maybe he should have upped and moved somewhere where nobody would be able to trace him. A village in the foothills of the Himalayas, or a hut on the beach of some remote Greek island. The idea did appeal to him, but he knew he didn't really have the courage to follow through. He was far too in love with the English landscape to ever think of giving it up. Glancing out of the windows now at the great gold-green flank of the down, he knew he could never leave England. But he was going to have to leave Winfield again today, he thought, and journey back into London. Maybe that was another reason he'd been short with Abigail the night before too. He'd been anxious about what was coming his way. An interview for a job.

Edward hadn't had a job interview for years. He'd been in his old position for so long that he'd forgotten what it was like to subject oneself to the rigours of an interview by a panel of total strangers. He'd happily forgotten the stresses of presenting a professional face to a team of people who might already have given the job to somebody within the company and were just going through the routine of interviewing others so they could tick a box. And he'd also forgotten how very nerve-wracking these things could be, forcing memories of every failure you'd ever had back into the forefront of your mind.

Why was it that one carried one's insecurities for years? Was there a physical place in the body where they were stored? Could you ever be free of them? Could you learn to purge yourself of them? Well, Edward had never managed it. He still remembered every single interview he'd messed up, every job he hadn't got and every test he hadn't passed. Those things were locked away inside him forever, he believed. Only he mustn't focus on them today – not if he wanted to project confidence and ability. It was a good job. He'd known the company for a number of years and they had a good reputation. The salary was good and the office was a short walk from a tube station.

But it wasn't his old job.

That's what a little voice inside his head kept saying. It wasn't his old job and his life would never be the same again. That old comfortable role he'd had with colleagues he'd trusted and worked with well. This new company, although he'd heard nothing but good things about it, wasn't the company he'd worked with for years. Mind you, he thought, that company had let him go, so why was he feeling so nostalgic about it? It was time to move on. The only thing that was certain in life was change – wasn't that what they said? Nothing stayed the same for long and, if you didn't adapt, you'd be left behind.

So, after making the journey into town and arriving in good time at the office, Edward took a deep breath before entering through the large glass doors, walking across a lobby filled with people he didn't know. He signed in and resigned himself to his fate.

~

It was an hour later when Edward came out of the office building and was hit by a wall of heat. There was a park nearby and he walked towards it, taking his jacket off and unbuttoning his shirt sleeves, rolling them up a moment later. It had been a ridiculous interview performed by three people who didn't have one smile between them. He'd been put through a series of silly questions to which the answers were clearly on his application form. He'd been relieved when the director had stood up to shake his hand, giving him the sort of look that promised nothing but a rejection in the coming week.

At least one thing had been gained by the whole sorry experience, Edward knew that he didn't want to work for anybody ever again. He couldn't put himself through the trauma of it all. He'd much rather focus on making his own way and building something that was his and he knew he could make things work even if money was tight for a while.

He'd still have to come into town every so often to meet with his London-based clients, but that was fine. He didn't mind that so much knowing that it would be on his terms and only for a few hours with the promised escape back to Winfield at the end of the working day.

Finding a bench under the shade of a large plane tree, Edward took a sip of water from his flask and ate a limp sandwich he'd bought from a shop outside the tube, wishing he was eating it on top of the downs with the summer breeze coming inland from the sea. There wasn't much air in the city and the shade from the tree above him was welcome but fleeting as the sun moved round so he got up to go. It was time anyway.

As if his job interview in a hot capital city wasn't enough to contend with, he had a doctor's appointment in an hour's time, but he was kind of regretting the second appointment now, wishing he could jump onto the train and get back to Winfield as soon as possible.

Edward had been seeing this doctor on and off for three years now and trusted him, so was hopeful he'd be able to help with the recent increase in pain he'd been experiencing. The clinic was just a short walk from Bedford Square and, mercifully, Edward didn't have to hang around in the hot waiting room for too long. He then had a series of tests and X-rays and was shown into a room and given a glass of iced water while he waited.

When the doctor came back with the results and started telling Edward something technical about what was going on inside his leg and hip, he did his best to understand.

'What does that mean in practical terms?' Edward asked.

'You don't need to make any drastic changes to your life. I'd still like you to maintain your current level of fitness.'

'And I can still swim?'

'Oh, yes. Swimming's good.'

'And the recent pain? What can I do for that?'

'We'll try these new painkillers. They're a little stronger than the last ones,' the doctor warned. 'Take them with food, and stop if you start hallucinating.'

Edward stared at him, half expecting him to laugh, but he didn't.

Great, Edward thought. Just what he needed in his life: another complication.

～

Life was also about to get complicated for Abi that day. She'd just set out several sheets of paper on her table and was about to embark on some preliminary sketches for a new pattern inspired by the photos she'd taken of the wildflowers on her recent walk, when her phone rang.

'Oh, god, Abi!' the voice cried.

'Ellen – are you okay?'

'No, I'm not! You're never going to believe what's happened! Can you come? Can you come right away?'

'Yes, of course I can,' Abi said, looking forlornly at the project she'd been so excited to dive into. But family came first, she told herself as she hung up the phone, wondering what on earth was happening with her sister. Ellen was one of those people who seemed to lurch from crisis to crisis, her life one big drama, and she'd had to manage without her little sister on her doorstep up until now. How had she coped? Was Abi being taken advantage of? She couldn't help thinking such thoughts and then feeling guilty for having them.

She left Winfield Hall in record time, driving towards Brighton, tapping her fingers nervously on her steering wheel and wondering what scene of devastation she would find once she got there. It was gone four in the afternoon so the girls would be home from school. Was it something to do with them, she wondered? A medical emergency or had something happened between Ellen and Douglas?

Finding a parking space outside her sister's house, Abi jumped out of the car and rang the bell.

'Ellen! Are you okay? I came as fast as I could.' She wrapped her sister in an embrace.

'I don't know what to do!'

'About what?' Abi could see that her sister's face was red with tears.

'This!' Ellen led her into the kitchen and sitting there in the middle of the floor was a tiny blonde and black dog, its liquid eyes gazing up at them both.

Abi's instinct was to laugh, but she knew better than to do that.

'Is *this* the problem?' she asked.

'Yes, *this* is the problem!'

'Who's is it?'

'It's ours apparently! Bloody Douglas had the bright idea to get a dog for the girls.'

'Where are the girls?' Abi asked, suddenly realising she hadn't seen them yet.

'Upstairs doing their homework.'

'And when did the dog arrive?'

'Douglas brought it home with him last night on a flying visit. He had it in this box and the girls were beside themselves when they saw what was in it.'

'Ellen,' Abi said, as calmly as she could, 'when you called me and asked me to come over right away, I thought Douglas was in hospital or something!'

Ellen frowned at her. 'What made you think that?'

'Er – you were crying down the phone.'

'I was desperate, Abi! I didn't know what to do. This dog's been terrorising me all day!'

'Well, he looks as if he's behaving himself now,' Abi said, watching as the puppy curled up in a tiny basket in a corner of the kitchen.

'But this is so typical of Douglas! He's away all the time and the girls are too young to take care of it. He *knows* the work will all fall to me!'

'It won't be all work, though, will it?' Abi asked. 'It'll be fun too, surely?'

'You call puddles of pee and piles of poo *fun*? And it's

already eaten its way through my handbag. Look!' Ellen said, grabbing hold of her bag from a nearby stool. 'Ruined!'

Abi chewed her lip. There was a tiny little bite mark on the strap, but it didn't look too bad.

'You'll have to get it some toys. Puppies chew things.' Then she thought of something. 'You keep calling the puppy "it". Hasn't he got a name yet?'

'I suppose,' Ellen said. Was it Abi's imagination or did her sister look embarrassed?

'What is it?'

'He's such a funny looking creature.'

'He's a pug, isn't he? He's meant to look funny.'

'Well, I took one look at him and said he was a pug ugly and Bethanne quickly said "Pugly".'

Abi laughed. 'You're calling him Pugly?'

'Actually, I think it's quite a good name!'

It was then that Bethanne and Rosie appeared in the kitchen, immediately running across the room to play with Pugly on the floor.

'Hi Aunt Abi!' Bethanne said.

'Hi girls.'

Rosie looked around and smiled briefly, but Abi could see that she'd been supplanted in their affections by the dear little creature.

'He's so cute,' Abi said, joining her nieces on the floor. 'He's barely bigger than my hand.'

'He pees everywhere!' Rosie informed her.

'So I've heard!'

'But it's okay because he's a baby,' Bethanne said.

'Where did he come from?' Abi asked.

'Douglas said a colleague of his posted a photo via social media. He couldn't resist apparently.' She rolled her eyes. 'The girls hadn't even been *asking* for a puppy!'

'Oh, every kid should have a pet, though,' Abi said. 'Remember when we tried to lobby Aunt Claire for a rabbit?'

Ellen groaned. 'She wouldn't even compromise with a hamster, would she?'

'Exactly! And you don't want to be remembered like that, do you? Well, Pugly is your chance to show your girls that pets are a wonderful addition to any family.'

'I can't help thinking Douglas is hiding something,' Ellen said under her breath.

'What do you mean?'

'I mean, he comes home with this puppy. Don't you think that's weird?'

'How is it weird to want to spoil his daughters a little?' Abi asked.

'Because it's like something somebody would do if they were trying to deflect attention from something else.'

'Like what, Ellen? You're not making any sense.'

Ellen grabbed Abi by the arm and led her out of the room and away from her daughters.

'Ellen, you're scaring me now,' Abi said when she saw tears sparkling in her sister's eyes. 'What is it?'

'I think he's having an affair.'

'Douglas? *No!*'

Ellen nodded. 'Why else is he away so often?'

'Because he's working. You know that!'

'He's hardly ever here, Abi! He doesn't want to be with his family.'

'That's nonsense! He adores you all! But you know his work's important to him and you knew the commitment he made to his company so that you could buy this place. And that means long hours away from home.' Abi looked closely at her sister. Surely she understood all this and was just getting herself worked up over nothing.

'I miss him so much!' Ellen cried.

'I know you do,' Abi said gently, 'and I'm sure the dog is nothing more than a gesture of kindness. Douglas is a good man and an amazing father. I think it hurts him to be away from you all just as much as it hurts you, and maybe this is his way of trying to make up for that.'

'You think?'

'Yes. I really do.'

They walked back into the kitchen together and Abi kneeled down on the floor again to fuss the puppy. For all the fun she was having watching her nieces' reaction to their new pet, Abi could see that Ellen looked absolutely exhausted with it all.

'Shall I take the girls out for a bit?' she asked kindly.

Ellen nodded, her face flooding with the relief of one being handed a lifeline.

'Will you take Pugly too?'

Abi was momentarily floored. 'Has he had all his injections and everything?'

'Yes. He was the cutest in the litter apparently and the owner kept him on as her own for a while, but then decided to sell him.'

'He's very easy to walk,' Bethanne piped up. 'But you can't let him off the lead yet. He's too little and silly. Like Rosie.'

Rosie hit her sister, but the teasing was all in good fun.

'And don't walk him too far,' Ellen said. 'He gets tired very quickly.'

'He likes being carried best of all,' Rosie said and Abi couldn't help wondering if that was a fact or if it was because the girls liked to carry him.

'Okay then. Let's see how far we get,' Abi said. 'Who's got his lead?'

Bethanne ran across the room to retrieve a pink lead. Of

course it was pink, Abi reasoned. Only the best for Pugly and it did match his very fetching collar, she noted. For all Ellen's complaints, she could see that this was going to be one very spoilt dog.

They left the house and walked to the nearest park. The girls knew the way and set up a merry banter all about the exploits of Pugly.

'He's so naughty!' Rosie said. 'He's even naughtier than me!'

'You mean he eats too many sweets and doesn't do his homework?' Abi said.

'Don't be silly!' Rosie cried. 'Dogs don't get homework!'

'Well, perhaps they should,' Abi said. 'Perhaps you should start training him.'

'I'm going to teach him to sit,' Bethanne said.

'That's a very good idea.'

'And not to eat things he shouldn't,' Bethanne added.

'Because we have to help Mummy love him more,' Rosie said and a little bit of Abi's heart broke at that.

'She'll come round,' she told Rosie.

'She's mad all the time,' Bethanne said.

'Oh, dear! Is everything okay?' Abi asked, knowing that you could always trust a child to tell you the truth.

'Mum and Dad have been fighting,' Bethanne confessed.

'Yeah – *big* fighting,' Rosie added.

'About Pugly?' Abi asked.

'Mostly. And some other stuff,' Bethanne said.

'What other stuff?' Abi said as they walked around the pond in the park, Pugly receiving admiring glances from passers-by.

'I just heard bits,' Bethanne said, 'but I kept hearing the name Rachelle. I think she's a friend of Dad's. Mum doesn't like her.'

'Has she been to the house?'

'No. Dad works with her but Mum was shouting at Dad and saying that Rachelle had answered his phone when she'd rung.'

Abi frowned. 'And what did your dad say?'

'That he was carrying a box or something and didn't want to miss the call.'

'I see.'

'Dad's away a lot,' Bethanne went on. 'Mum doesn't like that.'

'No, it's hard when the person you love is away,' Abi explained.

'She's been crying,' Rosie said.

'She always thinks we won't notice,' Bethanne said.

'But her face gets all red and blotchy,' Rosie added.

'Mine goes like that too when I cry,' Abi confessed.

'I get sad when she's sad,' Rosie said and Abi put her arm around her.

'I think that's maybe why Daddy got you Pugly – to help you be happy when he's away,' Abi told her.

'I love Pugly,' Rosie said, 'but he isn't Daddy, is he?'

'No, of course not,' Abi agreed, doing her best not to laugh at her niece's sweetness. 'But I think your daddy bought Pugly so you could cuddle him whenever you miss Daddy.'

'I'd better cuddle him now then,' Rosie said, scooping the puppy up from the ground and squashing her face into his wrinkled one.

'Me too!' Bethanne said, putting her arms around Rosie and pushing her face towards Pugly who looked delighted by all the attention.

After putting Pugly down and playing on the swings for a few minutes, they slowly walked back home, Bethanne scooping Pugly up when he started to lag behind.

'He's tired,' she explained.

Abi was beginning to feel tired too. She usually did when

she was worried. She couldn't stop thinking about the scenes her nieces had witnessed. How heartbreaking it must have been for them to hear their parents arguing and to see their mother in tears. It was bad enough that Douglas was away so often, but to spend the little time he was at home fighting with Ellen must make for a rather sad household.

Maybe there was something to Ellen's anxiety over Douglas, Abi kept thinking, and maybe it was time that she had a talk with him about it.

CHAPTER TWELVE

Abi had only fallen in love once in her life. But once had been enough. She'd managed to get through secondary school and art college without having a single long-lasting relationship. There had been a few casual boyfriends, a few dates that led nowhere in particular, but Abi really hadn't minded. She'd gone to college with the revolutionary motive to study and work. Work had always been her passion and she hadn't been one to sit in her student room mooning over the fact that she didn't have a date that night. Not having a date gave her more time to sketch, dream and study. Now *that* was something she could get really excited about.

After college, she'd dated a man called Billy for a few months. Billy was sweet and kind and, like Abi, was a dreamer. But he was a bit too much of a dreamer even for Abi to cope with. She remembered one day when they'd been walking around the National Gallery, taking in the enormous Constable's and Monet's, filling their eyes with colour and brilliance and Billy had talked and talked, and it had been so wonderful to listen to him, but there had come a point when

Abi realised that she couldn't listen anymore and that she could have been anyone standing there next to him. He really wasn't aware of her at all.

She often wondered what had happened to Billy. Was he still talking and dreaming? She hoped so. She hoped that enthusiasm hadn't been dampened by the realities of the world and that he wasn't wearing a navy suit and working in a cubicle somewhere.

And then Abi had lost herself to work, slowly building her company. Was that why she hadn't had a serious relationship? Well, she *had*, she told herself, just not one that had gone the distance.

'You're married to your work,' Ellen had once told her.

'No I'm not!' Abi had retorted, genuinely shocked.

'Yes, you are. Admit it – you'd rather be sat inside with your sketchbook than out on a date with a guy. Your work is your life.'

Abi mulled over this once again now as she sketched outside, her pencil flying freely across the creamy surface of the page. Her work was her life. Yes, she had to admit that there was a smidgeon of truth in that. But life *was* work, wasn't it? Her designs filled her with joy. Patterns made her feel passion and the endless possibilities of colour and form excited her more than anything else. Was it wrong to dedicate her life to such things? Especially now. After Dante.

Dante.

With a name like that, perhaps she should have realised he was an Italian tragedy just waiting to happen. Instead, she'd fallen for him hard. She'd always believed that she would be resoundingly practical when it came to matters of the heart, but it was all very well having theories about these things when one hadn't actually experienced the true turmoil of falling in love. He'd walked into her shop one day and had fixed those soft brown eyes on hers and she'd felt pinned to the spot. She still remembered the first time she'd heard him speak with that Italian accent which was all soft circles and melody.

'Your shop,' he'd said, 'is very beautiful.'

'Thank you,' Abi said.

'And so are you.'

Abi had felt herself blush. He didn't waste any time, did he? She quickly busied herself with something as he moved around the shop, but she could feel his eyes upon her and she caught them as she glanced up every so often, wishing he'd leave, but hoping he'd stay.

He'd admired many of her prints that day, asking if she was the designer.

'You have a good eye,' he told her when she said she was indeed the designer. 'And you have very beautiful eyes.'

The next thing she'd known, she was having coffee at a nearby shop with him. He told her he was teaching Renaissance art at University College, London, but how he missed his home on the Ligurian coast where his family of three sisters and four brothers lived.

'I'm one of two,' Abi told him.

'You have missed life!' he said.

She'd laughed at the joy in his face as he went on to tell her about his family and she knew that a little bit of her had fallen in love with him right there and then, listening to his stories and telling him just a few of her own. Unlike Billy, he listened as well as talked and that was a new experience for Abi. She felt like he cared.

Of course, he knew all the best Italian restaurants in London, guiding her to the ones with the freshest ingredients and the most authentic recipes. They ate out often, always chatting, always laughing. How wonderful it had been. Abi had felt like she was floating and that the feeling would last forever.

But then something had happened that had changed everything. Something unexpected and unplanned.

But not entirely unwanted, Abi thought to herself now. And that had been the problem.

The harsh cry of a seagull who'd flown inland suddenly brought Abi back to the present and she found that her face was wet with tears before she even realised she'd been crying. How long had she been crying for? She quickly wiped her tears away and reached for a tissue in her pocket, glad of the privacy in this corner of the garden. Why had she let her mind wander into the past? She'd come out to sketch the flowers, but had then fallen prey to memories. Perhaps it was because she was so concerned for Ellen and Douglas. Maybe thinking about their situation had reminded her of her own fateful relationship with Dante.

Abi sighed, trying to let the past go as she took some deep, stilling breaths of downland air. She looked up at the happy faces of her sunflowers. You couldn't feel sad when you looked at those and so she stared at each and every single one of them now, taking in their vibrant golden petals and the chocolate-brown centres. She got up to walk among them, thanking her lucky stars once again for the day she'd discovered Winfield and for the good fortune that Edward had chosen her to share it with. She had only guessed that she needed a place like this, but now she knew it for sure. This place was healing. It was a sanctuary away from the world. Of course that didn't mean you could completely shut the world out or protect yourself from everything, but it felt like a safe place. A place where one could rest and be at peace and she needed that so much right now. More than she dared to admit to anyone.

∾

Edward needed to find peace too. After a couple of stressful days dealing with issues from the builders, he needed a session in the river. His new medication, which only really took the edge off his pain, didn't appear to be making him hallucinate and so he deemed it safe to have a swim. He shut his laptop, switched off his phone and grabbed his things together.

It was a relief to get outside, away from the noise and dust of the building work. He crossed the driveway and that's when he saw Abigail. She was getting something out of the boot of her car and Edward nodded politely, but didn't stop moving.

'Hi Edward,' she said, a bright smile on her face.

'Hello.'

'It's a bit noisy today, isn't it?' she said.

'Yes.'

'Has it been disturbing you?'

'A little.'

She nodded. 'Going somewhere nice?'

He stopped by his car. 'Yes.'

'That's a very big bag,' Abi said. 'What's inside?'

He didn't answer for a moment.

'Sorry,' she said. 'It's none of my business.'

'It's a wetsuit and other bits and bobs.'

'Oh?'

'I'm going swimming,' he confessed at last.

'In the sea? How lovely!'

'No. The river actually.'

'Really?'

He nodded and it was then that he noticed her face. It looked pale and red all at once. Blotchy. Suddenly, he realised that she must have been crying and something inside him seemed to crack.

'Come with me,' he found himself saying.

'What?'

'Come swimming with me. It'll do you good. It's calming and energising all at once.'

'But I...' Abi's voice petered out as if she didn't quite know what to say.

'I've got a spare wetsuit,' Edward said. 'An old one of mine. It might be a tad big on you, but it'll help keep you warm. The water's still pretty cool even in the summer.'

'I'm not sure...'

'You can swim, can't you?' he asked.

'Oh, yes.'

'Honestly, you'll love it,' Edward told her. He wasn't quite sure why he was trying to persuade her so wholeheartedly. After all, he'd been looking forward to the solitude of his river swim. He wasn't looking for a companion.

'Okay,' Abi said.

'Really?' Edward found he was smiling. 'Let me get the other wetsuit. I won't be a minute.'

Abi couldn't quite believe that, just a little while ago, she'd been crying in the garden and now she was standing on the riverbank in Edward's spare wetsuit. How on earth had that happened? It had been a struggle to get into the ridiculous item of clothing even though there had been plenty of room to manoeuvre and Abi felt awkward wearing it now, teamed with a pair of old jelly shoes because Edward had insisted on something to protect her feet.

He'd given her some privacy to change, hiding himself behind a large oak tree where he got into his own wetsuit. When he emerged, Abi couldn't help laughing.

'What?' he asked innocently.

'I don't know. I guess I never imagined you wearing something like that. I'm so used to seeing you in business suits.'

Edward looked down at himself. 'You won't be laughing when you get in the water. You'll be thankful for your neoprene skin then.'

'Yes, about that...'

Edward frowned. 'You're not going to back out on me, are you?'

Abi looked down at the clear water flowing past. It looked beautiful in the afternoon sunshine. Beautiful and cold.

'I'm not sure. I might just watch you,' she said, feeling defeated before she'd even dipped a jellied toe.

'Come on, Abigail! When do you get a chance to do something like this? And it is summer. The water will be at its very best.'

That was true, she thought. If she didn't do it now in the middle of summer while dressed for the occasion and with a very patient teacher beside her, when would she? And there was a large part of her that was curious to have this experience – to immerse herself in another element and see the world from a completely new perspective.

'Okay,' she said.

'Great!'

'I'll follow you in.' She watched as Edward walked to the edge of the riverbank, sat down on it and then lowered himself into the water. 'Is it cold?' she dared to ask him.

'Not at all!'

Abi wasn't convinced, but she edged towards the bank and, like Edward, lowered herself in.

'I thought you said it wasn't cold!' she cried a moment later.

Edward laughed as he swam into the middle of the river, floating on his back and gazing up at the sky.

'Just keep moving. You'll soon acclimatise.'

Abi did as she was told. She couldn't remember the last time she'd been swimming, let alone wild swimming, but it must have been the trip to the seaside when Ellen's girls were very young. Bethanne had wanted to go paddling and Rosie had still been a babe in arms. The four of them had walked down to the sea together. It had been one of those scorching days which happily chase people into the sea to cool down and Abi had luxuriated in it, the salty waves breaking over her hot skin. But this was different. The river felt colder than the sea had that day, and the water was surprisingly deep so that she was soon able to swim and find her pace. And how deliciously odd it felt to be at eye-level with the surface of the water. This was a newt's view of the world, she thought, noticing how very high the sky seemed from the river and how very close the trees felt. This was so much more joyful an experience than swimming in the local community pool with the excited shouts of kids bouncing off the walls and the furious strokes of fellow swimmers knocking you off your own more sedate pace.

As she rounded a bend in the river, a heron took off from the bank. Abi gasped. Herons were big birds by any standards but seeing it from the vantage of the water made the predator look gigantic and Abi felt empathy for the fish that it preyed on.

Edward was still ahead of her, his body barely rippling the water around him. He seemed to glide so gracefully through it – like he was a part of this place. Abi was beginning to feel that too – as if she'd been accepted by this other element. She'd left the land behind and entered this other realm and it had welcomed her, enveloping her in its silky coolness until she could barely tell where her body ended and the river began.

She wasn't quite sure how long they spent in the water. Time became something that belonged to the world they'd left behind when they'd launched themselves off the bank and into the river. But they couldn't stay in there forever and, when Abi climbed out and sat on the riverbank, she felt the buzz of exhilaration.

Edward joined her a moment later.

'I didn't want to get out,' he told her. 'That often happens.'

'You come here a lot?'

'Not as often as I'd like, but I've promised that I will.'

'It's a special place,' Abi said, gazing down river at the trees that edged the water. It was a scene full of serenity.

'So, what did you think?'

Abi pondered. 'I'm not sure I was thinking. Not when I first got in. I think I was just surviving! But then I sort of felt absorbed by the water. Does that make sense?'

'Oh, yes.'

'It was like an extension of me and I felt this deep peace.'

He nodded as if in approval.

'How did you find this place?' she asked him.

'I've known about it for some time,' he said and Abi didn't push him for more. 'Listen, we'd better get changed.'

Edward disappeared behind his oak tree and Abi struggled out of the wetsuit, feeling the late afternoon sunshine warming her skin as she peeled the neoprene off.

When they were dressed, they walked back across the fields towards the road where Edward had parked and he put their gear into the boot before they got back into the car.

'I like this moment the best,' Edward revealed as he started the engine.

'What's that?'

'That mellow moment after a swim before you have to do anything else, before you lose the feelings you captured in the water.'

She looked at his face and saw that he was smiling although it was a very small smile. But his eyes were smiling and his face looked softer than normal, gentler, like he'd found his inner peace. And, in that moment, she couldn't help feeling a kind of kinship with him. They'd shared something rather special. They hadn't talked much. They hadn't confessed anything or revealed their pasts to each other, and yet there'd been a moment of connection through the water.

'Can you feel that?' he asked her.

She nodded and he pulled out into the road and drove home. They didn't speak after that, but Abi felt that something had shifted between them. That awkwardness had gone and, although they weren't exactly chatting and sharing life stories, she felt content to be with him.

'Thank you,' she said as they arrived back at Winfield. 'I had a really good time.'

'Good,' he said and, although he wasn't exactly smiling now, Abi felt that he was just as contented as she was.

CHAPTER THIRTEEN

Even a couple of days after seeing Ellen and her nieces, Abi couldn't shake what had been said about Douglas. She'd always adored her brother-in-law and they had a special understanding which arose from their relationship. From the moment Ellen had introduced him to Abi, they'd bonded and would often commiserate with each other in hushed voices when Ellen was becoming a little too much for them both.

So that's why she decided to call him. They'd always been so honest with each other and Abi couldn't let her sister's anguish go unchecked.

'Douglas?' she said when he answered his mobile that evening.

'Abi? What a lovely surprise. Are you okay?'

'I'm fine. Everything's fine,' she lied, 'but I was wondering if I could see you.'

'Yeah?'

'Yes. I just need to talk about something. Would that be okay?'

'Sure. Go ahead.'

'Erm, it would be better if you could come over for a visit.'

'Oh, okay. I'm heading back home tomorrow if that's any good.'

'That would be brilliant. You've got my address, haven't you?'

'The biggest house in Winfield, right?'

'That's the one. Just toot your horn when you get here and I'll come and get you.'

～

Time had a funny way of slowing down when you're waiting for a certain moment to reach you. Abi did her best to busy herself with her garden and her art. She'd been working on a new pattern inspired by the downland butterflies and couldn't decide which scale and repeat would work best and so she was filling sheet after sheet of paper experimenting. She wanted to use the fabulous Adonis Blue butterfly with its astonishing sky-blue colouring, and she knew she was going to juxtapose it with the Marbled White with its black and white markings. Black. White. Sky-blue. Those three simple colours made quite an impression together, she thought.

She worked quietly away, making herself a quick sandwich at lunch which she ate while gazing at her sketches, and repeating her meal at tea time because food was always the last thing on her mind when she was working on a new project.

It was after seven when she heard the toot of a car horn. Abi put down the sketch she was working on and blinked a few times. It was always a little disconcerting to be jolted out of such close concentration. She did some stretches, bending her neck from side to side and then raising her arms towards the ceiling. She always forgot how stiff she got while working. Until it was too late. In London, she'd had regular physiotherapy and was always being told off for mistreating her body so, but that was the price of her art, wasn't it? Fine work and plenty of it couldn't be achieved without making a few physical sacrifices.

Leaving her apartment by the French doors, Abi made her way towards the front of Winfield where Douglas was getting out of his car. She watched him cross the driveway towards her. By the sag of his shoulders, she could tell that he was stressed. He worked long hours and drove hundreds of miles every week in a job that was high pressured and relentless.

They embraced and he said something about how impressive Winfield was, but Abi brushed it off. Now wasn't the time for her to show off her new home. They had more important things to discuss. They were meeting without Ellen knowing which was a funny feeling for Abi, but she didn't know how else to go about it. She couldn't exactly ask him what was going on in front of Ellen and the children. She was also feeling guilty for taking up precious time that he could be spending with his family but, at the same time, she was hoping that this conversation would help.

'Blimey, Abi! This is some place,' he said as they walked into the walled garden and entered through the French doors.

'I can't believe you've not seen it yet.'

'I know. Work is crazy.'

'It always is, isn't it?'

'Yep!' He frowned. 'What's Ellen said now?'

'Oh, just the usual,' Abi said, easing gently into it. 'That she hardly sees you. The girls miss you too.'

'Just pile on the guilt, won't you?' he said with a hollow laugh.

'I'm sorry,' Abi said.

'Is that what this is about? My time away from home?'

'Sort of,' Abi said. 'Let's make some tea first, shall we? And we can sit in the garden.'

Abi made the tea, hot and sweet, in two large mugs and they walked out into the garden, sitting down on Abi's bench by the French doors.

Douglas let out a long sigh that seemed to deflate the whole of his body.

'Sounds like you needed that.'

'Ah, yes,' he said. 'One sometimes forgets just to sit down.'

'Is work really that crazy?'

'It's pretty full on,' he confessed. 'Some days just rush by me and it's hard to remember exactly what it was I did. I go from one training session to another. The conference rooms look the same with their lack of natural light and their hideously patterned carpets. I often wonder, if I ever have one of those near death experiences – you know the sort where your life flashes in front of your eyes?'

Abi nodded.

'I wonder if my visions will just be of hotel lobbies and corridors and conference rooms filling up with underwhelmed clients.'

'Oh, Douglas!'

He shook his head. 'I shouldn't complain. After all, I'm earning good money and it took me years to work up to this position.'

'And do you love what you do?' Abi dared to ask.

'Love is a pretty strong word, don't you think?'

'Not really. I mean, we spend a good proportion of our lives working. I think it's pretty crucial that you love how you're spending that time, don't you?'

He smiled. 'That's because you're an artist.'

'What's that got to do with anything?' Abi asked.

'It means you've got this romantic view of the world. You think we should all be happy, creative souls and I'm afraid most of us aren't. We just have to get on with things and play the hand we're dealt.'

'Is that what you really think?'

He closed his eyes for a moment. 'I don't know. I'm so tired, I can barely think straight.'

'You've got to take a break, Douglas. You're wearing yourself out and it doesn't seem to be making any of you happy.'

He took a sip of his tea and stared out over the garden.

'Look,' Abi said, 'I don't want to make you feel worse than you already do, I really don't, but we do have to talk.'

'I'm in trouble, aren't I?' he said. 'I can't seem to do anything right.' His shoulders slumped as he spoke. 'I took this job to bring in the money Ellen says we need for good schools and all those home improvements that seem so important to her. Honestly, you should see the stuff she buys. I don't know why we need all these things, but she keeps on buying them. Just last week, she bought this fancy new toaster. The old one was perfectly fine, but this one was shiny and new and she'd seen a couple of her friends had them. It was nearly two hundred quid, Abi!'

Abi gasped.

'And now you're telling me she hates me for doing the actual work that means she can buy this stuff and she resents me being away all the time. She can't have it both ways, you know.'

'I know. But I think it's time to reassess things.'

'What sort of things?'

Abi's fingers tightened around her mug until she felt sure it would explode into tiny fragments. There was no more delaying things.

'Douglas – are you having an affair?'

Douglas's head snapped around. 'What?' A deep frown creased his forehead as he stared at her in horror. 'No! God, Abi! Whatever gave you that idea?'

'Can you tell me who Rachelle is?'

'Where did you hear that name?'

'The girls told me.'

'The *girls*?'

'They overheard you and Ellen talking. Or rather shouting.'

Douglas closed his eyes and swore.

'Who is she, Douglas?'

He gazed down at the ground for a moment before answering. 'She's just a work colleague.'

'And she was in your hotel room?'

'Yes. But it's not what you think.'

'I promise you, I'm not thinking anything. I just want to make sure everything's okay with you and my sister.' She paused. 'So what was going on?'

'Nothing. We'd had a crazy long day with some tricky delegates and we just needed to sound off to one another for a bit. Wind down and have a laugh. I don't know. We ended up walking back to my room. I think Rachelle said hers was in a state. Not that I would've gone back to her room,' he added quickly. 'Anyway, I offered her a tea and she said we should raid the mini bar. I didn't think it was a good idea. I don't like drinking when I'm away, but she had the door open and brought out a bottle of something. I forget what.'

'Oh, Douglas,' Abi said, trying to picture the scene and hoping that the brother-in-law she thought she knew – the kind and decent man who loved his family – had stuck to his principles.

'Listen, she's a flirt and she's a very attractive woman. She's made some suggestive remarks too that led me to believe...' his voice petered off. 'I'm not that kind of man, Abi. I swear to you.'

'Then nothing happened?'

'Nothing happened.'

Abi breathed a sigh of relief. 'But you'll be working with her in the future?'

'Very likely.'

'And is there any way you can cut your hours back or work from home?'

'There really isn't. Not at the moment.'

They sat quietly, each one staring out into the garden while mulling over what had been said.

'Does Ells know you're talking to me about all this?'

Abi shook her head. 'She's no idea.'

'But she's spoken to you about it?'

'Not about Rachelle. But she's mentioned you being away a lot.'

'Have you met Pugly?'

'Oh, yes!'

'Isn't he adorable? The girls love him to bits. Ells, well, I'm sure she'll come round.'

Abi bit her lip, wondering if she should say something about his nickname for Ellen.

'Douglas?'

'Yes?'

'Must you call her Ells?'

He frowned, looking confused.

'But I've always called her that.'

'I know, but she doesn't like it. Nor does she like Ells Bells or...' Abi paused.

'What?'

'Elly Belly.'

'Ah!'

'She said that started when she was pregnant, but that you've never actually stopped calling her that.'

'It's a term of affection!' Douglas said.

'I know it is, but women are funny like that.'

'Did she ask you to tell me not to call her those names?'

'No, but she mentions her annoyance every so often.'

'You see? I can't seem to do anything right.'

'You know that's not true!'

'You know what I think?' Douglas said. 'I think she's addicted to drama. She's always creating these scenes. It's as if she feeds off them. Like they give her oxygen or something.'

'Well, there's definitely something in that,' Abi agreed.

'Has she always been like this? Chronically in love with high drama?'

'I suppose. Now I come to think about it.'

'There's no supposing about it. Honestly, every time I come home, there's some new drama to face. Nothing ever just seems to happen normally for Ells. I mean *Ellen*. It's always *a disaster* or *a catastrophe*.' He said the words in Ellen's voice and Abi didn't know whether to laugh or admonish him. It felt like a kind of betrayal to be listening to him berating her sister.

'I sometimes delay my returning home,' he then confessed. 'Isn't that awful? I actually stop off at places on the journey back – random places I pull into without really thinking about it like a garden centre or supermarket. The latest one was one of those massive antiques places where I wandered around aimlessly, just killing time. I'd no intention of buying anything. I don't even like antiques. But it just gave me a few more minutes of peace. You see, that's all I want – a peaceful life – a home I can relax in with my wife and daughters.' He paused. 'A happy home.'

'And it's not happy at the moment, is it?' Abi dared to ask.

'Not for me. It's stressful.'

Abi listened as he went on to tell her about the latest drama involving a decorator who apparently didn't know one end of a paintbrush from the other and how he'd made Ellen's life impossible for three straight days, and Abi couldn't help feeling increasingly uncomfortable as she realised that what Douglas was saying was true. Ellen did always seem to be in the midst of a drama even when doing the most simple of tasks. She was always fighting the whole world. Nobody else's problems got a look in.

'I came home from one trip away and I was going to tell her about a colleague I'd heard about. He'd been killed in a motorcycle accident. Horrible. Wasn't his fault. Just wrong place, wrong time.'

'I'm so sorry, Douglas,' Abi said, seeing the sadness in his eyes. 'Were you close?'

'Not really. We shared a few drinks after work. A few stories too. You know that strange camaraderie you can feel for someone for a few hours and then not see them for months at a time?' He sighed. 'Well, it was like that with me and Justin. But I liked him. He was a good sort and his death really shook me up. The thought that he'd gone and that I'd never see him again. Anyway, I got home and I was going to tell Ellen about it. She'd never met Justin, but I needed to talk about it all. And I said something like, 'Something awful happened,' and she stopped me. Literally stopped me with her hand in my face like some kind of irate lollypop lady.

'"Oh, you think something awful's happened to you, do you? Wait until you hear about *my* day!" And off she went.'

'What had happened to her?'

'Can't remember. I filtered it out as more noise and nonsense. But something to do with the washing machine, I think.'

'Oh, Douglas! Did you ever tell her about Justin?'

He shook his head. 'There really didn't seem any point.'

They sat quietly for a little while, watching the swifts dancing in the blue sky above the walled garden. The heat of the day had lost its sting and there was a bit of welcome shade in the garden.

'So, what are we going to do?' Abi began at last. 'You're working too hard and spending much too long away from home, but you're telling me part of that is because you're not happy at home. And Ellen and the girls are miserable when you're away, but then Ellen does nothing but cause drama whenever you do come home.'

'That's about the measure of it, and I don't think it's a problem we're going to solve anytime soon.'

Abi took Douglas's hand and squeezed it. 'I do know what you put up with when it comes to my sister,' she confided. 'And I know that you're a good and patient husband to her.'

'Thanks, Abi. That means a lot.' Douglas stretched out his legs and then yawned.

Abi smiled. 'I think you'd better head home.'

'Is it wrong to want to have a little kip right now?'

'Not at all. I take naps all the time during the day,' Abi said. 'It's one of the benefits of working from home.'

Douglas laughed as he got up and they walked back into Abi's apartment where they put their mugs by the sink. When he turned to look at her a moment later, he looked serious again.

'What is it?' Abi asked.

'Listen, if we're being honest with each other – absolutely honest – I think there's something I should tell you.'

'What?' Abi swallowed hard, wondering what on earth was coming next.

'I don't want to cause trouble between you and Ellen. That's the very last thing I'd want to do.'

'What is it?'

A pained look crossed his face. 'She sometimes says things. Cryptic things.'

'About what?'

'About you.'

'What do you mean?'

Douglas seemed to be searching for the words he wanted to say. 'She says you're the lucky one.'

'Lucky? How? You mean my business?'

'I guess that's a part of it. But there seems to be more to it than that. She says you've always had it easy. You've been sheltered from everything.'

Abi could feel her eyes prick with tears at that. 'I don't know what she means,' Abi said, feeling helpless. Ellen knew what she'd gone through, didn't she? She knew what a tough time Abi had had before she'd made the decision to sell her company.

'I don't know what she means either,' Douglas admitted. 'But it's something she says every now and then and, when I ask her more, she clams up and says it's nothing. But this happens over and over again so I'm kind of thinking it's *some*thing. I don't know. She always makes out that she's protecting you.'

'From what?'

Douglas shrugged. 'I really don't know. Maybe it's just her being a drama queen and a way to feel important. Who knows what goes through her head. I'm not sure if I'll ever work her out.' He approached her and gave her a heartfelt hug. 'I just thought you should know.'

Abi nodded, her throat still tight with emotion as they said their goodbyes.

CHAPTER FOURTEEN

Abi was sitting on the floor of her bedroom, her long fair hair covering her face in a curtain. A safety curtain. Like in the theatre. She'd seen those words when her mother had taken them both to see the panto just before Christmas. Abi remembered pointing at the words and asking what it meant.

'It's so the actors don't fall off the stage,' her mother had said with a giggle. Abi hadn't known whether to believe her or not, but had soon been swept away into the world of pantomime and had fallen in love with Cinderella. She wished she was there now in that safe world of the theatre where everything sparkled and shone. But she wasn't there. She was sitting on the cold floor of her bedroom while there were strangers downstairs and people shouting. Somebody was crying. She thought it was Ellen, but she couldn't tell. Maybe it was her mum. Abi had called downstairs for her, but Ellen had screamed up at her.

'Go to your room!'

Ellen was always bossing her around. It wasn't fair. Why should Ellen get to be downstairs where everybody else was and

Abi had to stay in her room? Well, she wasn't going to put up with that.

Abi got up from the floor and sneaked out onto the landing. The voices were louder now and she could see that the front door was open and two people were coming inside carrying something large and white between them.

'What are you doing?' Abi asked as she walked down the stairs, clutching the banister so hard that her little fingers hurt.

Ellen was standing outside the living room door and gasped as she saw her.

'I want Mummy!' Abi cried, reaching her sister just as the door was opened into the living room and the two men disappeared inside.

'No, Abi!' She felt a hand on her shoulder as she made to follow the men inside. 'Don't go in there. You *mustn't* go in there!'

Abi woke with a start, her face hot and her breathing ragged. Her hand fumbled for her bedside lamp and knocked her glass of water onto the floor instead. She cursed, finding the light switch at last and getting out of bed carefully to avoid the broken glass.

It took a full fifteen minutes in her nightmare haze to clean up the glass and calm down and she did what she was becoming driven to do more and more: opened the French doors into the garden to let the cool night air in. Her skin still felt hot and it took her a while before she felt like her normal self again, and only then did she let herself recall details of the nightmare.

It had all felt so horribly real and she still had the disorientating sense of having been lost inside her own head. But was it just a nightmare or was it a memory? As Abi stared into the soft darkness of the summer garden lit by a clear crescent moon and starlight, she really couldn't tell. But she knew one thing for sure – it had been her mother in the living room and the strange object that had been carried into the house had been a stretcher, hadn't it? Had her mother had an accident? Abi couldn't remember. All she knew was that her mother had died in hospital after a short illness and Abi hadn't been there. Her memories of that time were sketchy. She'd been so very young.

But why had she had the nightmare at all? Had it been because of the strange conversation she'd had with Douglas and how he'd told her that Ellen was always saying she was protecting Abi? Had that triggered a memory in her? Abi wished she knew. Perhaps she should talk to Ellen about it. They rarely talked about their mother because Abi knew that it was still a source of pain to Ellen. And so they always skirted around it, banishing it to the past.

Having spoken to Douglas, Abi now wanted to know exactly what it was Ellen believed she was protecting her from. Was it something from their childhood? Was it from the period when they lost their mother? And how easy would that be to bring up in conversation?

As Abi stared out into the moonlit garden, she knew she wasn't going to find the answers tonight and so she breathed the cool air deeply and gazed up at the stars. The sky was packed with them and she almost thanked her nightmare for giving her the chance to see them. As her eyes traced patterns between them, she suddenly became tired and decided to return to bed, hoping she would sleep through the rest of the night.

When she woke up, she was relieved to see that morning had arrived and, although the remnants of the nightmare were still swirling around her head, she felt that she could push them into a little corner, a place where she wouldn't disturb them and where, with any luck, they might just dissolve into nothing and be forgotten.

'And I can get on with my day,' she thought, looking out at the sunny garden.

It still felt strange for Abi to be at home during the day with no meetings to attend and no pressure on her time. In London, she'd become a kind of machine, churning out designs on demand because the shopping season demanded them. Here, however, she was free to choose her work and that was very liberating.

Something else that was liberating was being able to down tools and head into the great outdoors whenever she wanted to and she felt in need of that today – to lose herself in the bright and airy landscape and embrace the freedom of it all. So she quickly packed a little bag with a sandwich made with slightly stale bread because she hadn't been shopping for ages, a flask of water and her sketchbook and camera in case she was lucky enough to spot some more butterflies.

She walked. It was a loose-limbed sort of a walk, so unlike her walking in London which had been stifled and stymied by other people she'd had to dodge. And the longer she walked , the more her nightmare receded as did her anxiety about Douglas and her concerns for Ellen. One's perspective on life switched up here. This was a place where the clouds lived and Abi watched as they chased one another across the sky, their great shadows darkening the landscape below. For a moment, Abi was caught underneath one and felt the brief chill on her limbs after the warmth of the sun. But the sun soon returned and she was grateful for it.

The higher Abi climbed, the more she felt a part of it all – as if her physical body was melting away and she was becoming a creature of the air. She stopped to inhale, knowing now that, if the breeze was from the south, it would hold something of the sea.

She followed a footpath which skirted a wood and then found a patch of ground studded with wildflowers. Taking care sitting down, Abi ate her meagre lunch, vowing to do better next time, but it didn't matter because she really wasn't thinking about her food; she was thinking about the landscape before her and how it made her feel. Maybe if she could get Ellen and Douglas up here, they'd feel it too. Maybe the downland air would help to blow away some of the tension between them.

Slowly, after she'd finished her lunch, Abi descended, becoming more aware of the heaviness of her body now as her knees strained. She felt the vital pump of her heart from her exertion and the unmistakable joy of just being alive.

Leaving the downs behind her, she crossed a field which came out at a small unmetalled road lined with the sort of cottages Helen Allingham might have painted over a hundred years ago. It really did feel as if Abi had stepped back in time and she smiled as she looked at the farm workers' cottages, their gardens spilling over with flowers. The air was hot and still for she'd left the refreshing breeze on the downs now and she suddenly realised how tired she was. And that's when she saw the cottage. It was a ramshackle sort of place with a red-tiled roof and a long low brick-and-flint wall running the length of the garden which was an impressive size and full of towering hollyhocks in shades from the palest pink to the deepest red. A row of tall canes stood sentinel and masses of beans scrambled up their height, and there were enormous bramble bushes too, their blackberries green and bullet-hard at present, but promising gorgeous fruit pies later in the season.

But it was an old blackboard propped up against a wooden crate by the wall that caught her attention. It was advertising goods for sale. There were pots of raspberry and gooseberry jam and beetroot chutney, and there were freshly-cut flowers in a galvanised bucket. There was also a piece of paper tacked to the bottom of the board which, in sloping letters, read:

Drinks served daily. Tea and Coffee – £1. Squash – 50 pence.

How could Abi resist? She picked up a jar of the beetroot chutney and opened the gate into the garden, following the path around the house. The casement windows on the ground floor of the property looked as if they were about to fall out of their frames. They were all open and Abi had the feeling that they were the sort of windows that were all very well on a hot summer's day when they let the fresh air in but, come winter, they would do nothing to keep the cold out.

Just to the left of the path, there were three old wooden tables, each with a few rickety chairs with sun-faded cushions upon them. Abi looked around the garden and then back at the house and then noticed that there was a small brass bell on the centre of each table. She approached the one nearest to her and picked it up, ringing it gingerly and looking around to see if it had any effect. Sure enough, a moment later, an old man came stumbling up the garden path. He was small but sprightly, with a shock of white hair stuffed under an old green hat with a feather sticking out of the left hand side, and a pair of bright eyes which fixed themselves on her immediately.

'Not been waiting there long, have you?' he asked anxiously.

'Not at all. I've just got here,' Abi told him.

'I got stuck for a minute,' he said. 'Was trying to tackle some thistles down by the river. I can't think how they got so big.'

Abi smiled, remembering the state of the walled garden when she took it on and the jungle of thistles that had greeted her.

'So, are you after a cup of tea?'

'Actually, I'd love a squash,' Abi said.

'Don't blame you. Too hot for tea, ain't it? So, what sort of squash? I've got orange, lime or elderflower.'

Abi pondered, feeling like a child again with far too many tempting things to choose from.

'Lime,' she said.

'Good choice. Ice?'

'Please.'

'Take a seat. I'll pop a brolly up for you.'

Abi watched as he added a pretty shade to one of the tables and she took a seat. He reminded her of a teddy bear with his friendly face and white fluffy hair – the sort of bear a child would never want to be parted from – one that would follow you around for years, gradually losing bits of stuffing and having to be stitched up time and time again, but one that was loved above all other toys.

A moment later, he disappeared into the dark interior of the house, coming back with a tall glass of lime cordial, clinking with ice cubes.

'Come over the downs, did you?'

'How did you guess?' Abi asked, patting her cheeks with the back of her hand, guessing them to be a little pink.

'Used to be a big walker myself. Went everywhere on foot. Loved it. Doesn't do for my knees these days, though. Mind you, this garden is all the exercise I need now. Keeps me busy enough.'

'It's wonderful.'

He lifted his hat off his head and had a scratch. 'Yeah, well, it could do with an army of young folk to help me, but I get by.'

'I don't suppose you sell any kind of food, do you?' Abi dared to ask. 'I've only had a very poor sandwich all day.'

'Well now, my wife used to serve cakes, but she died a year back. But I've been told my scones are pretty good. I could get you one of those with some home-made jam?'

'Sounds delicious.'

He gave her a funny little salute and disappeared again, leaving Abi to enjoy the peace of the garden at her shady table. It was a beautiful spot and she couldn't understand how she had the place to herself, and then she realised that it was the middle of the week and that most people would be at work. Again, she felt a twinge of guilt about that, and yet she was kind of at work too, wasn't she? She'd been gathering material and inspiration up on the downs.

And now she was relaxing because, as every sensible person knew, relaxing was just as important as working, wasn't it? It was just that Abi had forgotten that over the last few years.

She was just watching a bee on a nearby snapdragon when the old man appeared with a little floral tray on which sat a china plate with a large scone, a chunk of butter on a side dish and a pot of raspberry jam.

'Hope this is all right for you,' he said.

Abi nodded in delight and handed him some money.

'Let me get you some change,' he said.

'No, no. This is all priceless,' she told him and he chuckled, popping the money in to a deep pocket of his trousers.

'I'll be over there if...' he said, pointing vaguely into the garden and wandering off, his sentence unfinished. Abi smiled as he ventured into an overgrown patch of wildflowers and grasses towards a dilapidated greenhouse. She looked back at the house. It was as run down as the greenhouse, with a buddleia sprouting out of the drainpipe on the first floor, but there was an immense charm about the place. It was loved, Abi could sense that, and – like her own garden at Winfield – it was just the place to ease you gently back into yourself if you'd had a rough time of things, and Abi could still feel that jangly sensation from her nightmare, its feelers gripping hold of her, although the sunshine and her surroundings were forcing it to lose its grip a little.

She sat there for a while, feeling the garden work on her senses, giving her that wondrously drowsy sensation that only a summer garden can give. She finished her scone and jam which was delicious, the raspberries tangy and so very fresh, and then she got up and dared to wander into the garden, her legs slicing through the long grasses either side of the path. She noticed how dry and feathery they were, soft to the touch and blowsy to the eye. A small orchard lay ahead with apple and plum trees and she walked among it for a while, marvelling at the lushness of it all and the view back to the cottage.

'You all right?' the owner's voice came from somewhere to her right, making her jump.

'Oh, yes!' she said. 'I couldn't resist a quick look around. Is that all right?'

'Fine by me,' he said.

'The scone was wonderful, by the way. I loved the jam.'

'Right from this garden.'

'Yes. That must be so gratifying. I've just bought a place with a bit of a garden,' Abi confessed.

'Oh, yes? Near here?'

'Winfield Hall.'

'You bought the hall?' He looked surprised.

'Well, half of it, but I got most of the garden in my lot. Do you know it – the walled garden?'

'I know of it, yes. Impressive place.'

Abi smiled. 'I'm Abigail,' she said, thinking it only right to introduce herself at this point. 'Abi.' She held out her hand towards him and he looked down at his own rather dusty ones, giving them a wipe on his equally dusty trousers before shaking hers.

'Ronnie,' he said. 'Well, it's Ronald really, but that's awful, ain't it?'

Abi smiled. 'I think it's regal.'

'Do you now?'

She nodded.

'Would you like to look around then? I mean, it's not as impressive as Winfield.'

'I'd love to and I think it's charming.'

He led her through a grassy patch. 'Wildflowers,' he explained. 'Good for the pollinators. You must never cut your grass too short.'

She listened as he told her about the things he was growing and the issues he'd had with too much rain and then too much drought. He pointed out his favourite flowers and told her to come back in September when there'd be a glut of produce.

'I sells a bit, but it's more fun to give it away. Anyway, everyone around here has their own.'

Abi was looking forward to the day when she too would have gluts.

She listened to him as he talked on, envying him his knowledge. He knew so much about plants and was so in love with the world around him. He knew the precise week when the celandine would shine like golden coins in the woodlands, he knew the moment when the nightingale would sing in the valley each evening, and he knew when to listen out for the first cuckoo, the first swallow and where to search for the first delicate harebells growing up on the downs. It was a lifetime of knowing, of being there, of taking in each breath of nature and making it a part of your own soul.

'I don't know what will happen to this place when I've gone,' he said once they were back at the house. 'I've got no kids, see. We – well – it wasn't meant to be. The missus couldn't carry long-term.' He shook his head and a dagger of pain flickered through his eyes. It was an old pain, but it was still there.

Suddenly, it was as if the sun had been swallowed up by a

big dark cloud and Abi started shivering.

'Are you all right, love?'

'I...' Abi's vision was blurring and she stumbled.

'Here – let's get you inside, okay?'

She let herself be led into the cottage where it was cool and dark after the heat and brightness of the garden, but Abi welcomed its comforting atmosphere. She could still smell the earth and the foliage through the open windows, and the scent of jasmine too.

'Sit here,' Ronnie said, easing her down into a worn armchair near the open window where she could feel the faint breeze coming in. Although it was warm, it was still soothing. Abi dared to close her eyes for a moment, but felt swimmy again and so opened them.

'Here,' Ronnie said. 'A cup of tea with plenty of sugar.'

'Thank you,' she said. 'You must let me pay you, only I seem to have dropped my bag.'

'No need to pay. We're friends now, aren't we?'

She smiled. 'You're very kind. And I feel so silly.'

'No, no. Not silly.'

'I'm not sure what happened.'

'Probably a bit too much sun. It sneaks up on you like that.'

'Yes. I've been out in it all day. I'm not used to it, I guess.'

'Just take your time and have your tea.'

Abi sipped at the sweet tea as she glanced around the room. Like the garden, it was full of plants – on the windowsill, on the mantelpiece and on the tops of every other surface. There was an old clock ticking on a dresser that was stacked with newspapers and seed packets and another couple of armchairs heaving with cushions. It wasn't the neatest room by any means, but it was one of the most welcoming that Abi had ever seen.

She watched as Ronnie walked over to the dresser and picked up a packet of seeds.

'Oh, blow. I should have planted another row of these last week.' He shook his head. His old thick fingers picked through the other packets and brown envelopes and he made a small pile to his left. 'Jobs to be done,' he muttered. 'Always something to do when you have a garden.'

She listened to him, his gentle voice easing her back into her body until she was feeling calm once again.

'I'd better get back,' she said, feeling that she was taking up his precious time. She stood up and wobbled slightly.

'Hey, now!' He was by her side in an instant.

'I'm okay.'

'I'll run you back.'

'Oh, no – there's no need.'

'You're really planning on walking back over the downs in this heat, are you? The way you're feeling?'

Abi sighed. He was right. She felt completely washed out.

She followed Ronnie out of the cottage and found her bag. He then led her into the lane where his old car was parked and he opened the passenger door for her, quickly bending inside to remove a heap of netting which he put on the backseat.

'For my cabbages,' he explained.

Abi got in. 'Thank you,' she said as he started the engine a moment later and headed down the lane.

'How are you feeling?'

'Embarrassed.'

'No need, my dear.'

'I'm putting you to so much trouble.'

He chuckled. 'Are you kidding? This is the most excitement I've had in weeks. Months, probably.' He tutted. 'Sorry. Shouldn't have said *excitement*. Wrong word.'

'It's okay. I guess I know what you mean.'

'I don't get out much. That's what I mean.'

'Neither do I,' Abi told him.

'You don't?'

'I recently gave up a job in London and I've sort of... well, I've been enjoying some time at home.' She smiled.

'Time alone?'

'Yes.'

'We all need that,' Ronnie said, 'but not too much. Not too much.'

She turned to look at him and saw the sadness in his face again. Was he lonely, she wondered? Perhaps they could be friends. Perhaps they could be each other's go-to when one was feeling that they'd reached their personal quota of alone time.

'Well, here we are,' Ronnie said a few minutes later.

Abi was grateful to see Winfield Hall, but she was a little sad too because she was going to have to say goodbye to Ronnie.

'Would you like to come in for a cuppa? My turn to repay you for your kindness?'

'No, no – you should rest.'

'But you'll come and see the garden some time?'

He seemed to perk up at that and nodded enthusiastically.

'Thank you for everything,' she said as she got out of the car.

'And thank you for your company.'

'I'll come and see you again, okay?'

'You bet! I'll make sure there are plenty of scones.'

Abi laughed as she closed the car door and watched as he drove away.

It wasn't until she started walking towards the front door that she saw the car parked behind her own. It was her sister, Ellen's. Abi sighed. She felt emotionally and physically drained. The very last thing she wanted was an encounter with her sister, but there she was, sitting on the doorstep. She got up, red-faced and impatient when she saw her approaching and, before Abi could say anything, she dropped her bombshell.

'I've left Douglas,' she announced.

CHAPTER FIFTEEN

Abi had hoped that she'd be able to sneak into Winfield Hall, wash her face with cold water, draw the curtains and slip between the cool sheets of her bed for a little while, but there was no chance of that now.

'I've been waiting here forever!' Ellen went on. 'Where have you been?'

'Just walking in the hills.'

'In the middle of the day?'

It was on the tip of Abi's tongue to ask when else would she walk in the hills, but she decided it would be best not to.

'And who was that who dropped you off? Are you seeing somebody?'

Abi almost laughed out loud at the thought of her seeing Ronnie, but why not? And why not tease her sister a little?

'Maybe,' she said.

Ellen didn't appear to be listening; she was too wrapped up in herself.

'Come on in,' Abi said. It was her turn to make some sweet tea.

'Did you hear what I said?' Ellen asked as soon as they were in Abi's apartment. 'I've left Douglas.'

Abi nodded as she switched the kettle on. At this moment, she wasn't too perturbed by the news because Ellen had delivered it before. Several times in fact.

'He's home at the moment?' Abi asked.

'No.'

'Where are the girls?'

'At a friend's.'

'And Pugly?'

'He went with them.'

Abi quickly made the tea and gestured towards the garden. Ellen shook her head.

'I feel like I've been sitting outside forever,' she complained, rubbing her bottom. And perhaps it was best that Abi stayed indoors for a while. She'd had more than her quota of sunshine for one day.

They sat down on the sofa together and Ellen sipped her tea.

'So tell me what's going on,' Abi said.

'What's to tell? I've left him,' Ellen said dramatically, her tone scaring Abi slightly. This had happened before, but there was something in the way Ellen was speaking now that made Abi think it was more serious this time.

'Did you have a fight?'

'Of course we had a fight! We do nothing *but* fight these days!'

'Oh, Ellen!'

'Don't say that like it's my fault.'

'I'm not!'

'You always have that tone of voice with me, Abi.'

'What tone?'

'Like I'm making things out to be worse than they are.'

'Well, you do seem to have this way of attracting drama into your life.'

Ellen's mouth dropped open and Abi wished she could take her words back. She really couldn't face a confrontation right now.

'Listen, Ellen – I just worry about you. I worry about how you respond to things.' She rested her hand on her sister's arm, doing her best to placate her. 'Like this thing with Douglas. I know how hard it is on you and the girls with him always being away. I can't imagine how you must feel.'

'No – you can't. You've never been married or had children.'

Abi swallowed hard, doing her best to ignore the cruel barb. Her sister was upset and she was lashing out. Now wasn't the time to start arguing with her. So she took a deep breath.

'Douglas is doing his best – he really is,' she told Ellen. 'You just need to listen to him more when he is home.'

'What do you mean?'

'He said...' Abi stopped, biting her lip.

Ellen frowned. 'Have you been talking to him behind my back?'

There was no point in trying to fudge her way through this, Abi thought.

'He came to see me.'

'Why didn't you tell me?' Ellen's face was even redder now.

'Because I was hoping you guys would work things out.'

'Was it his idea or yours?'

'I suggested having a chat with him.'

'So you've *both* been talking about me behind my back? Well, that's nice, isn't it? My own sister and husband!'

'Ellen – it's because we both care about you. We're trying to help.'

Something in Ellen seemed to crack then. Maybe it was that word 'help' or even 'care', but tears glittered in her eyes.

'Oh, Ellen!'

'I'm just so scared he's going to leave me, Abi, just like Dad left us!'

'Well, he will if you keep pushing him away like this,' Abi told her as gently as she could. She put their cups of tea down and pulled Ellen in for a hug. They didn't often hug as sisters. Ellen was usually far too busy for hugs, but Abi instinctively knew that her sister wouldn't pull away from her now.

'Douglas adores you. You *know* that, don't you?'

'But he's away all the time. How can he love me if he's away?'

'Because he's working hard for you all,' Abi said. 'He said this was something you both agreed to – that he should take this work so that you could have a nice home and clothes for the children and all those little things you love to buy.'

Abi did wonder how her sister could have forgotten about that. She clearly remembered Ellen saying how important it was to have nice things – the right house in the right neighbourhood, a decent car and proper clothes for the girls to wear. Then there were all the things that came from just having a big house like the extra work which meant Ellen had hired a cleaner, and the garden which needed maintaining. To say nothing of the expensive holidays they took each year – sometimes twice. All those things cost money.

'But I miss him.'

Abi could feel the genuine pain in Ellen's voice.

'Ellen? When was the last time you were happy?'

Ellen leaned back with a sniff and mopped her eyes with a tissue. 'What do you mean?'

'I mean, when were you and Douglas in a good place together? When were you not fighting?' Abi asked. 'Can you even remember?'

'I'm not sure,' Ellen said, and then she frowned as if she were genuinely trying to recall. 'It was at The Ridings.'

'The terrace house?'

She nodded. 'Number Eight The Ridings.' She gave a hollow little laugh as she remembered it. 'I thought I hated it there. I thought it wasn't good enough for us. It was so small and pokey and the garden was overlooked.' Ellen took a deep breath. 'But we didn't fight there. I mean, we used to have our little disagreements about whose turn it was to take the rubbish out, but that's normal isn't it? Anyway, it certainly wasn't like it is now.'

'And Douglas didn't have so much pressure on him there because it was a smaller home to run. This mortgage is crippling him and he's feeling the pressure of all the new stuff that's being bought all the time. Stuff that, perhaps, isn't always needed,' Abi said as delicately as she could while still trying to get Ellen to really hear her.

Ellen frowned. 'But he hasn't said anything to me.'

'No, he wouldn't,' Abi told her. 'He just wants you to be happy.'

Ellen sighed. 'But I can't give up our home, Abi! Don't ask me to do that!'

'You'd rather give up your marriage?'

'No!'

'And that would amount to the same thing anyway – if you and Douglas split up, you'd have to sell the house.'

'Don't talk like this! Why are you torturing me like this?'

'Because something's got to change – *that's* why! You can see that, can't you? The pressure's he's under and how miserable all this is making you and the girls?'

Ellen stared down at the floor, not answering for a moment. Abi reached for her tea again and handed it to her.

'Do you want another?'

Ellen shook her head.

'Why don't you go home, okay? And call Douglas and just talk.'

'I don't know what to say. I feel so embarrassed. I really shouted at him!'

'Just talk. Tell him how you feel. *Calmly*, though, okay? And listen to him. He's in so much pain over this.'

'Really?'

'Of *course* he is!' Abi said, feeling a little frustrated at how very focussed Ellen was on herself. 'He doesn't want to live like this. He's miserable in his job the way it is at the moment.'

'Is he?'

Abi nodded. 'You need to talk to him.'

Ellen seemed to understand at last. 'I don't want our girls growing up not knowing their father like we did,' she told Abi.

'I know.'

'And having him around is more important than having expensive things, isn't it?' she asked, as if she needed confirmation that this was true.

'I think it is.'

Ellen nodded. 'I think we might have taken on more than we can cope with – the house, the new car...' her voice petered out. 'I thought I wanted those things. I thought they were important, but they're not, are they?'

Abi shook her head and they sat in silence for a moment.

'Do you remember our parents?' Ellen suddenly asked, surprising Abi.

'I was too young when Dad left,' Abi told her, 'and I've only a vague memory of Mum. Sometimes, she feels more like a dream than someone who was really in my life.'

'That's sad,' Ellen said.

'I guess it is,' Abi agreed. 'There's just this big gaping hole where my parents should be.'

'And I'm afraid Aunt Claire didn't fill that gap very well, did she?' Ellen said with a tiny grin.

'She certainly wasn't the parental type.'

They smiled at one another. It was good to see Ellen smiling again.

'Listen, Ellen–' Abi began as they left her apartment.

'What?'

Now that they were talking – really talking – Abi was thinking about something that Douglas had told her. Something about Ellen saying she was protecting Abi. Was now the right time to broach it – while they were being so open and honest with each other?

Abi looked at Ellen's face. It had been so red when she'd first arrived and while she'd been crying. Now, it looked pale. She looked exhausted – as if life had wrung every little bit of strength out of her, and Abi's concerns about what Douglas had told her suddenly didn't seem important anymore.

'It's nothing,' she said.

'No?' Ellen said. 'Are you sure?'

'Another time.'

Ellen nodded and the two of them embraced. It was nice to feel this closeness with her sister again. It didn't happen very often and Abi didn't want to ruin it by bringing something up that might cause friction between them.

'Let me know how it goes, okay?' Abi said. 'And send my love to Douglas.'

'I will. I think I'd better send him some of mine too,' Ellen admitted.

Abi hugged her again. It was rather miraculous to get this self-recognition from Ellen and Abi only hoped that it wasn't too late.

Since seeing her sister waiting for her on the doorstep of Winfield Hall, Abi hadn't had time to think about what had happened to her in the garden at Ronnie's, but that's what her thoughts turned to as soon as Ellen's car was out of sight. She'd blamed the heat and Ronnie had found that easy to believe. After all, she'd been walking in the sunshine for hours and her fair complexion was apt to make her a little more vulnerable to sunshine than some. But it hadn't been the sun, had it? Well, maybe that had played its part, but Abi knew what had cut into her with such precision. It had been something Ronnie had said.

Abi closed her eyes now as she remembered it, seeing once again the pain in Ronnie's face. She'd recognised it because she'd seen it in her own face all too recently, hadn't she?

It was the pain of loss that no amount of time can erase.

CHAPTER SIXTEEN

Something felt different that night in London. That was Abi's first instinct although she wasn't at all sure what it was that felt different and so she ignored it. She went about her daily tasks, getting up, making fresh orange juice, walking along the river to the tube and going to work, and yet the space she inhabited in the world, the space within her was changing.

She was pregnant.

Her initial response had been one of joy because, somewhere in her future, Abi had always known that she'd wanted children only the future had hijacked her and arrived a little earlier than anticipated. For this had not been planned. She and Dante had been so careful. At least, they thought they had, but these things weren't one hundred percent, were they? Life could sometimes surprise you no matter how many precautions you took.

Abi tried to be philosophical about it. It might not be planned, but some of the greatest adventures in life weren't planned, were they? And, yes, it was going to be difficult running her company and being a mother, but it wasn't impossible, was it? Women had babies all the time and still managed to work and Abi was young and fit.

'And determined,' she whispered to herself. Yes, she was determined to make this work.

For those first few heady hours after finding out for sure that she was expecting, she carried her secret with her, sitting in meetings at work, wondering what they'd all say if she told them. Her head of marketing would be thrilled as she'd just had a baby. But her account manager was likely to complain and tell her it wasn't advisable – it was the wrong time, the wrong season. She should really have planned things better. This wouldn't make financial sense. Abi couldn't help smiling inwardly at that.

A baby. She was going to be a mother. Ellen would be thrilled too, wouldn't she? Abi couldn't wait to tell her sister although she knew Ellen would be full of warnings too – warnings about what she should eat and what she should and shouldn't do because, when Ellen was pregnant, she'd read every single book and blog on the subject.

Abi waited a few days before telling Dante. She wasn't quite sure why. They didn't see each other every day and perhaps she felt it was the kind of news one didn't send in a text or via a phone conversation. But there was something else which held her back if she was being absolutely honest: she wasn't sure how he would respond.

They'd only been seeing each other for a year and it still felt so early in their relationship. Certainly rather early to turn them from a couple into a family of three. They weren't even living together. How would it all work? So many thoughts and fears swirled through Abi's mind, but the overriding one was of joy because she felt that this was meant to be happening.

When she called Dante, he was in a good mood and she

suggested meeting at hers after work. It seemed funny that he arrived carrying a large bunch of flowers. It was as if he knew they had something to celebrate. She listened to him telling her about his day as she put the flowers in a glass vase and placed them on the coffee table in the living room. There'd been some mishap with one of his students, apparently.

'Got herself pregnant, the idiot!' he laughed. 'In her final year too. Can you believe it? What a waste. Why do they do that, huh? Start a course and put all that work in, wasting their time and money and the resources of the tutor if they're just going to go and get pregnant?'

Abi didn't say anything. Instead, she went through to the kitchen to put the kettle on.

'It's so commonplace, don't you think? Anyone can have a baby, but an education, study, following your passion – now that's something to strive for.'

Maybe now wasn't the right time to tell him, Abi thought. Maybe she'd wait. Maybe...

'You okay, Abi?' he asked, making her jump as he placed his hands on her shoulders from behind her.

'I'm pregnant!' she blurted, her eyes wide.

'What?'

'We're going to have a baby,' she said, feeling her heart racing wildly. 'You and me.' She wasn't sure why she added that. She just wanted to make things absolutely clear.

Dante stared at her, his dark eyes not giving anything away.

'Aren't you going to say something?' she prompted him.

He nodded, but didn't speak.

'Dante?'

'You're sure?'

'Yes.'

'How?'

'I did three tests,' she told him with a little laugh, remembering her own disbelief as she'd done test after test.

'Have you seen a doctor?'

'No. Not yet.'

'I think you should. To be absolutely sure.'

'I am absolutely sure.' Abi was starting to get a little anxious now. 'You are happy about it, aren't you?'

'No, no,' he said. 'I mean – of course.'

Abi looked closely at him and could see the fear in his eyes which looked darker than normal. He said he was happy, but they were just words and they felt empty and hollow.

'I know we didn't plan this,' she said as calmly as she could, 'but we can make it work, can't we? I mean, people have babies all the time. How hard can it be?'

He nodded, but he had a faraway look and Abi had a feeling that he wanted to be far away too at that moment.

'It's just... unexpected,' he said at last.

'I know it is.'

'How did it even happen? We've been so careful.'

'We're a blip,' she said. 'A blessed blip!'

Dante walked through to the living room and stood looking out of the window towards the Thames. Abi left him for a moment as she made the tea and then joined him.

'At least we have a few months to prepare,' she told him, 'and to get used to the idea. I think that's why pregnancy takes so long. It's so that the parents are totally ready for when the baby arrives.'

'Parents,' he said. 'I'm not even used to being a partner yet.'

'Dante!' she said, shocked by his admission.

'Sorry,' he said quickly. 'I want to be honest with you. I can, can't I?'

'Yes, of course.'

'Because I don't want to lie to you, Abi. This is a shock.'

'I know. It is for me too.'

'I'm just finding my feet here in London. My teaching...' he paused and gazed out across the river again. Abi wished she could read his mind although perhaps it was best that she couldn't. She might not like what she'd discover.

'I very nearly didn't tell you,' Abi said.

'What do you mean?' He sounded angry now.

'I was scared of your reaction.' She gazed up at him. 'Tell me I was right to tell you because you're making me nervous.'

He raked a hand through his dark hair. 'Of course you were right to tell me. Just give me a little time, okay?'

She nodded. 'Okay.'

He glanced around the room as if looking for an excuse to leave.

'Why don't you go home?' Abi said gently, giving him the excuse he needed. The truth was, she couldn't bear to look at him when he was like this. It was better that he left.

He walked out of the room, stopping at the front door and then returning to kiss her cheek as if in afterthought. Not once had he asked her how she was feeling. It just hadn't occurred to him. Her being pregnant was totally about his own response, wasn't it?

She watched him from her living room window, his shoulders sagged in despondency as he walked along the river towards the tube and she felt as if something had closed inside her. She had been anxious about telling Dante the news of her pregnancy, but she had kind of hoped for just a little bit of elation. Was that so totally unreasonable? She was carrying a new life inside her. Surely that was to be celebrated for the miracle that it was.

As Dante disappeared round the corner, Abi stepped away from the window, her hands instinctively touching her tummy although there was obviously no physical change as yet. But there would be, she thought, wondering how soon the changes would come.

I'm going to be a mother.

She smiled at the inner voice that kept repeating those words. Even if Dante wasn't smiling at the thought, she absolutely was.

CHAPTER SEVENTEEN

Edward had had a good morning. He'd hired somebody to design and set him up with a website, he'd been in touch with several of his former clients and had secured two new clients as well from word of mouth. It was all looking very positive. He could make this work, couldn't he? He didn't need a big company behind him. He was all the company he needed. It just required a little bit of confidence and a good input of time and effort.

He was just about reward himself with a pub lunch when his mobile rang. He looked at the screen and saw the name. Oscar. For a moment, Edward debated ignoring the call, but he knew his brother would only persist and he didn't want to run the risk of him actually turning up at Winfield Hall again for fear of him running into Abigail. Abi was just the sort of sweet and trusting person that Oscar would prey on and he didn't want his brother to have anything to do with her. So he took the call even though speaking to him was the last thing he wanted to do.

'It's Dad,' Oscar said without preamble.

'What about him?' Edward said, equally abruptly.

'He's in bad shape.'

'He's always in bad shape.'

'This is worse than normal.'

'Tell him to stop drinking then.'

Edward heard Oscar swearing.

'I can't get to see him. You should go over.'

'Don't ask me to do that,' Edward said.

'I'm asking. You need to check on him. I spoke to him on the phone and he sounded odd and he was crashing around the place before.'

Edward sighed. He might have known that his good morning was too good to last.

'Are you going to go or do I need to phone a neighbour to break in?' Oscar threatened.

'I'll go,' Edward said and Oscar hung up.

Edward ran a hand through his hair. He was feeling wretched and he hadn't even left the safety of his home yet. This was not something he was looking forward to, but he'd do it. What choice did he have? Derek Townsend was still his father.

He picked up his car keys and the key to his father's home and left the hall, driving the short distance to the old family home. Parking outside and getting out of the car, he walked quickly to the front door and inserted his key.

'Dad?' he called as soon as he was inside. The hallway was dark and there was a dreadful noise coming from the front room. Edward stumbled in the dark, treading on something as he made his way to open the curtains which were still shut even though it was midday. As soon as they were open, he walked towards the television which was pumping out some dreadful chat show where one of the presenters was shouting his opinions and his colleague, even more intent on being heard, was shouting hers right back at him. Edward switched it off and a blissful silence descended, and that's when he began to survey the room. It was not only filthy, but the coffee table had been knocked over and there were cans, bottles and fast food cartons littering the floor, one of which he'd stepped inside. He checked his shoes now and, sure enough, his right shoe had half a slice of pizza stuck to its sole. Edward grimaced as he pulled it off and wiped the sole with an old piece of newspaper he found. How could anybody live like this, he wondered?

The smell of stale alcohol hung in the air. It was a far cry from the light and airy rooms at Winfield and the world that Edward was trying to create for himself there.

His father had always enjoyed a drink, but he'd never held it well. It made him angry and, on occasion, violent. And he liked it. For him, it was his right at the end of each day's work. Edward had once challenged him about it and had been soundly cuffed round the ear.

'Let him be,' his mother had said and not in defence of her son. She knew when to leave Derek alone with his drink.

Then Linda had died and Derek had gone downhill fast, sinking his sorrow in bottle after bottle. She hadn't been there to give him her gentle guidance. It hadn't always worked, of course, but at least she'd had some influence over him and had stopped some of his scenes in their tracks before they'd escalated out of control. Like the time Oscar had come home late from a party at sixth form. He'd been exactly ten minutes late, and Derek had worked himself up into a good alcoholic lather about it. If Linda hadn't been there that night to literally hold her husband back while Oscar ran up to his bedroom and locked the door, Edward dreaded to think what might have happened.

'Dad?' Edward called now, making his way upstairs and passing the very room Oscar had escaped to that drink-fuelled night. Sure enough, his father was in bed or rather on it – face down, his hair a sweaty mess on the pillow. The room smelled awful and Edward moved to open the curtains and then the window, letting in a blast of much-needed fresh air.

He heard his father swear from the bed. So, he hadn't killed himself with the drink yet then, Edward couldn't help thinking. But it was on the cards for some time soon.

'Dad?' he said. 'You awake?'

His father mumbled something that wasn't very clear, but sounded awfully like a curse to Edward, but he was used to that.

'Have you eaten today?' Edward asked. Silly question. His father's kitchen wasn't a place to cook or eat – it was merely used as a store for his alcohol. His fridge hadn't seen anything approaching food since Linda had died.

There was another groan from the bed. Edward stared down at the sorry state of the man who'd given him life.

'I'll make you something to eat if I can find any actual food in your kitchen,' Edward said now, backing out of the room and returning downstairs.

Edward made his way to the kitchen and grimaced at the state of it. He opened the fridge and, just as he'd thought, there was nothing but a stack of beer cans, bottles of wine and some mouldy cheese. He sighed and started looking in the cupboards. He found a box of eggs that wasn't yet out of date and there was a plastic container of home-grown tomatoes on the kitchen table, possibly a gift from the kind neighbour who kept an eye on Derek. Tomato omelette it was then. But first, he'd do a bit of tidying up.

Rolling his sleeves up, he tackled the stacks of dishes that lay in the sink and on the draining board and table. It was clear his father hadn't washed up for days. Edward had once paid for a home help to clean and shop for him, but the company he'd used had rung him up to complain that his father had been verbally abusive and that their services would no longer be available to him. When Edward had confronted his father about it, he'd got some of the same abuse. He hadn't really been surprised as he'd grown up with it, and yet it still had the power to shock him because he always hoped that, somehow, his father would change – that, one day, he'd wake up and miraculously see all the damage he'd done. Edward gave a hollow laugh as he thought about that now. His father was never going to change. His behaviour was entrenched.

Even when he'd been sober, Derek Townsend had not been the best of fathers. He was too wrapped up in himself to care much for others and yet he had adored his wife. In his own way. Edward could still hear their arguments. They used to wake him up from his childhood dreams. You never forgot the sound of your mother crying, did you? Or the sound of glass breaking when a bottle was thrown across the room and the harsh words his father would scream whether he'd been drinking or not.

There wasn't a single trace of his mother left in the house anymore. His father had hired one of those house clearance companies shortly after she'd died – the sort that paid you a pittance to come and take all of a person's things away. His so-called love of Linda had been eclipsed by his need for money for alcohol. Edward remembered seeing him take his mother's jewellery out to sell. He'd been appalled when he realised what was happening and had gone into the room after his father had left the house. There on the dressing table, Edward had found a hair slide. It was just a cheap thing which glittered with paste stones, but he remembered how fond his mother had been of it and had pocketed it, keeping it safe from the ministrations of his father. He still had it, tucked away in a drawer.

His father had been devastated by Linda's passing. Edward hadn't quite realised how very dependent he'd been on her, but she had run the house, making sure everything was neat, tidy and clean and that there was never a shortage of fresh, wholesome food. They might not have had much money, but she made the very best of what they had, even growing a bit of fruit and veg herself in the tiny back garden. Of course, the garden had been neglected since her passing and was now a wasteland of grasses and rubbish bags that hadn't found their way to the bin. Edward went outside and dealt with a few of them now, wondering how his father could bear to live in such a tip.

It pained him that he couldn't talk to his father, but how could you have a relationship with a man who'd never showed you any compassion? You couldn't just switch it on in yourself the moment that they needed you, not if you'd never had anything from them in the past. But Edward did try and help.

Tossing as many bin bags as he could from the garden into the plastic dustbin and wheeling it round the front of the house, he returned inside to tackle the mess there. He found a bin bag under the sink and got to work in the front room, clearing the floor of debris and setting the table upright. He wasn't sure why he was bothering really – it would only return to this same state in a few days' time.

Once that was done, he washed his hands and made the omelette for his father, taking it upstairs with a glass of water. His father was sitting up on the bed now, a dazed look on his pale face.

'I've brought you something to eat,' Edward said. 'It's not much. I couldn't find a lot in the way of food in the house.'

'I'm not hungry,' his father growled, swinging his legs out of bed. He was wearing a long stained T-shirt and socks and his thin, pale legs looked both pitiful and menacing.

'You should eat,' Edward told him, glancing away, as if he shouldn't be looking at his father's partial nakedness.

'What do you care?'

It was on the tip of Edward's tongue to say that he didn't, but the last thing he wanted to do was antagonise the old man. He looked around the room for a clear surface on which to put the plate and glass, but couldn't find one.

'I'll put these in the kitchen.'

'You can put them in the bin for all I care.'

Edward sighed. He'd done his best and it wasn't good enough, and now it was time to go. He walked down the stairs, each step sending him deeper and deeper into himself. He hated how he felt when he was around his father and he tried to switch those feelings off by chanting to himself.

I'm leaving now. I'm leaving now. I'm leaving now.

That thought kept him sane. He could leave. He was no longer trapped there as he had been when he was a boy. He had his own life now and it was a good life, and yet this old one kept dragging him back, forcing memories to resurface and making him feel as if he'd regressed to that anxious boy who'd felt so helpless when living there.

'You worry too much,' his mother had once told him when he'd asked if she was okay. 'Your father just has a bit of a temper, but he's got a good soul.'

Well, Edward had never seen any evidence of this good soul and, as he'd grown older, he'd begun to think that his mother was delusional – she had a severe blind spot when it came to his father. But Edward wasn't under any illusions. His father was a mean man when sober and an even meaner one when drunk, and that was all there was to it.

It was with great relief that he left the house. He'd done his bit as best as he could and now it was time to return home. He breathed a few great lungfuls of fresh air as he drove away with his windows open, trying to dispel the expression of sheer hatred on his father's face when he'd offered him something to eat. Why had he let Oscar convince him to go over? Was it fear that had driven Edward to do it? Fear of his father crashed out on the floor, helpless? Or was it humanity – his compassion for a man who'd never shown him any? Edward didn't want to analyse it. All he knew was that he felt deeply unsettled whenever he had to have anything to do with the old man and it wasn't just because of the way his father treated him, but the way he'd treated his mother during her lifetime.

Linda Townsend had once told Edward that she remembered the first time she'd seen Derek. He'd been propping up a bar. Of course he had. But he'd had this twinkle in his eye, this certain magical charisma that drew her to him. It was unstoppable, she'd said, and it had engulfed her completely and, although she came to learn that he had his faults, she loved him with an affection that made the soul weep to see because he was no good for her. Edward had been a witness to it growing up, and it had made him ache. He couldn't understand how she could put up with his father's behaviour – the drinking, the swearing, the violence, the inability to hold down a job. Instead, she accepted him for what he was, defended him when others went the attack, and she made do with her lot, taking two jobs on at once in order to bring in the money that the household needed. And she learned to hide any money she had because she knew what would happen to it if her husband got hold of it.

There was a part of Edward that had admired his mother for how she'd borne things, but he'd also wished that she'd made her escape. He wouldn't even have minded if she hadn't taken him and his brother with her – as long as she'd got away to lead a better life somewhere. But running had always been the last thing on her mind.

'I chose him,' she'd once told Edward. 'This is my life.'

Was that loyalty or foolishness? Edward had never really decided, but he thought about it now on the short drive back to

Winfield where he saw that Oscar was waiting for him. There was no escaping his family today it seemed.

'I tried calling you,' Oscar said as soon as Edward got out of the car.

'My phone was off.'

'How is he?'

'He was upright when I left him.'

'What did he say?'

'He said, "What do you care?"'

Oscar frowned. 'Is that all?'

'There were some other disparaging remarks, but we didn't have a full-blown conversation if that's what you mean. I went in, made sure he was okay, tidied up, made him a meal which he didn't eat and left.'

'And he'd been drinking?'

'What do you think? Of *course* he'd been drinking!'

'All right! No need to get shirty with me.'

Edward sighed. 'I'm not getting shirty. I'm just frustrated that this is still going on.'

'You think he's going to change?' Oscar said incredulously.

'No, I don't. That's what's so frustrating. And you could learn a thing or two as well,' Edward told his brother.

'What do you mean?'

'Your drinking.'

'What about it?'

'It's pretty out of hand.'

'Are you kidding me?'

'What was that, then – the other night?'

'I'd had a few to celebrate you moving back home.'

Edward didn't like Winfield being referred to as "home" – not in the way Oscar meant it. Yes, Edward might well have returned to the county of his childhood, and Winfield might be in the village adjacent to his old stomping ground, but it was a million miles away in terms of feeling.

'You're becoming like him, you know,' Edward said in a low voice.

'Me? Like Dad?'

Edward nodded. It was a little unfortunate that, growing up, Derek had been a bit of a role model for young Oscar. Where Edward had instinctively felt that his father's behaviour was wrong, Oscar had idolised him and they'd soon become drinking buddies, laughing and poking fun at Edward who always refused to join in. Now, Oscar was more reliant on alcohol than he cared to admit and Edward had seen the very worst of it.

'What can I say? I like a drink,' Oscar said with a little laugh, 'but I know how to handle it. I don't go overboard like Dad.'

Edward could have said all manner of things to that, but he chose not to. He didn't want to fight. He already felt emotionally drained from having been in his father's company for so brief a time.

'So, are you going to give me a tour?' Oscar asked, gazing up at the golden facade of Winfield.

'No.'

'No?' Oscar sounded genuinely shocked. 'Why not? I want to see your new place. I've only seen the entrance hall.'

'I've got to work. And shouldn't you be at work too?'

'God, you're always bloody working!' Oscar said, not answering Edward's question as to why he wasn't at work. 'Dad was right.'

'What do you mean? What's he said?' Edward really didn't want to know, but felt compelled to find out.

'He said you're uptight and boring and haven't any time for fun in your life. You're always working.'

Edward sighed inwardly. 'And what would Dad know about

work? I can't remember a single year when he didn't give up on some job or was fired from one.'

'Yeah, but at least he knew how to have a good time.'

'You call it a good time *now*? Have you seen the state of his house?'

'Of course I have. I see it more than you do.'

Edward caught his brother's barb.

'You should try clearing up after him when he's had an all-nighter,' Oscar went on. 'I can only stomach it if I've had one or two myself.'

Edward silently cursed. At least, he thought it was silent.

'What did you say?' Oscar caught Edward's arm.

'Nothing!'

'Yes you did. You said something about me drinking, didn't you?'

Edward started walking towards the front door, but Oscar blocked his path.

'What *is* your problem?'

'Seriously? You want to know what my problem is?' Edward said, disbelief in his voice that his brother didn't realise.

'Yes, I want to know.'

They stood staring at each other for a heated moment. Oscar was the first to speak.

'If you're not going to invite me in, why don't we go out somewhere – have a couple of drinks and chill out.'

'You're kidding, right?'

Oscar looked wounded by this which was typical of him. 'No, I'm not kidding.'

'Haven't you done enough damage?' Edward asked him, but Oscar didn't have time to answer because it was then that Abi appeared from the walled garden, a basket full of flowers over her arm. She was heading towards her car when she saw them.

'Hello,' she said with a wave.

Edward watched as Oscar ran a hand through his sandy hair and waved back at Abi, casually walking towards her.

'How are you, Abigail?' he asked.

'I'm very well. How are you?'

'All the better for seeing you,' Oscar said.

Edward rolled his eyes and hoped Abi had the good sense not to be taken in by his brother's charm. Unfortunately, he'd inherited that dubious charm from their father and Oscar knew exactly how to reel women in.

'Edward giving you a tour?' Abi asked him.

Oscar laughed out loud, causing Abi to frown. 'Something like that,' he said. Edward willed Oscar not to mention their father. Not to mention anything.

'Well, I've got to get on,' Abi said and Edward sighed in relief.

'See you later maybe?' Oscar said, hope in his voice.

Edward watched as Abi left and then Oscar turned towards him.

'So, do I get to see this place or yours then?'

'Not today,' Edward said and made his way inside, firmly closing the door between him and his brother.

CHAPTER EIGHTEEN

As Abi drove away from Winfield, she couldn't help thinking about the little scene she'd walked into between Edward and Oscar, and why Oscar had laughed so maniacally when she'd asked if Edward was giving him a tour. It all seemed rather odd, but who was she to judge? If Edward ever stumbled upon her having one of her family discussions with her sister, goodness only knew what he'd make of it, and so she did her best to put it to the back of her mind. It was none of her business. Anyway, she had other things to think about that day because she was on her way to see her new friend.

Arriving in the little village at the foot of the downs, Abi took a moment to settle her thoughts. Ever since Ronnie had dropped her off at Winfield after her little incident, she'd wanted to thank him for his kindness. So she'd picked a few flowers from her garden, trying to choose blooms that she couldn't remember seeing in his own.

She parked on the unmetalled road outside Ronnie's cottage, marvelling at the heat of the afternoon as she got out of the car with her basket in one hand and a sun hat in the other.

As she entered the garden, she saw a woman sitting at one of the tables, a yellow Labrador by her side. The dog was looking up at its owner patiently, its head tilted hopefully.

'Boo, you've already had half of my scone when I dropped it!' she said.

The dog's attention didn't waver and the woman chuckled, breaking off some more of the scone she'd been attempting to enjoy herself and feeding it to her companion. Abi smiled at the scene and then went in search of Ronnie.

Of course, Ronnie was in the garden. Where else would he be on such a beautiful day?

'Abi! How are you?' he said, a huge smile dividing his face in two when he saw her as he emerged from the greenhouse, a pair of terracotta pots in his dusty hands.

'I'm well,' she said as she walked up the path towards him. 'How are you?'

'Can't complain. Had a flurry of activity this morning – a walking group came along. Kept me on my toes.'

She smiled. It was good to see his friendly teddy bear face again.

'I know you don't need any flowers, but I wanted to bring you something from Winfield to say thank you for the other day.'

'You didn't need to do that,' he told her, putting his pots down and taking the flowers she gave to him, 'but I'm kind of glad you did. Come on inside while I put them in some water.'

She followed him into the house, the warm scent of potted geraniums filling the air.

'Have a seat,' he said and Abi sat on the chair she'd occupied last time, by the window overlooking the garden. Once again, the window was open.

'I'm afraid they've wilted a little,' Abi said.

'When did you pick them?'

'Just before leaving.'

'Ah, you see the best time to pick them is first thing in the morning or last thing at night, when the day is cooler and the stems are full of water.'

'Oh, dear. Have I failed at the first hurdle in growing flowers?' Abi asked.

'Not at all. We all have to learn and these are beautiful,' Ronnie told her.

'I was actually hoping you'd tell me what the pink ones are. I'm afraid I didn't label them,' Abi confessed, wincing at another of her amateur errors.

'It's cosmos rose bonbon.'

'I love its fluffy flowers.'

'They're called doubles,' Ronnie told her as he placed the flowers in an earthenware container. 'Beautiful. But make sure you don't go all double in your garden as some doubles are impossible for the pollinators to access. You want plenty of open flowers too.'

Abi nodded. It was all so fascinating and she was lapping up his knowledge.

'Cup of tea?' he asked. 'If you've time?'

'Oh, I've time. If you have?'

He nodded. 'Always plenty of time here. The world moves slowly in the summer in this place.'

Abi shifted uncomfortably in her chair. 'Actually, there was something I wanted to talk to you about,' she said, her voice whisper soft.

'Oh? About your garden, is it?'

'No. Not about the garden.'

He turned to look at her as he placed the vase of flowers on the table and, seeing something in her face, he nodded.

'Let's get that cup of tea, shall we?'

~

Abi hadn't told Dana or her other work colleagues about her pregnancy for a few weeks, anxious in her early stages for everything to go smoothly. Luckily, she didn't suffer from morning sickness – much to the chagrin of Ellen who had gone through it with both her pregnancies.

'You have *no* idea how wretched I felt!' Ellen told her.

Actually, Abi *did* know how wretched Ellen had felt because she'd texted her sickness updates every single day. But Abi felt lucky all the same as she read through blog posts and online forums about pregnancy, hearing women's experiences and wondering if things would change for her.

After telling Dante her news, she only saw him twice during that first month. He was busy at work, he told her. Abi had tried to hide her disappointment in him, wondering if he was making any plans for their future together. He certainly hadn't made any suggestion that she should move into his flat or that he could move into hers. It was as if he was just getting on with his normal life. So much for Italians and their love of family life, Abi thought, typecasting horribly, but feeling better for a brief moment of giving her frustration free rein.

But she delighted in her new-found state. Pregnancy was something she'd never really imagined unlike her sister. Even as a child, Ellen had always been one for dressing up dolls and brushing their hair; Abi had been far more interested in her coloured pens and little paintbox. But why shouldn't she be a good mother? Just because she was creative and had been wed to her art for so long didn't mean she couldn't do a good job of raising a child. And perhaps her creativity would give her a little extra edge too, she thought, imagining her future self sitting at a table with her daughter or son, sharing with them the magic of colour, the splendour of pattern – just as she had with Bethanne.

And then it happened. In the middle of the night. Abi woke alone and in pain and screamed as she realised what was happening to her.

Dante came over immediately and held her as she wept. His hands stroked her hair which was tear-soaked and he rocked her back and forth like a baby. They didn't say anything. There were no words which could possibly have filled that void.

Abi didn't go into work for the rest of the week, but Dante did. He rang her and texted her, but didn't come over until three days later.

'You look pale,' he said when she opened the door to him. There was a part of her that wanted to scream at him, 'Really? I wonder why!' He seemed surprised that she hadn't pulled herself together already.

She sat on the sofa and watched as he moved around her kitchen, prepping the vegetables that he'd brought with him.

'I thought we'd try a new recipe,' he said, pulling a pan out of a drawer. 'Something warming. It's been so cold today.'

Abi wasn't normally one to hate people, but she couldn't help hating him in that moment. How could he be so focussed on ordinary things when something so tremendous had happened to them? Had it not touched him at all? She wanted to scream at him and beat her fists against his chest, but she had the feeling that wouldn't make a bit of difference. He still wouldn't understand. And so she ate the meal he made for her and drank the wine he'd brought with him. Then, as they sat on the sofa together, he put his arm around her and kissed her cheek. She was ready to hear it then – the sweet, gentle words that would express his sadness.

'Maybe it's for the best,' he told her. 'It's just us again.'

Abi couldn't believe what she was hearing. How could losing a baby be for the best?

'You know how I've always admired your talent and I think you'd be throwing it away having a baby. You'd probably never design anything else ever again.'

Abi stared at him in bafflement. 'Dante, women can have a family and a career as well. This isn't the Dark Ages anymore.'

'I know, but I think you can only do one thing really well in this life and perhaps yours is your design work.'

She could feel tears pricking at her eyes, but she was determined not to cry in front of him.

'I think you should go.'

'What?' he said, genuinely baffled.

'I want you to go, Dante.'

'Are you tired?'

Abi nodded because she didn't have the strength to tell him exactly how she was feeling in that moment, but she knew things had shifted between them and that they'd never get back to that sweet place they'd once shared.

'I love you,' he told her as he left. But how could he? How could he truly love her without loving the little being she had held deep inside her albeit for so brief a time? How could he love her without feeling the pain that she felt? Dante may have spoken the words of love, but Abi had felt none of the feeling behind them.

~

Now, after telling Ronnie what had happened to her, Abi looked at his gentle face which was full of concern.

'When you mentioned your own loss the other day, I guess I had a moment...' Abi began, but her voice petered out.

Ronnie nodded and his rough hands reached across the space between them to hold Abi's.

'I'm so sorry, Abi. It's a terrible thing to go through. And, if I may say so – that chap of yours didn't deserve you by the sounds of things.'

Abi smiled weakly, like a piece of sun trying to break through the clouds.

'I don't think he ever wanted any sort of commitment, which was kind of fine for a while because I was so obsessed with my work,' Abi confessed. 'He was one of life's free spirits and I loved him because of that and I suppose there was a part of me that knew he'd resent me if I pushed him into any sort of serious relationship. Maybe that's why I didn't push. Not even when I found out I was pregnant. But I couldn't go on after seeing that relief in him. It was unmistakable. He never wanted a child. Not then. Not with me at least. He wanted us to continue being together, but things had changed between us and I couldn't bear to be with him any longer. Was that wrong of me? Was I unfair?'

'No, no, my dear. You were just two very different people who wanted different things.'

Abi sniffed, keeping the tears at bay as she nodded.

'And how are you now?' Ronnie asked gently.

'I don't know,' Abi said honestly. 'I thought moving out of London away from where it all happened would help, but I'm still having nightmares. Sometimes, I'll wake up in the middle of the night and feel that pain and it's like it's happening all over again.'

'It'll take time,' Ronnie told her. 'It's something nobody wants to hear, but it will take time.'

Abi looked out of the window into the green depths of the garden.

'When it happened to us, we didn't know how we'd ever get

over it,' Ronnie said. 'It seemed insurmountable. But time passes, doesn't it? And the raw edges get smoothed away a little.'

'Just a little?'

'A little enough so that you can go on living.'

Abi nodded. There'd been a few dark days when she'd wondered if she even wanted to do that, and then Dana would show up at her home with a tub of ice cream, a bunch of freesias and a shoulder to cry on. When she'd reached out to her friend with the news, she'd been round in a heartbeat. Abi wasn't sure what she would have done without her in those first couple of weeks, especially after she'd broken up with Dante. It had all been too much and that's when she'd decided to sell her company. A fresh start. A new beginning. And here she was in Sussex, sitting in a stranger's home telling him the most intimate details of her life. Only, he didn't feel like a stranger. He felt like the very dearest of friends even though she'd only known him a short time.

She looked at his face now, creased and kind, his eyes warm and gentle.

'How about a walk around the garden?' he asked her. 'It's a good cure-all, I find.'

Abi nodded. 'That sounds like a very good idea.'

Later, once Abi was back at Winfield, she sat in her living room with the French doors open, tears streaming down her face. She hadn't realised that she was still carrying around so much grief inside her, but talking to Ronnie had helped to release it.

It was strange, but she'd found it so easy to talk to him. Much easier than talking to her sister. She still remembered the awkwardness she'd felt when Ellen had visited her just after the miscarriage. Ellen had gone into mother mode – tidying and going out shopping, preparing a meal for Abi and making sure she had everything she needed. It was kind of her, of course, but the one thing she didn't do – very much like Dante – was to just sit and talk to her. Or not talk. Just to be with her in that same emotional space for a while.

Even up to when she was leaving, Abi was expecting Ellen to say something, anything.

'You have everything you need?' Ellen had said, her hand on the door, ready to go, and Abi had nodded dumbly at her, wishing she had the courage to ask her sister to stay and to talk and talk until all the hurt was talked out of her.

But, even now, they still hadn't really talked about it and Abi suspected that they never would. Ellen probably just assumed that Abi was over it by now. After all, she'd moved house and, to Ellen's mind, that showed strength and survival. Abi must therefore be fine. But was she? She still felt so prone to tears and strange spells like she'd experienced at Ronnie's. She thought about him telling her that it would take time. It's what everybody said, wasn't it? Time will heal. Let time do its thing. This too shall pass.

And what did you do in the meantime? Abi gazed out into her garden. You planted sunflowers, that's what you did. Huge, happy sunflowers with chocolate and yellow faces that smiled down upon you. You couldn't feel unhappy when you looked at a sunflower. Or a cosmos for that matter. Abi really shouldn't give all the glory to the sunflower. Her garden was becoming her therapy, her escape, her joy, and she felt so grateful to have it. She would get through this, she told herself. With time and her garden and with friends like Ronnie, she would heal.

CHAPTER NINETEEN

It was the beginning of August and the books weren't balancing. That was the conclusion Edward came to after a morning of number crunching. He knew he could make his business work, but it was going to take time to make a regular income that could be relied upon to run a house the size of Winfield. Even with Abi having shared the burden, Edward was still struggling to make ends meet and that meant one thing. He was going to have to start renting his apartments out much earlier than he'd anticipated.

The trouble was, the builders were far from leaving. There was still so much work to be done and that might put a potential tenant off. Still, it hadn't put him off moving in. You just had to find the right person, he reasoned. The right person wouldn't mind a bit of hammering or dust. Or walls being knocked down. Well, that's what Edward hoped anyway.

There was one apartment that was almost ready to let and Edward went to see it now. It was the one adjacent to his own and he'd asked the builders to prioritise work on it over his although his was very nearly finished now. Opening the door into it, he couldn't help smiling. It was a wide open space with huge white walls, beautifully finished floorboards and the same marvellous view of the downs that he enjoyed from his own apartment. Who wouldn't want to live in such a place? It was a place one could dream in. Dream and breathe. That's what he'd been able to do most in his short time at Winfield. Although he'd been horrendously busy with everything, there had been some magical moments when he'd just stood in the middle of his living room, breathing in the beauty of the scene.

He smiled to himself. Winfield was turning him into a romantic. Well, he'd just have to find someone with the same sort of sensibilities to share it with.

The first viewer was most certainly not a romantic. He was called Mr Basildon and he owned his own company manufacturing something expensive in the car industry. He was a sprightly sixty-year old who said he was looking for a country retreat that he could escape to at weekends. He'd sounded very pleasant on the phone but, when he arrived, Edward wasn't sure that he wanted this man as his neighbour. There was just something about him – a restlessness. He was one of life's fidgeters and he also liked to clear his throat, very noisily, at regular intervals. Edward began to count the time between the throat clearings and it was less than thirty seconds. No, he would not do as a neighbour.

The next person was a Mrs Asprey who was a head teacher at a very nice school for girls who wore green blazers and straw hats in the summer.

'Does it come furnished?' she asked.

'No, it's unfurnished,' Edward told her. He'd thought the advertisement had made that clear, but obviously not.

'Oh,' she said. 'And the garage?'

'No garage. But plenty of room to park on the driveway.'

'Oh.'

Edward tried to hide his frustration at the fact she hadn't yet praised anything she *was* getting.

'And the walled garden – that bit over there?' she asked when they were outside.

'That's somebody else's,' Edward said, 'but you'll have access to this part.'

'Oh,' she said again with a derisive sniff this time.

Honestly, he thought as she drove away, some people were never happy – no matter what you gave them, they always wanted something else.

The third viewer was a Mr Harry Freeman who seemed like a nice guy. He did something in advertising for a large company in London, had family close by in Sussex and, most importantly, really seemed to understand Winfield.

'These sash windows are great,' he said.

Edward smiled. 'They are, aren't they? They were one of the things I first fell in love with.'

'And the views!' Harry gave a long, low whistle.

'You're in London at the moment?'

'Suburbs. A bit cheaper, but the commute's a pain.'

'But won't commuting from here be worse?'

'Actually, I'm going to be opening up an office in Brighton.'

Edward nodded. 'An easier commute than London.'

'Just a bit.'

Edward continued the tour, answering Harry's questions and giving him all the information he thought of interest.

'Thank you,' Harry said when he came to leave. 'You've got my number?'

'I have. You're interested then?'

'Oh, yes!'

They shook hands. 'I've got one more person coming, but I hope to get back to everyone soon after that.'

'I look forward to hearing from you.'

Edward watched as Harry Freeman drove away, noticing the way he glanced back at the hall. He was just as smitten with the place as Edward had been after he'd viewed it for the first time all those months ago.

The next viewer arrived a little late, but Edward soon forgave her when she got out and smiled at him. Tamara Wakefield was nearly six foot tall with raven-black hair down to her shoulders and a smile that was pure sunshine. She was a business consultant and had had enough of her noisy flat in Eastbourne and wanted some peace and quiet.

Edward gave her the tour.

'And there's just the one apartment?'

'At the moment.'

'So there'll be more in the future?'

'No more than eight in the whole building.'

He was just about to tell her something else when she smiled at him and the thought completely left his head. And so he showed her the garden, thinking that some fresh air might shake him back to his old self.

Abi was just returning from shopping when she saw a woman walking out of the hall with Edward. She was tall with plenty in the way of legs and hair, Abi couldn't help thinking. Rather like a fine racehorse and probably just as expensive to maintain.

She watched as the woman got into a sporty-looking car and drove away and then Abi got out of hers.

'Ah, Abigail!' Edward called over to her. 'Time for a chat?'

'Of course.'

They walked round his side of the hall and sat on the bench in a spot of sunshine.

'I meant to tell you,' Edward began. 'I'm going to be renting one of my apartments out. I hope that's okay. I should have run it by you first.'

'You don't need to do that. It's your half of the hall. You can do as you see fit.'

'Still, it's only polite to tell you my plans. After all, you'd soon notice a stranger walking around.'

'A tall, willowy stranger?' she asked with a grin and, to her delight, she saw Edward blushing.

'Well, we'll have to see.'

'She looked...' Abi paused, 'expensive.'

A tiny smile tickled the corner of Edward's mouth. 'I know we suggested spring before renting out, but I could use the income,' he confided.

'Oh, dear. Is everything okay?'

'It will be if I can get an apartment let.'

Abi stood up. 'Well, let me know how it goes.'

'I will.'

She smiled at him. 'I'll see you later,' she told him as she left to get her shopping out of the car.

Later that evening, Edward sat with a glass of wine on his bench in the garden, the light in the sky was turning from gold to royal blue and the heat of the day had finally exhausted itself, leaving but a shadow of its memory behind in the walled garden.

As he sat there, Edward thought about the two viewings which had gone especially well: that of Harry Freeman and Tamara Wakefield. How could he possibly choose between them? On the one hand, he had a like-minded businessman who appreciated the beauty of the place just as he did. On the other, he had a beauty he could appreciate. Edward tutted at himself. He had to be professional about this. You couldn't make a business decision based on looks. It wasn't ethical or politically correct. Still, the facts couldn't be ignored. Miss Wakefield had been very beautiful, smart and personable. It was a shame he didn't have two apartments ready to go.

Edward couldn't remember the last time he'd even contemplated going out with a beautiful woman or when he'd had a proper relationship. Well, he could. It had been with Lucy and it had been a disaster. Edward shook his head as he remembered. She'd been as married to her job as he had been to his and the time they'd made for one another had been pitiful really, squeezed between meetings with them both looking at their phones all the time. It was doomed to fail.

Then there'd been Samantha. That had lasted a while, but mainly because they'd hardly seen one another. Theirs had been a digital affair comprising of texts, emails and phone calls and not very much in the way of actual physical contact.

But here at Winfield, time had slowed down a little. He had room to think about such luxuries as love, didn't he? Of seeing somebody. Of spending quality time with them.

As he thought of romantic relationships, he couldn't help thinking of Abigail and then chastised himself for doing so because it would never do to mix business and pleasure. Abigail was his neighbour and renovation partner. Theirs was a special, unique bond. They'd been brought together by Winfield Hall and they were only just slowly developing a friendship. And friendships were good; they were vital. Yet, he couldn't help thinking of the moment he'd watched her cross the driveway towards him earlier that day, the sun full on her face, bringing out those freckles. She'd raised a hand to shield her eyes and a collection of bangles had jangled down her arm in a pleasing sound.

He shook the image from his mind. Abigail Carey was to be nothing more than a friend.

It was then that his phone buzzed with a text. It was Tamara Wakefield. She thanked him for his time today, but had found something else that suited her better. Well, Edward thought, that solves that little conundrum.

He called up Harry's number and sent a quick message.

Would you like the apartment? It's yours if you do.

The reply came back within a minute.

Definitely! Would love it! Haven't been able to stop thinking about it all day.

Edward smiled.

I'll send over the paperwork in the morning.

Edward switched his phone off and leaned back on the bench, gazing up into the blue and gold sky. It had been a good day.

The next day, Abi was out in the garden re-staking some sunflowers when her phone rang.

'Hey, Abi!'

'Douglas – how are you?'

'I'm good. *Really* good! I just wanted to ask you what on earth you said to Ellen?'

Abi laughed. 'I take it things are better between you?'

'Better than better – they're *great*! We're going to sell the house!'

'What?'

'Yep! We had a long talk – several long talks actually – and we both think that it's putting too much pressure on us so we've just had an estate agent round.'

'Douglas – this is huge!'

'I know. Unlike our next house.' He laughed and Abi could hear his relief.

'So where are you going?'

'Just out of town. We've got our eye on a cottage actually. It's a semi with this great garden for the girls. It's a bit of a doer-upper, but nothing insurmountable, you know? Just a bit of tarting up which we'll do as and when we can.'

'Oh, Douglas – I'm so pleased.'

'It means I won't have to work away anymore. I can take a job in Brighton and be home each night to see the girls.'

'That's going to make such a difference,' Abi said, thrilled to hear how happy he was at reclaiming his position as a real member of his own family again.

'It really will and I think I've got you to thank for this, haven't I?'

'I don't know about that.'

'Well, when I left Ellen that day, she was spitting knives at me saying this was the end and, when I got back, she was all sweetness.'

'Well, we did have a little talk,' Abi confessed at last. 'You know, sometimes you just need to state the obvious, and the obvious isn't always obvious when you're living in the middle of it. Does that make sense?'

'I think so!'

Abi laughed. 'You know what I mean. I think Ellen had taken on way too much – both for herself and for you – and it had become the new normal and she couldn't see a way out of it all.'

'Well, we can now.'

'I'm so pleased.'

'Oh, and she asked me to tell you to come round tonight. If you're free.'

'I can do that.'

'She says she's got a favour to ask.'

'Sounds interesting.'

'Yeah, don't get too excited,' Douglas said. 'She had a shifty sort of look about her when she asked me to tell you.'

~

Abi was so excited to see Ellen after Douglas's news even if there was something slightly shifty going on, and it was a brand new sister who opened the door to her when she arrived. There was a brightness in Ellen's face and she was smiling, actually smiling. The habitual frown had vanished and there was what looked like true joy in her eyes.

'Did he tell you we're moving?' Ellen asked as Abi walked through to the kitchen with her.

'He did! I'm so proud of you, Ellen.'

'We're really going to make it work, aren't we?'

'I know you are.' The two of them embraced just as the girls ran through. Rosie was carrying Pugly and they all had a group hug.

'You know what this is called now?' Bethanne said a moment later. 'A hugly!'

Everyone laughed.

'Oh, they're driving me crazy!' Ellen said, but she was half-laughing instead of the old complaining. 'Everything is "ugly" at the moment. They want their drinks served in a *mugly*. If anyone sneezes, they have a *bugly*, and I've even started calling Douglas *Dougly*!'

Abi laughed again and watched as the girls left the room in fits of giggles, Pugly in tow.

'Talking of Dougly,' Ellen said as she switched the kettle on, 'I've had a brilliant idea to take the pressure off him a little.'

'Oh?'

'I'm going to start sewing. You know – taking little jobs.

Mending, making children's clothes. Maybe even open my own Etsy store.'

'That sounds exciting!'

'Isn't it? I might even rival you in a few years and have my own shop!'

'I'm sure you could if you put your mind to it,' Abi told her.

'So, I was thinking. There's something I really need to get started.'

'Right?' Abi said, wondering if her sister was going to ask for a small sum of money or even a large one. She never had before, but times had obviously been testing for her sister and she was happy to help.

'I've got a favour to ask.'

'Ask away.'

'Do you remember our old sewing machine?'

'No.'

'Well, I kind of need it now,' Ellen said. 'But there's only one problem. It's at Aunt Claire's and I want you to get it for me.'

Abi's mouth dropped open in horror. 'Oh, *don't* ask me to go there!' she cried, wishing her sister had asked for a huge sum of money instead. 'Why can't you? You could take the girls.'

'Aunt Claire doesn't want to see them.'

'Well, she won't want to see me either,' Abi said bluntly.

'But you could be in and out in five minutes.'

'Let me buy you a new machine. A more modern one,' Abi begged.

'There's no point spending when we already have one.'

'But it would be my gift to you – to wish you well in your new venture.'

Ellen shook her head. 'But this one was Mum's. Don't you remember? She used to mend all our clothes on it.'

'I don't remember that,' Abi said sadly.

'It's special and I'd love to use it.'

'Are you even sure Aunt Claire will still have it?' Abi tried.

'Of course she will. She never threw anything out, the old miser. She'll have it and you're going to get it for me.'

Abi sighed. She knew when she was beaten.

The next day, after a sleepless night because she knew what she was heading towards, Abi pulled up and parked in a neat London suburb where the houses all looked exactly alike. She had found a rare parking space outside number seventy-three and sat for a moment, staring at the red-bricked house. She'd rung her aunt the night before to make sure she'd be in. Their conversation had been brief, functional.

'Well, I'm not doing anything with the old machine,' Aunt Claire had said. 'You might as well use it. It's just taking up room.'

Abi sighed as she tried to remember the last time she'd been in the house. She hadn't been there since graduating from art college but, even from the outside, she could tell that it hadn't changed a bit with the old curtains at the windows, neat but faded, and the two identical pots with their identical evergreens standing either side of the door. Everything was neat and tidy, but a little bit soulless. Abi had definitely not been inspired by her aunt's choices yet perhaps her own need for colour and pattern had stemmed from being stifled in this house.

She got out of the car and walked up the path, knocking on the door. As she waited, a part of her couldn't help wishing that Aunt Claire had been called away unexpectedly and wasn't at home at all, but that would just be postponing the pain. It would be best to get in and out as soon as possible.

The door opened and Aunt Claire's dour face greeted Abi.

Her hair, once fair, was threaded through with grey now and she wore it tied back from her face which was free from make-up and remarkably young-looking. Abi wondered how old she was now – late-fifties? Perhaps even early-sixties. She'd been older than her sister, Abi's mother, that's all she knew.

'Come in,' she said.

Abi closed the door behind her and felt the oppressive atmosphere of the old house again. The wallpaper in the hallway was the same – a very dull cream and grey stripe, a little faded with age now, and the carpets hadn't been replaced. Aunt Claire believed in using things up until they were completely dead, and there was still a little life clinging on to the décor and furnishings at number seventy-three.

'How are you?' Aunt Claire asked, her voice clipped as if she'd forced the question out.

'I'm good. How are you?'

Aunt Claire nodded. 'You want the old sewing machine?'

So, this was purely business, Abi thought. In and out. No nonsense.

'Yes please,' she said meekly and she followed her aunt into a room at the back of the house. Although the sun was shining, it never quite made it round to this part of the house. Abi remembered always being slightly afraid of it during her childhood. It had been her aunt's domain, a very adult room with glass ornaments and fine furniture. Looking at it now, Abi wished she could take a paintbrush to the whole place, giving it a much-needed make-over and filling it with soft yellows and pretty fabrics to lift the mood.

'Well, there it is,' Aunt Claire said with a sigh. 'I gave it a dust last night after you called.'

'Thank you.'

'It's not been used for years so I don't know if it's still working.'

'I guess we'll find out,' Abi said.

There was a pause. An awkward, dread-filled pause when Abi half expected Aunt Claire to offer her a cup of tea, but of course she didn't. Abi had come for a specific reason and there would be no niceties.

'I'll take it out to the car,' Abi said. The machine came in its own case and the whole thing was bulky and heavy, but Abi managed it, placing it on the floor behind the passenger seat. Her aunt watched from the door as if to make sure she was leaving, but then called her back with a quick motion of her hand.

'You might as well have all the other bits and bobs that went with it,' Aunt Claire said. 'I won't use any of it.' She returned to the room at the back of the house and Abi followed, watching as her aunt pulled a box out of a corner cupboard. It was full of ribbons and buttons and reels of different coloured thread. It was all so pretty and Abi couldn't believe she'd never seen it before. It had lived its life in the darkness of a cupboard.

'Thank you. Ellen and the girls will love this.'

Aunt Claire nodded as Abi took the box from her, but didn't say anything. She wasn't interested in her niece or her great-nieces.

It was then that Abi spotted a silver photo frame on the sideboard. She put the box down and walked towards it, her hands reaching to pick it up. It was of her mother and aunt as teenagers, their two faces full of the family freckles. They were both so beautiful and so alike. Just as Abi and Ellen were today, she couldn't help thinking. But one thing struck her above all else: her aunt was smiling. The young Claire Carey had been happy.

'Aunt Claire?' Abi began. 'I'd love to know more about my–'

'Put the picture down please,' Aunt Claire interrupted before Abi had a chance to complete her sentence. She'd known what was coming, hadn't she? She'd known that Abi had been about to say "mother".

'I don't remember much about her at all,' Abi said sadly as she carefully placed the picture frame back on the sideboard.

'I have to go out now,' Aunt Claire said in that clipped, brook no opposition way she had and Abi found herself nodding in meek acquiescence and leaving the house with the box of threads and ribbons. She placed it alongside the sewing machine on the floor of the car and, when she looked up to wave goodbye, she saw that her aunt had already closed the front door.

Abi couldn't get away from that house quickly enough. But there was one thing she couldn't shake from her mind as she left the suburbs and that was the photo of Kristen and Claire Carey: two beautiful young women with shining futures ahead of them. Except one of them was dead and the other as good as.

CHAPTER TWENTY

Abi wished that she'd somehow managed to take a photo of the picture of her aunt and mother, and she would have been able to if she'd been left alone in the room but, of course, she hadn't. Her aunt had stood sentinel and had more or less escorted Abi off the premises.

Abi wondered if Ellen remembered the photo and she did her best to recall it now. Maybe she could do a sketch of it, capturing her mother's smiling, sun-filled face before it faded from her memory forever.

Quickly grabbing a drawing pad and pencil once she was back home, she did just that, holding the features of her mother in her mind's eye as she sketched from memory. It didn't take long before she had a likeness that pleased her, and also one that touched her heart with both joy and pain.

Abi put down her pencil and her fingers reached out to touch the soft lines she'd drawn on the page before her, wondering if Ellen would recognise the image as their mother. Perhaps she'd take it with her when she delivered the sewing machine that afternoon.

It was around lunchtime when Edward's phone rang. He recognised the number as a local landline, but couldn't think who it might be.

'I'm sorry to bother you, son,' a man's voice said. 'I'm Mr Howard. I'm ringing about your father.'

Edward was on immediate alert. He'd left his mobile number with a couple of his father's neighbours in case of emergencies and now it sounded like that time had come.

'What is it?' Edward asked anxiously.

The man sighed and Edward braced himself.

'He was out in the street in the middle of the night. Drunk to his eyeballs, yelling his head off and crashing into dustbins.'

Edward's eyes closed. On the one hand, he'd been expecting even darker news, but this really wasn't much better.

'You've got to have a word with him. He doesn't listen to us and we've all had polite words to him whenever he does manage to answer the door to anyone. We just can't take it anymore. Have a word with him, son, before the police have to be involved.'

'Look,' Edward said as politely as he could, 'I'm sorry, but we're just not that close. He doesn't listen to me any more than he does you.'

'But he's your father.'

Edward sighed. It was the common refrain of society – if you were related to someone, you were expected to care for them or at least be responsible for them. People didn't understand when a child didn't care for their parent. There was a kind of taboo around the subject.

'I'll give him a call, okay?' Edward promised, hoping that would be enough to deflate the situation.

'Good.' The neighbour hung up.

Edward felt all his energy draining out of him as he rang his father's landline a moment later, but it was his brother who picked up the phone.

'Oscar?'

'Ed?'

'How long have you been at Dad's?'

He heard Oscar sigh. 'What's the time?'

'Just after one.'

'PM?'

'Of course PM!'

'I've lost track since eight last night.'

'What's happening?'

'What do you mean?

'I've just had a neighbour on the phone complaining about the noise last night.'

'What noise?'

'Dad shouting and crashing around the street?'

'Ah, right.'

'And you were there?'

'I might have passed out by that point.'

'God, Oscar. What the hell is going on? I thought you were worried about him drinking and getting into a mess.'

'I am!'

'So what do you think you're doing going over there and joining in?'

'We were having a laugh! Anything wrong with that?'

'There is when it involves an alcoholic causing chaos in the middle of the night,' Edward cried.

'I thought it would be better if he had someone with him,' Oscar said.

'Not someone who's going to pass out.' Edward sighed again. 'Look, make sure he's okay, will you? And tell him that the neighbours are on the verge of calling the police if he doesn't sort himself out.'

'Nosey bloody parkers!'

Edward hung up, switching his phone off in case his brother tried to ring him back. He'd had enough. He'd tried so many times in the past to reach out to both his father and brother to explain how he felt and how they could be living better lives, but it always ended in misery. For him at least.

He gazed out of the window to the downs beyond. He'd go walking if he had the energy, but he felt exhausted. Perhaps he'd sit in the garden later. He'd just try and do a little bit of work first so that the day didn't feel like a total waste of time.

When Abi reached her sister's, she pulled the sewing machine out of the car, taking it to the front door and putting it down before returning for the box of ribbons and threads. When she turned around, the front door was open.

'I heard you arrive,' Ellen said. 'You got it!'

'I certainly did!'

'You're brilliant, Abi! You must tell me all about it.'

'Oh, I will.'

The two of them went inside, placing the machine on the kitchen table together with the box and then Abi bent over the dog basket to give Pugly a stroke.

'The girls went to a friend's after school so we've got some time to ourselves,' Ellen explained as she opened the carrying case of the sewing machine and smiled.

'Don't you think it should be in a museum?' Abi asked.

'Nonsense! I'm going to make good use of this.'

Abi watched as Ellen patted the top of the machine. 'Aunt Claire never used it, did she?'

'I don't think so.'

'I remember her always sewing by hand if we had a torn sleeve or a hem down.' Her fingers gently touched the sides of it and Abi guessed what her sister was thinking: the last hands to touch this, to work it, would have been their mother's.

A lump formed in Abi's throat and she swallowed hard. 'I can't wait to see what you make with it,' she said, trying to lighten the mood.

'So what's in the box?' Ellen asked.

'Take a look.'

Ellen opened it and gasped. 'Were these Mum's?'

'Well, can you imagine Aunt Claire keeping coloured ribbons?'

'Er, no!' Ellen said, her hand delving inside and bringing out spools of rainbow-bright thread. 'I had no idea this existed.'

'It was shut away in a cupboard in the back room,' Abi told her.

'I used to hate that room. Aunt Claire would make me clean it sometimes and it was always cold and dark. She never put the radiator on in there.' Ellen turned to Abi. 'So how was the old harridan?'

'Pretty much like that room – cold and dark,' Abi said.

Ellen groaned. 'So you didn't have a cosy chat over tea and cake?'

'She marched me in and marched me out,' Abi said.

'Did she ask after me and the girls?'

'I'm afraid not.'

Ellen shook her head.

'But there's something I wanted to show you,' Abi told her. 'Just a minute.'

She ran out to the car and came back a moment later with her sketch. 'There was a photo in the back room,' she said. 'It was of mum and Aunt Claire as teenagers. I'd never seen it before and I picked it up, but Aunt Claire flipped and told me to put it down. I should have got a photo of it on my phone, but she kind of frogmarched me off the premises at that point.'

'Old cow!'

'So I tried to sketch what Mum looked like in it when I got home.' Abi showed Ellen the sketch now.

'Oh, Abi! That's so beautiful,' Ellen said, taking the picture from her. And then she gasped. 'She looks just like you!'

'You think so?'

'You don't see it?'

Abi looked at the picture again. 'I suppose. A little.'

'God, does that make me Aunt Claire?'

Abi shook her head. 'Never!'

'I see you didn't draw her.'

'I don't really need to see her miserable face,' Abi said. 'Although she was actually smiling in the photo.'

'She can smile?'

'She obviously used to in the dim and distant past.'

Ellen shook her head. 'Mum was so beautiful, wasn't she?'

Abi nodded, unable to trust herself to speak at that moment. Instead, the two of them stood with their arms around each other's shoulders, gazing into the face of the mother who was no longer with them.

Later that afternoon, once Abi was back at Winfield, she walked the length of the walled garden. The sun was warm on her bare limbs and she wasn't surprised to see Edward sitting outside on his bench, his eyes closed against the sun. She didn't want to disturb him and was about to turn away when he opened his eyes and saw her there.

'Hello,' he said.

'Hi.'

'You okay?'

She nodded as she approached him. 'How about you? Had a good day?'

For a moment, she thought she saw a pained expression dance across his face, but he smiled.

'Sure,' he said.

He looked tired and Abi couldn't help feeling sorry for him because tired seemed to be his default setting. But there was something else in his face today – a kind of weariness, as if life had played its worst with him.

'How about you? Good day?' he asked.

Abi thought about the cold, dark room at Aunt Claire's and the cold, dark reception she'd given her, and she thought about the sweet face of her mother in the photograph and the warmth of her smile and how she'd never see that smile this side of heaven.

'Yes. A good day,' she said, keeping her feelings locked inside.

She sat down beside him and the two of them enjoyed the peace of the garden together for a few moments. It was a strange companionship, she thought. They were sharing this special place, making a home there for themselves, so close to each other and yet knowing so very little about one another. Abi couldn't help wondering what Edward would make of her problems if she confessed them to him now. He would probably run a mile and, in truth, she didn't want to tell him. It would spoil the strange quiet friendship that they shared. Although could they really be considered friends if they didn't share their thoughts and feelings? Or maybe that made for the best friendships, Abi pondered. Maybe not knowing too much about each other was better.

She glanced at him and for all her protestations about it being better to know little about each other, she couldn't help wanting to ask him if he was okay – *really* okay. She just couldn't help it. It seemed like he was in pain and she wanted to reach out to him.

'Hey you!' she found herself saying.

'What?'

'Fancy a swim?'

His eyebrows rose. 'Now?'

'Why not?'

'In the river?'

She nodded and he smiled. It was good to see him smile.

'Well, okay then,' he said, getting up. 'Wetsuits?'

'Do you think it's warm enough for just swimming costumes?'

'We could give it a try. Meet you out the front in five?'

She nodded.

Twenty minutes later, they'd driven to the river and walked across the field. The sun was lower now and Abi was wondering just how wise it was to be there without wetsuits. Had she made a terrible mistake? No, she thought. She was going to do it – she was going to swim properly with as little as possible between her skin and the water.

'It's a beautiful afternoon, isn't it?' she said, her hand outstretched as she touched the tall grasses that they passed. 'Just look at this landscape. It's all lacy and golden.'

Edward paused for a moment. 'You really have it, don't you?' he said.

'Have what?'

'The secret of life unlocked, unpacked and laid at your feet.'

She frowned, surprised by his summation of her. 'You *think* so?'

'I do. You have this way of moving through a landscape – of seeing its colours and feeling its textures.'

Abi looked confused. 'And you don't?'

'Well, I have to make a conscious effort,' Edward told her. 'I can see it all when I look, but my head is very often elsewhere. I find it hard to relax into the moment in front of me.'

Abi nodded. 'But you're learning, aren't you?'

He smiled and it was such a lovely, warm and unexpected smile that Abi found herself smiling right back at him.

'Come on – I'll race you to the river!' Edward said.

Abi was a little astonished by the playfulness of his tone. This was a different Edward she was seeing now and Abi began to laugh – a nervous little giggle at first, but quickly rolling into something approaching hysteria as she began to run.

'Come on, Abi!' he called as he tore across the meadow. 'Last one in cleans up after the builders this weekend!'

Abi might not have been relishing the idea of jumping into the cold river water, but she wasn't going to be left behind and so she ran as she hadn't done since she was a child, screaming in excitement as she did so and quickly catching Edward up.

'I'm going to win!' she cried.

'No you're not!' Edward answered, picking up speed.

For a few wonderful moments, Abi forgot the stresses of the day as she gave in to the joy of living in the present and, together, they raced across the meadow to the river as it made its sparkling progress towards the sea.

END OF BOOK ONE

HIGH BLUE SKY

What would you sacrifice to be with the person you love?

Summer has arrived and it's over a year since strangers Abigail and Edward bought Winfield Hall at auction and restored it together. Now, two new tenants are about to join them at their beautiful Georgian home.

Workaholic Harry Freeman has forgotten what it is to relax so when he meets healer, Aura Arden, and learns to meditate with her, he can't believe how good he feels and he soon finds himself falling for her. But, with her bare feet and crystal beads, Aura's not a big hit with Harry's old-fashioned parents, and he finds himself torn between the people he loves most in the world.

It isn't just Harry and Aura finding love. Summer has woven its spell over Edward and his brother Oscar, and both are making a play for Abi. But Abi isn't happy at having to choose between these two very different men and, when Oscar's behavior spirals out of control, she realizes that some decisions can have devastating consequences.

High Blue Sky is the second novel in the heart-warming trilogy from the bestselling author of *The Rose Girls* and *The Book Lovers* series.

ACKNOWLEDGEMENTS

Huge thanks to Jacky Radbone who made the winning bid on my 'Name a Character' auction in aid of CLIC Sargent. It was my total pleasure to feature Jacky's beautiful dog, Boo, in my novel.

Thank you to my editor, Catriona. And thanks also to the amazing Lisa Brewster who designed the covers for this trilogy.

As ever, thank you to Roy for letting me bounce ideas off him and for all the help on the techie side.

ALSO BY VICTORIA CONNELLY

The House in the Clouds Series

The House in the Clouds

High Blue Sky

The Book Lovers Series

The Book Lovers

Rules for a Successful Book Club

Natural Born Readers

Scenes from a Country Bookshop

Christmas with the Book Lovers

Other Books

The Beauty of Broken Things

One Last Summer

The Heart of the Garden

Love in an English Garden

The Rose Girls

The Secret of You

Christmas at The Cove

Christmas at the Castle

Christmas at the Cottage

The Christmas Collection (A compilation volume)

A Summer to Remember

Wish You Were Here

The Runaway Actress

Molly's Millions

Flights of Angels

Irresistible You

Three Graces

It's Magic (A compilation volume)

A Weekend with Mr Darcy

The Perfect Hero (Dreaming of Mr Darcy)

Mr Darcy Forever

Christmas With Mr Darcy

Happy Birthday Mr Darcy

At Home with Mr Darcy

One Perfect Week and Other Stories

The Retreat and Other Stories

Postcard from Venice and Other Stories

A Dog Called Hope

Escape to Mulberry Cottage (non-fiction)

A Year at Mulberry Cottage (non-fiction)

Summer at Mulberry Cottage (non-fiction)

Secret Pyramid (children's adventure)

The Audacious Auditions of Jimmy Catesby (children's adventure)

ABOUT THE AUTHOR

Victoria Connelly is the bestselling author of *The Rose Girls* and *The Book Lovers* series. With over half a million sales, her books have been translated into many languages. The first, *Flights of Angels*, was made into a film in Germany. Victoria flew to Berlin to see it being made and even played a cameo role in it.

A Weekend with Mr Darcy, the first in her popular Austen Addicts series about fans of Jane Austen has sold over 100,000 copies. She is also the author of several romantic comedies including *The Runaway Actress* which was nominated for the Romantic Novelists' Association's Best Romantic Comedy of the Year.

Victoria was brought up in Norfolk, England before moving to Yorkshire where she got married in a medieval castle. After 11 years in London, she moved to rural Suffolk where she lives in a thatched cottage with her artist husband, a springer spaniel and her ex-battery hens.

To hear about future releases and receive a **free ebook** sign up for her newsletter at victoriaconnelly.com

Printed in Great Britain
by Amazon